The Music of Antônio Carlos Jobim

The Music of Antônio Carlos Jobim

Peter Freeman

intellect Bristol, UK / Chicago, USA

First published in the UK in 2019 by
Intellect, The Mill, Parnall Road, Fishponds, Bristol, BS16 3JG, UK

First published in the USA in 2019 by
Intellect, The University of Chicago Press, 1427 E. 60th Street,
Chicago, IL 60637, USA

A catalogue record for this book is available from the
British Library.

"Águas de março" and "Saudade do Brasil"
by Antônio Carlos Jobim
Reproduced by kind permission of Corcovado Music Corporation
Administered by Fairwood Music (UK) Ltd for the UK & Eire
© 1972 and © 1976 Corcovado Music Corporation.

Copy-editor: MPS Technologies
Cover designer: Alex Szumlas
Production manager: Tim Mitchell
Typesetting: Contentra Technologies

Print ISBN: 978-1-78320-937-8
ePDF ISBN: 978-1-78320-939-2
ePUB ISBN: 978-1-78320-938-5

This is a peer-reviewed publication.

Contents

Acknowledgments   xv
Abstract   ix
List of Musical Examples   xi

Chapter 1:   Introduction   1
             Antônio Carlos Jobim: Introduction and Background   3
             The Perception of Jobim: Reviews, Impressions, Quotations, Influences 3
             Discussion of Sources   15

Chapter 2:   Influences   21
             Historical Background and Development   23
             The Birth of Bossa Nova   24
             Instrumental Pieces and Film Music   26
             Rhythmic Influences: *Samba, Maracatu, Baião, Frevo*   27
             Folk and Popular Music Influences: *Modinha, Choro*   33
             Western Art-Music Influences: Villa-Lobos, Chopin,   39
                 Debussy, Ravel, Stravinsky, Gnattali, Gershwin
             Jobim's Aesthetics and Philosophy   47

Chapter 3:   Harmonic Language   53
             Introduction   55
             Harmonic Techniques: 'Chega de saudade'   56
             Melodic Sequence with Non-Sequential Altered Harmonies   57
             Major-Minor Mode Changes   61
             Descending Linear Chromatic Harmonic Relationships   65
             Contextual Use of Extended Harmony   70
             Parallel Harmonic Progression   77
             Tonal Ambiguities   79
             Guitar-based Sonorities   79
             Chords for Harmonic Effect   82

Bitonal Influences and Chordal Superimposition 84
Comparison of Whole Works and Parts of Jobim's Works: *Saudade do Brasil* 90
Bird Calls 94
Female Choir as an Orchestral Instrument 95
Arquitetura de morar 97
Conclusion 100

Chapter 4: **Rhythmic Techniques** **107**
Samba 109
Clave Rhythmic Patterns 112
Polyrhythmic Techniques 115
Rhythmic Accent 116
Hypermetre 117
Pedal Tones 122
Melodic Timing 124
Conclusion 129

Chapter 5: **Thematicism and Structural Design** **131**
Self-Referential Attributes of Bossa Nova 133
Juxtaposition of Static and Shifting Musical Material 135
Motivic Design Restrictions 138
'Insensatez' 141
Descending Minor Second Motive 148
Musical Inter-dependence and Understatement 150
Transposed Motive Repetition 150
'Águas de março' (Waters of March) 152
Melodic Tributes 166
Melodic Contour 168
Whole-Tone Scales 170
Choro Structural Form 171
'Dindi' 172
Alternative Melody 174
Conclusion 177

Chapter 6: **Conclusion** **183**
Bibliography **193**

Acknowledgements

I wish to acknowledge my appreciation of the meticulous critical feedback and support that my colleagues Dr Simon Perry and Professor Philip Bračanin provided during the course of my studies on stylistic diversity in the music of Antônio Carlos Jobim. I am also very grateful to Luiz Roberto Oliveira who sent me the *Tom Jobim Songbooks*, the CD *Urubu* and much encouragement and information from Brazil. Luiz's launch of the outstanding *Clube do Tom* website coincided with the start of my research, and I am indebted to him for the many valuable research paths that I explored that were revealed by his comments to me and his web postings. The support and help of my colleague, Nathan Warfe has also been entirely welcome. Nathan's interest, knowledge and enthusiasm for Brazilian music and the Portuguese language has been infinitely reassuring.

In Rio de Janeiro in February 2015 Paulo Jobim (Antônio Carlos Jobim's son) was very accommodating and encouraging towards my publishing endeavours. I remember with fondness our walk in the Jardim Botanico and his kind guidance particularly in relation to the musical presentations in this book. Antônio Carlos Jobim's grandson, Daniel Jobim, has also been very supportive and constructive, a wonderful source of information and recollections of life with his grandfather. Daniel's international performances and upholding of the bossa nova tradition are uncannily reflective of the original gift of music handed down to him. In Ipanema, Carlos Alberto Afonso at the centre for bossa nova, *Toca de Vinicius*, has also been a fount of knowledge and encouragement. I owe Carlos so much for his enthusiasm and dedication in promoting Antônio Carlos Jobim's music. He is a treasure.

My musician friends among the Brazilian community in Brisbane, interstate and overseas particularly Mauricio Hosi, Eddie Gazani, Mike Bevan, Heloise McMillan, Doug de Vries, Yamandu Costa, Anna Paes, Adriano Giffoni and André Gonçalves have been very encouraging, as has Eliane Costa in editing my Portuguese. My 'companheira de viagem', Kay Sullivan, who accompanied me to Brazil in 2013 and 2015, has been an enchanted godsend. Her embracement of Brazilian music has been a most welcome tonic and a catalyst to not only further musicological exploration but also to the discoveries and joys of playing together.

Finally, and most importantly, my wife Julie provided exceptional strength in her support of my undertaking of this book. Living with my pre-occupation for such an extended time required her to make considerable sacrifices, which she accepted without complaint. Instead her positive suggestions, encouragement and wise counsel often helped to overcome some of the more awkward aspects of my writing and helped me to look at things more objectively. Her dedication to my endeavours reached even to the extent of her learning introductory Portuguese. This in turn gave me the confidence and support to undertake what initially seemed like a formidable research task – that of persisting with the interpretation of many Portuguese sources. I now know it was worth the effort. Her passing in 2012 makes her support of my work even more poignant and meaningful.

Abstract

Antônio Carlos Jobim has been called the greatest of all the contemporary Brazilian songwriters. He wrote both popular and serious music and was a gifted piano, guitar and flute player. His songs have made a lasting impression worldwide to the extent that many are now standards of the popular music repertoire. Jobim was also attracted to languages – not only did he write the lyrics to many of his songs in his native Brazilian/Portuguese, but he showed a command and love of English, particularly its musical Anglo-Saxon sounds.

Jobim's profound melodic and lyrical sensibility was enhanced and complemented by his inventive and peculiar harmonic idiom. This idiom, not the norm in either popular music or jazz, is characterized by dissonant and highly coloured chords that sound entirely natural and fit effortlessly into a personalized musical context.

'Tom' Jobim, as he was called by his friends, was trained in classical music and was well acquainted with the works of Bach, Beethoven, Chopin, Debussy, Ravel, Stravinsky and the techniques of the twentieth-century serialist composers. His most important musical influence, however, was Heitor Villa-Lobos, whose works combined influences from classical, native Indian, folk and popular Brazilian styles. In the early 1960s, Jobim became the most important identity in the creation of the new, internationally recognized, popular music style called 'bossa nova'. As well as this, Jobim's musical works reveal a wide range of stylistic influences: from classical piano and French impressionism, samba rhythms from Rio de Janeiro and Bahia, American Tin Pan Alley songs, to popular Brazilian music composers such as Pixinguinha, Ary Barroso and Dorival Caymmi.

His success as a popular music composer is so well recognized that many of his songs form the heart of the 'Latin' jazz music repertoire and have been recorded by such celebrities as Frank Sinatra, Miles Davis, Ella Fitzgerald, Stan Getz, Sarah Vaughan, Sting and Diana Krall. Jobim also composed larger-scale orchestral works such as *Sinfonia do Rio de Janeiro* (1954), and *Brasilia: Sinfonia da Alvorada* (1960), as well as film scores and other orchestral pieces, such as the tone poem *Saudade do Brasil* (1975).

This book examines a selection of Jobim's most important songs and instrumental pieces and attempts to elucidate not only the many musical influences that formed his musical output, but also the stylistic peculiarities that were as much the product of a gifted composer as of the rich musical environment and heritage that were so much a part of his life.

List of Musical Examples

Chapter 1: Introduction

Ex. 1.1.   System of registral designations.   16

Chapter 2: Influences

Ex. 2.1.   Basic rhythmic cell of many Brazilian melodies of African origin.   31

Chapter 3: Harmonic Language

Ex. 3.1.   Antônio Carlos Jobim, 'Chega de saudade', introduction, measures 1–8.   57
Ex. 3.2.   Antônio Carlos Jobim, 'Chega de saudade', main theme (upper voice),   58
            measures 9–16.
Ex. 3.3.   Antônio Carlos Jobim, 'Não devo sonhar', measures 5–12.   58
Ex. 3.4.   Antônio Carlos Jobim, 'Engano', measures 1–16.   60
Ex. 3.5.   Pixinguinha, 'Ainda me recordo' (*choro*), opening measures.   60
Ex. 3.6.   José Maria de Albreu, 'Tomando sereno' (*choro*), opening measures.   61
Ex. 3.7.   Heitor Villa-Lobos, *Choros No. 1*, measures 1–8.   61
Ex. 3.8.   Antônio Carlos Jobim, 'Chega de saudade', measures 17–24.   62
Ex. 3.9.   José Maria de Abreu, 'Aguenta o leme' (*choro*), measures 1–16.   62
Ex. 3.10.   Antônio Carlos Jobim, 'Oficina', measures 13–24.   63
Ex. 3.11a. Antônio Carlos Jobim, 'Discussão', measures 13–21.   64
Ex. 3.11b. Antônio Carlos Jobim, 'Chega de saudade', measures 30–39.   64
Ex. 3.12.   Antônio Carlos Jobim, 'Chega de saudade', measures 79–83.   66
Ex. 3.13.   Antônio Carlos Jobim, 'Samba de uma nota só', measures 6–13.   66
Ex. 3.14.   Antônio Carlos Jobim, 'Corcovado', measures 13–28.   67
Ex. 3.15.   Antônio Carlos Jobim, 'Diálogo', measures 5–12.   68
Ex. 3.16.   Antônio Carlos Jobim, 'Diálogo', measures 13–20.   68
Ex. 3.17.   Claude Debussy, 'Jardins sous la pluie' (Gardens in the rain),   69
            measures 90–95.
Ex. 3.18.   Antônio Carlos Jobim, 'Eu te amo', measures 9–18.   70

Ex. 3.19. Maurice Ravel, 'Jeux d'eau', introduction, measures 1 and 2.   71
Ex. 3.20. Frédéric Chopin, *Nocturne, Op. 15 No. 1*, measures 29–31.   72
Ex. 3.21. Frédéric Chopin, *Nocturne, Op. 27 No. 1*, measures 64–65.   72
Ex. 3.22. Claude Debussy, 'Pour les Sonorités Opposées' from *Douze*   73
    Études, last eight measures.
Ex. 3.23. Antônio Carlos Jobim, 'Passarim', final measures.   74
Ex. 3.24. Antônio Carlos Jobim, 'Surfboard', measures 17–32.   74
Ex. 3.25. Antônio Carlos Jobim, 'Surfboard', measures 49–52, second repeat.   75
Ex. 3.26. Antônio Carlos Jobim, 'Sabiá', opening measures (piano reduction).   76
Ex. 3.27. Claude Debussy, 'Hommage à Rameau', measures 65–70.   77
Ex. 3.28. Maurice Ravel, 'Pavane pour une infante défunte', measures 24–27.   78
Ex. 3.29. Antônio Carlos Jobim, 'Você vai ver', measures 21–24.   78
Ex. 3.30. Antônio Carlos Jobim, 'O morro não tem vez', measures 23 and 24.   78
Ex. 3.31. Antônio Carlos Jobim, 'Chora coração', measures 36–40.   79
Ex. 3.32. Heitor Villa-Lobos, *Choros No. 5*, measures 29–32.   80
Ex. 3.33. Antônio Carlos Jobim, 'Insensatez', final measures.   80
Ex. 3.34. Antônio Carlos Jobim, 'Se todos fossem iguais a você'.   81
Ex. 3.35. Heitor Villa-Lobos, *Etude No.4*, measures 1–4.   82
Ex. 3.36. Heitor Villa-Lobos, *Choros No. 8*, final chord.   82
Ex. 3.37. Heitor Villa-Lobos, *Bendita Sabedoria, No. 2*, Andante, measures 45–46.   83
Ex. 3.38. Antônio Carlos Jobim, complex chord structures in the final   83
    cadences of three songs: 'Bebel', 'Bangzalia' and 'Trem de ferro'.
Ex. 3.39. Darius Milhaud, inversions built on (the first eight notes of) a chromatic   84
    scale of the chord consisting of three major triads (C, D♭ and D major).
Ex. 3.40. Antônio Carlos Jobim, *Arquitetura de Morar*, measures 74–78,   84
    including his superimposed chordal designations (nomenclature)
    above the staff.
Ex. 3.41a. Antônio Carlos Jobim, 'Trem para Cordisburgo', measures 24–27,   85
    including Jobim's designation of his superimposed chordal voicings.
Ex. 3.41b. Antônio Carlos Jobim, 'Borzeguim', final measures.   86
Ex. 3.42. Darius Milhaud, 'Ipanema', *Saudades do Brasil*, vol. 1, no. 5, final chord,   86
    measures 84–85.
Ex. 3.43. Antônio Carlos Jobim, 'A correnteza', measures 3–6.   86
Ex. 3.44. Antônio Carlos Jobim, 'Falando de amor', measures 10–11.   87
Ex. 3.45. Maurice Ravel, *Sonatine*, third movement, measures 60–63.   88
Ex. 3.46. Antônio Carlos Jobim, 'Noites do Rio', measures 181–85.   88
Ex. 3.47. Comparison of harmony and melody between Satie's 'Je te veux'   89
    and Jobim's 'Imagina'.
Ex. 3.48a. Antônio Carlos Jobim, *Saudade do Brasil*, main theme.   91
Ex. 3.48b. Antônio Carlos Jobim, *Saudade do Brasil*, secondary theme.   91
Ex. 3.48c. Antônio Carlos Jobim, *Saudade do Brasil*, introduction.   92

Ex. 3.48d. Antônio Carlos Jobim, *Saudade do Brasil*, measures 16–33.   93

Ex. 3.48e. Antônio Carlos Jobim, *Saudade do Brasil*, measures 42–43.   93

Ex. 3.48f. Antônio Carlos Jobim, *Saudade do Brasil*, measures 54–57.   94

Ex. 3.48g. Antônio Carlos Jobim, *Saudade do Brasil*, measures 106–12.   94

Ex. 3.49.   Maurice Ravel, *Oiseaux Tristes*, measures 13–14.   95

Ex. 3.50.   Heitor Villa-Lobos, *Bachianas Brasileiras No. 5* (first movement),   96
            measures 14–19, soprano melody.

Ex. 3.51.   Antônio Carlos Jobim, 'Canta, canta mais', measures 67–74,   96
            female vocal melody.

Ex. 3.52.   Antônio Carlos Jobim, *Arquitetura de morar*, measures 19–30.   97

Ex. 3.53.   Claude Debussy, *Les sons et les parfums tournent dans l'air du soir*,   98
            measures 8–10.

Ex. 3.54.   Claude Debussy, *Feuilles Mortes*, measures 11–15.   98

Ex. 3.55.   Antônio Carlos Jobim, *Arquitetura de morar*, measures 88–99.   99

Chapter 4: Rhythmic Techniques

Ex. 4.1.   Typical samba rhythm as played by G.R.E.S. Unidos do Porto da Pedra.   110

Ex. 4.2.   Classical samba rhythms.   110

Ex. 4.3.   Antônio Carlos Jobim, 'Matita Perê', measures 92–95.   110

Ex. 4.4.   Antônio Carlos Jobim, 'Samba do avião', measures 41–44.   111

Ex. 4.5.   Typical samba and bossa nova bass accompaniment.   111

Ex. 4.6.   Classical samba rhythm.   111

Ex. 4.7.   Antônio Carlos Jobim, 'Samba de uma nota só', measures 1–13.   112

Ex. 4.8.   Bossa nova clave rhythm and its retrograde.   113

Ex. 4.9.   Antônio Carlos Jobim, 'Insensatez' introduction, guitar accompaniment   113
            showing a typical bossa nova 'clave' rhythmic figure.

Ex. 4.10.   Bossa nova rhythmic formulae.   114

Ex. 4.11.   Clave rhythm from Jobim's 'Samba de uma nota só' and   114
            'Garota de Ipanema'.

Ex. 4.12.   Clave rhythm from Jobim's 'Vivo sonhando', *A Arte de Tom Jobim*.   114

Ex. 4.13.   Antônio Carlos Jobim, 'Meninos eu vi', introduction, measures 8–11.   115

Ex. 4.14.   Heitor Villa-Lobos, 'Abril', introduction showing two-measure   116
            polyrhythmic guitar figure with unevenly accented percussion
            accompaniment.

Ex. 4.15.   Heitor Villa-Lobos, *Choros No. 5*, measures 3–8.   116

Ex. 4.16.   Antônio Carlos Jobim, 'Chega de saudade', introduction measures 1–4.   117

Ex. 4.17.   Igor Stravinsky, *Petrouchka*, first movement, measures 81–85.   118

Ex. 4.18.   Antônio Carlos Jobim, 'Surfboard', opening measures.   119

Ex. 4.19.   Antônio Carlos Jobim, 'Vivo sonhando', introduction.   120

Ex. 4.20. Claude Debussy, 'Passepied', measures 24–29.   120

Ex. 4.21. Antônio Carlos Jobim, 'Remember', measures 23–34.   121

Ex. 4.22. Antônio Carlos Jobim, 'Deus e o diablo na terra do sol', measures 24–27.   121

Ex. 4.23. Antônio Carlos Jobim, 'Trem de Ferro', measures 40–42.   122

Ex. 4.24. Heitor Villa-Lobos, *Suite Populaire Bresilienne No. 5*, 'Chorinho',   122
measures 31–40.

Ex. 4.25. Heitor Villa-Lobos, *Étude No. 10*, measures 57–63.   123

Ex. 4.26. Antônio Carlos Jobim, 'Surfboard', measures 1–4.   123

Ex. 4.27. Antônio Carlos Jobim, 'Pois é', measures 15–23.   124

Ex. 4.28. Claude Debussy, 'La soirée dans Grenade', measures 38–52.   125

Ex. 4.29. Antônio Carlos Jobim, 'Pato preto', measures 54–66.   126

Ex. 4.30. Antônio Carlos Jobim, 'Two kites', measures 213–36.   127

Ex. 4.31. Antônio Carlos Jobim, 'Triste', measures 17–19, *Tom Jobim Songbook*.   127

Ex. 4.32. Antônio Carlos Jobim, 'Triste', measures 17–19, *Cancioneiro Jobim*.   127

Ex. 4.33. Antônio Carlos Jobim 'Este seu olhar', *Tom Jobim Songbook*.   128

Chapter 5: Thematicism and Structural Design

Ex. 5.1. Antônio Carlos Jobim, 'Samba de uma nota só' first verse lyric,   133
with Portuguese lyric by Newton Mendonça and English lyric by Jobim.

Ex. 5.2. Antônio Carlos Jobim, 'Vivo sonhando', measures 9–16.   134

Ex. 5.3. Antônio Carlos Jobim, 'Soneto de separação', measures 1–12.   135

Ex. 5.4. Antônio Carlos Jobim, 'Bonita', measures 9–23.   136

Ex. 5.5. Heitor Villa-Lobos, *Prelude No. 1*.   136

Ex. 5.6. Heitor Villa-Lobos, *Gavota-Choro*, measures 24–28.   137

Ex. 5.7. Claude Debussy, *La Cathedral Engloutie*.   137

Ex. 5.8. Antônio Carlos Jobim, 'Se todos fossem iguais a você', measures 41–48.   138

Ex. 5.9. Antônio Carlos Jobim, 'Retrato em branco e preto', measures 1–8.   139

Ex. 5.10. Frédéric Chopin, *Étude Op. 10 No. 6*, opening measures 1–6.   139

Ex. 5.11. Frédéric Chopin, *Op. 34 No. 3*, measures 8–17.   140

Ex. 5.12. Antônio Carlos Jobim, 'Tempo do mar', measures 8–15.   142

Ex. 5.13. Frédéric Chopin, *Prelude in E minor, Op. 28 No. 4*.   143

Ex. 5.14. Antônio Carlos Jobim, 'Insensatez'.   144

Ex. 5.15. Antônio Carlos Jobim, 'Insensatez', measures 1–11, melody   145
and guitar accompaniment.

Ex. 5.16. Frédéric Chopin, *Prelude in E minor, Op. 28 No. 4*, right-hand (melodic line). 146

Ex. 5.17. Antônio Carlos Jobim, 'Insensatez', melody.   146

Ex. 5.18. Frédéric Chopin, *Prelude in E minor, Op. 28 No. 4*, measures 1–11, reduction. 147

Ex. 5.19. Heitor Villa-Lobos, *Choros No. 5*, measures 3–8.   149

Ex. 5.20. Antônio Carlos Jobim, 'Falando de amor', measures 11–19.   149

Ex. 5.21. Heitor Villa-Lobos, *Hommage á Chopin*, measures 1–8. 151
Ex. 5.22. Antônio Carlos Jobim, 'Eu te amo', measures 9–18. 152
Ex. 5.23. Antônio Carlos Jobim, 'Dinheiro em penca', measures 168–73. 152
Ex. 5.24. Antônio Carlos Jobim, 'Águas de março' (Waters of March), 157
           Portuguese and English lyrics. Text translation from Jobim,
           Cancioneiro Jobim: Obras Escolhidas, 1971–1982, 330.
Ex. 5.25. Antônio Carlos Jobim, 'Águas de março', the set of constituent melodic phrases. 158
Ex. 5.26. Antônio Carlos Jobim, 'Águas de março', opening sequence of melodic 159
           phrases (Portuguese version).
Ex. 5.27. Antônio Carlos Jobim, 'Águas de março', measures 40–43. 160
Ex. 5.28. Antônio Carlos Jobim, 'Águas de março', overall sequence of melodic phrases. 160
Ex. 5.29. Antônio Carlos Jobim, 'Águas de março', chord sequences comprising 161
           four-measure, structural harmonic blocks.
Ex. 5.30. Antônio Carlos Jobim, 'Águas de março', the sequence of four-measure, 162
           structural harmonic blocks throughout the complete song.
Ex. 5.31. Antônio Carlos Jobim, 'Águas de março', measures 12–13. 163
Ex. 5.32. Antônio Carlos Jobim, 'Águas de março', Cmajor7 guitar chord voicing. 163
Ex. 5.33. Antônio Carlos Jobim, 'Águas de março', final measures 111–24. 164
Ex. 5.34. Antônio Carlos Jobim, 'Águas de março', measures 5–11. 164
Ex. 5.35. Antônio Carlos Jobim, 'Águas de março', harmonic reduction final measures. 164
Ex. 5.36. Claude Debussy, 'Rêverie', measures 3–5. 166
Ex. 5.37. Antônio Carlos Jobim, 'Chovendo na roseira', measures 23–28. 166
Ex. 5.38. Heitor Villa-Lobos, 'Abril', measures 5–12. 167
Ex. 5.39. Antônio Carlos Jobim, 'Chovendo na roseira', measures 23–34. 168
Ex. 5.40. Heitor Villa-Lobos, 'Abril', three-measure phrase played on the guitar. 168
Ex. 5.41. Antônio Carlos Jobim, 'Quebra pedra (Stone Flower)', measures 87–90, 168
           three-measure phrase played on flute.
Ex. 5.42. Antônio Carlos Jobim, 'Modinha', measures 5–12. 169
Ex. 5.43. Antônio Carlos Jobim, 'Wave', measures 1–17. 170
Ex. 5.44. Antônio Carlos Jobim, 'As praias desertas' (Deserted beaches), 170
           introduction, measures 1–5.
Ex. 5.45. Antônio Carlos Jobim, 'Choro' (Garoto). 171
Ex. 5.46. Antônio Carlos Jobim, 'Meu Amigo Radamés', measures 1–10. 172
Ex. 5.47. Antônio Carlos Jobim, 'Dindi', opening measures 1–4. 173
Ex. 5.48. Claude Debussy, 'Les collines d'Anacapri', measures 62–65. 173
Ex. 5.49. Antônio Carlos Jobim, 'Dindi', alternative conclusions to the song, 175
           from *Tom Jobim Songbook 3* and *Cancioneiro Jobim*.
Ex. 5.50. Antônio Carlos Jobim, 'Retrato em branco e preto', normal melody 176
           (upper staff) and alternative melody (middle staff).

Chapter 1

Introduction

Antônio Carlos Jobim: Introduction and Background

Antônio Carlos Jobim came to prominence at a pivotal point in Brazilian cultural history. In 1959, Heitor Villa-Lobos, Brazil's most internationally recognized composer, died, bringing to an end a significant era of Brazilian nationalism in art music. Three years earlier, the reformist Kubitschek government had come to power with its optimistic mandate of '50 years in 5', promising rapid industrial expansion and capitalist modernization. A new capital, Brasília, was planned, international companies invested heavily in the country's infrastructure and the results were soon seen in full employment, political support for the arts, architecture, interior and fashion design, technology and the media. Under Kubitschek's leadership there was a national sense of well-being and positive self-assertion. It was in this confident social environment that bossa nova developed as a new musical expression of Brazilian identity.[1]

A key aspect of this new musical expression was the struggle for legitimacy in creating 'true and high-quality' Brazilian music.[2] The author and musicologist, Martha Tupinambá de Ulhôa, referred to this struggle as a search for *verdadeira música brasileira* (Brazilian musical truth) and *música de qualidade* (music of quality), and stated that this search was embodied in Brazilian popular music of the latter half of the twentieth century.[3] The products of this pursuit for quality and truth were found most notably in the music of Antônio Carlos Jobim.[4] Ulhôa identifies these qualities as the possession of a 'proper' social circle and active relationships within it, a disposition for conquering and maintaining a leadership position, a capital of intelligence and a richness in cultural understanding. Ulhôa also identifies a familiarity with the standards of art music, such as linguistic 'innovation', literary lyrics and a distanced attitude in relation to commercial ends. With this background, Jobim's work was able to be widely acknowledged and respected throughout his life in the realm of both popular and art music.

The Perception of Jobim: Reviews, Impressions, Quotations, Influences

Jobim's death in December 1994 initiated a number of biographical publications, tribute recordings and scholarly articles on his life and musical achievements. In a comprehensive article, Reily refers to Jobim as 'one of the most talented musicians Brazil ever produced' and to the bossa nova movement, of which Jobim was an acknowledged leader, as having 'reformulat[ed] the language of Brazilian popular music'. Acknowledging that Jobim was not alone in the creation of a distinctive musical style, Reily maintained that 'just as bossa nova was the product of an era, it was also the product of the genius of those involved in its creation'.[5] Later publications included references to Jobim's 'rich harmonic progressions' and identified the *bolero* and *samba canção* influences in bossa nova as belonging to the 'sophisticated segment of Brazilian popular music'.[6] Even as early as the 1960s, the critic Robert Farris had made an often repeated comparison between Gershwin and Jobim, claiming that '[Jobim's] creations are among the most enchanting and most melodic of our times'.[7] Frank Sinatra had also said: 'The work I did with Tom Jobim gave me the most personal and professional satisfaction of my career. He was a genius who made anyone who worked with him feel good'.[8] Perhaps one of the most concise appraisals of Jobim and his music was given by Béhague, who wrote:

> During the last 25 years of his life the worldwide recognition of his talents was unprecedented for a Brazilian popular musician: his music was recorded in the best studios of New York and Los Angeles and released on the largest multinational labels. He toured with his Banda Nova in several continents, received several further Grammy awards and was awarded many honours, including honorary doctorates from Brazilian and Portuguese Universities. [...] His output, which numbers some 250 titles, reveals his talents as a profoundly creative composer whose innovative and inspiring melodies, harmonies and rhythms and inventive orchestration always expressed his passionate love for his native city and its people with simplicity and honest emotion.[9]

The composer/arranger Clare Fischer highlighted Chopin's influence in Jobim's music, stating in a video interview in 1993, that,

> Tom is very influenced by Chopin. He has that lyrical quality which Chopin had. I don't know if he's aware of it or not, but it is definitely there. Now nobody is saying that somebody is copying, because [...] see, music is like everything else. Nothing comes from nothing. Something always comes from something. We are all influenced by different people and we do different things with it.[10]

In his later years Jobim received many accolades and awards for his music and worked with some of the world's best orchestras. He had worked with the New York Symphony Orchestra in 1975 for his album *Urubu*, which included mainly orchestral works. After the last recording session for the tone poem *Saudade do Brasil*, he was awarded a standing ovation by the members of the orchestra.[11] In 1984, Jobim and his ensemble *Banda Nova* began a tour of Europe, beginning in Vienna's Konzerthause performing with the Austrian Radio (ORF) Sinfonietta. The group followed this initial success with performances in other European venues, including Rome's Teatro Olimpico.[12] Carnegie Hall was also the venue for five of his concerts. He performed there for the first bossa nova celebration concert in 1962, then again in 1985 with the Banda Nova, and subsequently in 1989, 1992 and in 1994.[13] The critic George W. Goodman of the *New York Times* wrote, amongst other things, of 'the appearance and influence of bossa nova as part of American popular music'.[14]

On the few occasions that Jobim's orchestral music was performed in public during his lifetime, it was generally well-received. The performance of *Sinfonia da Alvorada* during the National Commemoration of Independence week in September 1985 in the Praça dos Três Poderes in Brasília was enthusiastically received, in marked contrast to other planned events.[15] Jobim was pleased and honoured to have two of his former teachers perform – Radamés Gnattali, playing piano, and Alceu Bocchino, as conductor of the choir and the Orquestra Sinfônica de Brasília. The official acceptance of the *Sinfonia da Alvorada* was reflected in Jobim being granted the title of Grand Commandeur des Arts et des Lettres by the French Minister of Culture, Jacques Lang, while he was in Brasília.[16]

Hodel's description of Jobim's Carnegie Hall concert in 1985 concluded that Jobim's music 'goes far beyond the standard harmonic formulae and pasted-on melodies that make up much popular romantic music'.[17] He added that Jobim's songs 'are so well-structured that most of them would be appealing if arranged for piano solo or for any combination even up to a large chamber orchestra', and affirmed that, 'It was a delight to hear Antônio Carlos Jobim put sensuous flesh on the bones of songs we only get to hear these days in the muzak of banks and dentist's offices'.[18] In a review of Jobim's concert at New York's Avery Fischer Hall in 1987, Stephen Holden hinted at Jobim's eclecticism:

Much as Ray Charles crystallised American pop-soul by fusing gospel, blues and pop in the early 1960s, Mr Jobim's bossa nova wedded Brazilian samba and soft-edged European pop with classical and jazz influences ranging from Chopin to Debussy to Miles Davis in his cool jazz phase. The fusion resulted in a pop style that remains unmatched in its delicate sensuality, especially when the music is interpreted in the caressingly guttural intonation of the Portuguese language and played on the guitar.[19]

In the last decade of his life, Jobim received many awards in recognition of his work. These include the Medalha do Mérito Alvorada in Brasília, the EMI Major Performer and Composer Trophy, the Honors Diploma of the Inter-American Music Council, the title of Rector of the Universidade de Música de São Paulo and honorary doctoral degrees awarded by the Universidade do Estado do Rio de Janeiro (UERJ) and the Universidade de Lisboa, and the Medalha Pedro Ernesto, given by the Rio de Janeiro State Legislature. He was also named as a member of the National Academy of Popular Music's Hall of Fame, alongside Cole Porter, the Gershwin brothers, Irving Berlin and Michel Legrand.[20]

In the light of the endemic poverty and lack of opportunity for millions of Brazilians, it is surprising that the reception of Jobim's sophisticated music throughout Brazil has generally been positive, especially considering a predictable envy and occasional resentment of his educated, middle-class background. The most profound manifestation of this acceptance came from a *favela* (slum) in Rio de Janeiro, home to one of the most traditional and beloved samba schools, G.R.E.S. (Grêmio Recreativo Escola de Samba) Estacão Primeira de Mangueira. In 1991 the school chose Jobim as the theme for the following year's carnival parade. Prior to the carnival, several CD recordings were made featuring the Mangueira percussionists and 30 major names in Brazilian popular music. Later, 'in the parade Jobim appeared on the tallest of Mangueira's floats, wearing a white suit, beside his piano, waving his panama hat at the audience of 100,000 people. "I felt as though I had been awarded the Nobel Prize for peace", he confessed, still moved by the ovation the crowd had given him, after the parade had come to an end'.[21] The significance of this accolade was not only that it was a manifestation of the recognition of Jobim's music by the mulatto and lower socio-economic classes of Rio de Janeiro, but that the urban middle class had also responded to an indigenous element in Jobim's music – samba.

Another observation of the extent of Jobim's approval in Brazil was given by Martha de Ulhôa Carvalho. In her research into style and emotion in Brazilian popular song she made the observation that, 'The Brazilians that I interviewed are very critical of the "quality" of performance. When asked why they keep buying records by Tom Jobim, who has been singing "poorly" of late, they say that his melodies are so beautiful that it does not matter if his performance is bad'.[22]

Not all Jobim's music, however, was well-received. Stroud recounts the controversy that overshadowed the third *Festival Internacional da Canção* (International Song Festival) of 1968. The event was held at the Maracanãzinho Stadium in Rio de Janeiro with a capacity crowd for the occasion. After all the individual performances had taken place, the consensus of the audience was that the winning song should be Geraldo Vandre's leftist protest song 'Pra não dizer que não falei de flores' (Not to say I didn't mention the flowers). The festival ended in uproar as the winner of the national section, after covert governmental pressure, was judged to be Tom Jobim and Chico Buarque's 'Sabia', despite continued noisy audience support for Geraldo Vandre's rendition of his own song.[23] After the tumult of booing that lasted 23 minutes, the jury had to flee from the venue under police protection. Commenting on the outcome, Jobim later stated that he had never wanted to win the competition at all, but had merely entered the competition to avoid being on the judging panel. 'I refuse to judge my peers' he said.[24] Ironically, the lyrics of 'Sabia' allude to the issue of exile, a topical subject in the light of the fact that the military dictatorship had forced many Brazilians into exile during its preceding four years in power.

Béhague also takes an ambivalent attitude towards Jobim and bossa nova by referring to debates that arose immediately after the height of bossa nova's success. Encapsulating these debates was the influential publication by Brazilian critic José Ramos Tinhorão who wrote a particularly controversial article in 1966.[25] This much-quoted work polarized critical opinion about the extent of American influence in Brazilian music and bossa nova in particular. In extending this argument Béhague cites Tinhorão, who had previously highlighted 'foreign influences coming from North American jazz and "internationalized" pop music' as the reason for many of the controversies surrounding bossa nova.[26] Béhague continues:

Debates grew from questions involving the alleged disruption of the traditional samba or the lack of authenticity of the new samba style because of 'Yankee Imperialist' domination of Brazilian composers and performers. For many Brazilians, these appeared as mere suppliers of raw material and specialised, musical labor to the big international recording industry, movie music and show business. Some reactionary critics went as far as suggesting that one of the most serious problems confronting bossa nova arose from the basic concern of musicians such as João Gilberto and Antônio Carlos Jobim of attempting to impose a popular cultural product abroad.[27]

Béhague's rhetoric suggests that, in order to appeal to an international audience, Jobim and his fellow musicians would have to renounce their Brazilian stylistic peculiarities and accommodate others, thereby losing their authenticity. As an example of the impact of the economic power of the United States on the course of the bossa nova movement, Béhague also cites the 'Americanisation of *Sergio Mendes and Brasil 66*' and the 'unfortunate combination of A. Carlos Jobim and Frank Sinatra'.[28]

Realizing that the circumstances that led to this critique were not without precedent, Dário Borim nevertheless sees the very existence of bossa nova's critics as the inevitable result of its continued success, not only in Brazil but also worldwide. Their voices, he maintains, keep alive the tradition of denunciation of anything that is not authentic. Borim maintains that, 'for the dramatist, all the bossa nova musicians do is to corrupt and vulgarise the popular music of Brazil under the pretense of renovating it'.[29] According to Borim, not only do the critics denigrate the style but they have also mistakenly heralded the imminent demise of this 'refined' and 'subtle' music for some time, without any evidence for this assumption becoming apparent. Borim also identifies another bossa nova critic and opponent, Ariano Suassuna, a columnist for *Folha de São Paulo*, who is seen as blindly espousing Tinhorão's exacerbated nationalist views on foreign influence in bossa nova. Borim surmises that any criticism of Jobim and bossa nova would be welcomed as a reinforcement of Suassuna's stance. 'The critic would only need to call Jobim a detestable quack of the popular baton in order to deserve Suassuna's eulogy a little further'.[30]

Another side to the cultural-alienation argument espoused by Tinhorão, Béhague and Suassuna, particularly in relation to the influence of American jazz, is expressed by Perrone. He asserts that bossa nova cannot be simplified as the commonly argued combination of samba and jazz, because of their pronounced stylistic differences, even though Brazilian musicians had undeniably heard American jazz in the 1950s. Instead, Perrone attributes Tinhorão's contention of American musical infiltration to a 'disdain for jazz'.[31] This negative attitude was also evident in an earlier critic, Gilberto Freyre, a passionate promoter of samba as 'a vibrant expression of the real Brazil'.[32] Freyre also detested jazz and expressed anxiety about its influence on Brazilian music. He wrote referring to the influence of jazz in Brazil of the 'detritus that comes to us from the United States and Europe' and referred to jazz and ragtime as 'horrid stuff' and its dances as 'barbarous'.[33]

Perrone and Dunn point out that one of the unfortunate consequences of bossa nova's introduction in America in the early 1960s was its rapid and crass commercialization:

There was no process of gradual assimilation of musical concepts by composers and performers. Instead, the style was exploited for quick turnaround in hastily conceived jazz albums and in thoughtless pop renditions. Even though it was not dance music, promoters tried to make of bossa nova another dance craze, complete with schools and shoe styles. Falsehoods were propagated in such songs as 'Blame it on the Bossa Nova', in the voice of Edie Gormé, and 'Bossa Nova Baby', recorded by Elvis Presley and Tippy and the Clovers. In view of such treatments, the music critic of Saturday Review called industrial bossa nova-ization: 'one of the worst blights of commercialism ever to be inflicted on popular art'.[34]

A significant part of this commercialization and an important determinant of its reception outside Brazil was the adoption of bossa nova (particularly in America in the 1960s) as pleasant, unobtrusive and accessible 'muzak' – that is, background elevator music and lounge music to be played in public spaces such as shopping malls, airport lounges, restaurants and bars. Acknowledging its powerful universal attraction, Lanza refers to 'Antônio Carlos Jobim's Brazilian beat' as having 'just the right amount of ethnic anomaly to render it disturbingly alluring and ambiguous'.[35] Certainly the multiplicity of its musical elements, strong melodies, sophisticated harmonies and complex rhythms made available an unpretentious aural smorgasbord that could divert the ear and one's immediate presence of mind. Bossa nova's attraction was found powerful enough for it to be included in advertisements for Yardley cosmetics and Benson & Hedges cigarettes, for instance, while its influence was felt in numerous recordings that included songs like Burt Bacharach and Hal David's 'The Look of Love', the Beatles' 'The Fool on the Hill' and the songs of Sergio Mendez and Brasil 66.[36]

In recalling bossa nova's early days in the late 1950s and early 1960s, Cabral puts in context the effect of imported American recordings on bossa nova artists. He explains that groups of musicians and composers used to meet in clubs in Copacabana, in shows and in friends' houses, and were socially and culturally different from the bulk of the producers of Brazilian popular music.[37] They belonged to the middle class, were educated and knew about musical techniques.

[…] one of their aims was to make Brazilian popular music as sophisticated as the music they heard on records imported from the US. It certainly was not their intention to slavishly copy whatever came in from outside, but to use resources in our samba that, in their opinion, would improve it greatly. As it was not a movement that had set rules, the bossa nova was the result of individual contribution from each of its members.[38]

Grasse points out that bossa nova's 'sophisticated amalgam of diverse sources reflects, for lack of a better term, "white" cosmopolitanism specific to a *zona sul* upper-class milieu'.[39] He continues by referring to the style's inclusion in the 1959 Marcel Camus' film *Orfeu Negro* (*Black Orpheus*) as not only '[lending,] in its luxurious quietude of modernity, a certain commercial "wholesomeness" and marketability to the film' but also that in doing so 'bossa nova gains cultural currency as a music of "the people", as a national music, a status never truly realized despite its easily recognized "Brazilian-ness".

However, not all artists associated with these early collectives shared the same ideals. The pianist and composer João Donato, long associated with bossa nova through his songs and collaborations, said that he had nothing to do with bossa nova. 'The bossa nova is Tom Jobim, João Gilberto and all my friends, but I don't like it. They want me to be one of the founders, one of the popes, but that's all bullshit. If they ask me what I think of the bossa nova, I say I think it's sickly, it's rather boring. It just goes on and on'.[40]

As well as local anti-bossa nova sentiments, Jobim had to contend with accusations of plagiarism. Cabral identifies Jobim compositions that had been singled out as examples of plagiarism by the music commentator Antônio Maria. Jobim's 'Este seu olhar', (Look to the sky) said Maria, had been copied in essence from the music of the film *The Moon is Blue*. 'Demais' (Too much) was a copy of not only the music but also the words to 'The End of a Love Affair'. 'Dindi' mimicked the start of the song 'Love for Sale', 'Samba de uma nota só' (One note samba) copied the first part of 'Night and Day' and 'Eu sei que vou te amar' (I know that I'm going to love you) was largely inspired by 'Dancing in the Dark'. Cabral reports Maria as defending Jobim, on the one hand, but pointing out that no-one, despite their status, is exempt from temptation:

Não adianta dizer que Tom é excelente pessoa. Eu também acho (bom amigi, pai extremoso, esposo amantíssimo), tanto que, se viesse a ter um novo filho, convidá-lo-ia para padrinho. Mas ótimas pessoas também se influenciam pela música dos outros. Em outros casos, como dá menos trabalho, copiam direto.[41]

(One cannot say [simply] at the outset that Tom [Jobim] is an extraordinary person. One could also include good friend, outstanding father, loving husband, to the extent that if I were to be a father again, I would invite him to be my child's godfather. But extraordinary people are influenced by the music of others. In similar situations, because it is less effort, they have copied directly.)[42]

Accusations of plagiarism and musical similarities aside, Jobim remained unfazed by this and maintained a cordial relationship with Maria. Other commentators have also nominated the same compositions as examples of plagiarism, but, as indicated by Tiso, musical plagiarism is not without precedent. 'They say that Chopin's Prelúde in E minor was plagiarized for "Insensatez", but all great composers do similar things at the start. Villa-Lobos did the same. You can find the same in George Gershwin and Cole Porter'.[43]

Another hindrance to a wider acceptance of Jobim's music is the problem of misleading statements about of the nature of bossa nova and Jobim's role in it. For instance, in *World*

Musics in Context, Fletcher attempts a rather cursory definition of bossa nova by pointing to several of its musical characteristics and its derivation as an offshoot of samba.[44] However, his statement that 'the style was initiated during the late 1960s by Antônio Carlos (Tom) Jobim (composer and pianist), with João Gilberto (guitarist and vocalist), and a group of university students in search of a "cooler" form of samba' is both presumptuous and chronologically inaccurate by at least ten years.[45] Fletcher goes on to state that, 'The laid-back ambience of the style is typified by such enervating tunes as "The Girl from Ipanema"', a song that subsequently sold over 25 million copies, and contends that bossa nova was 'essentially élitist music'. Writing in the *New Grove Dictionary of Jazz*, Flanagan states that 'Jobim acknowledges the songs of Cole Porter and the playing of Gerry Mulligan as decisive influences on his style' but does not acknowledge his sources for this specific contention.[46] In the absence of any other stated influences, these comments seem selective, if not speculative, particularly the ascription of Mulligan's influence, as Jobim actively rejected suggestions that he was influenced by American jazz.

Jazz is often regarded as one of Jobim's major sources of inspiration in the creation of his bossa nova classics. Jobim said, however, that the stimulus for bossa nova came more from local Brazilian styles and classical music than jazz, that jazz had very little influence. In the foreword to the series *Cancioneiro Jobim*, Jobim's son Paulo recalls his father talking about the origins of bossa nova:

Bossa, all right, but not all that Nova (new), really, Tom Jobim used to say. He also vigorously denied any suggestions that the style derived from jazz: 'bossa nova is not jazz samba; it's an old rhythm that has always been around in the samba schools of Rio and Bahia. The pa-tah-pa-tah beat is accurately described in a French book published in the 1940s called *La Musique, des origines à nos jours*'. If it were in fact a purely American music, Jobim argued, Americans wouldn't have taken it up. 'It's Brazilian, and it's deeply influenced by Villa-Lobos'. And also by Custódio Mesquita, Caymmi, Ary Barroso and Vadico, he would later add. The harmony of bossa nova, with its three-note chords, the fourth note being implied or else supplied by the singer's voice, did have foreign antecedents, particularly Debussy and Ravel.[47]

In an interview with Almir Chediak, the publisher responsible for the three-volume *Tom Jobim Songbooks*, Jobim told of his early musical influences, again giving much credit to classical composers:

As for jazz, real jazz, I never had much access. [...] Real jazz here was something for collectors, for rich playboy types. I'm not much of a connoisseur of jazz. Later on, I saw that purists here were saying that bossa nova was a copy of American Jazz. When these people would say bossa nova's harmony was based on jazz, I thought it was funny because this same harmony existed in Debussy. No way was it American. To say a ninth chord is an American invention is absurd. These altered eleventh and thirteenth chords, with all those added notes, you can't say they're an American invention. This kind of thing is as much South American as it is North American. Americans took to bossa nova because they thought it was interesting. If it was a mere copy of jazz, they wouldn't be interested.[48]

The writer and commentator Tárik de Souza also pointed out: '[…] using as a cornerstone the recording by Stan Getz (sax) and Charlie Byrd (guitar) that sold a million copies of "Desafinado" in the early 1960s, Jobim's influence on jazz became proportionately greater than the other way around'.[49] In the documentary film *Bossa Nova*, Henry Mancini expressed his views about bossa nova's attraction to jazz musicians and its timeliness:

> The jazz people came in after bossa nova, not before. A rhythm of that sort is very attractive to play if you're a jazz musician or a singer, because it keeps you afloat, it keeps you like this [demonstrates with his hands] […] you float on it. And that's what Stan Getz saw in it – he saw a nice carpet that would suit him – you know he could roll around on the carpet.[50]

Carlos Lyra, another of the early bossa nova pioneers, protested about what he thought was an inordinate jazz influence on the emerging style by pointedly writing a song entitled 'Influência do jazz' (Influence of jazz). The song 'parodied the excessive intrusion of North American jazz techniques in Brazilian music by exaggerating their presence in the piece itself'.[51]

With this evidence refuting the extent of the influence of jazz, there remains nevertheless considerable doubt about its lack of effect on bossa nova. 'The maestro Lindolfo Gaya, who did the arrangements for many songs at the beginning of the bossa nova also thought that the young composers of the 50s were highly influenced by the harmony and melodic development of the song "Laura" (Johnny Mercer and David Raskin)'.[52] Chediak maintains that, 'There was a clear connection with jazz', but that jazz was not the only influence.[53] Jazz certainly had an influence on such pre-bossa nova popular music composers as Dorival Caymmi and the *choro* guitarist Garoto, who used such jazz elements as four-note, dissonant chords and occasional chromaticism.[54] The level of jazz influence on bossa nova remains contentious. On the one hand there are definite similarities, especially in the use of altered and extended harmonies, and on the other, there are differences in idiomatic harmonic progressions, in the importance placed on improvisation and in the basic rhythmic accompaniment of pitched and purely percussive instruments.

Jobim is remembered principally for his songs, of which he wrote over 250. But he also wrote orchestral works and music for film. In the late 1950s, Jobim co-wrote the music for the film *Black Orpheus* with the guitarist Louis Bonfá and later wrote the soundtracks to the films *Porto das Caixas* and *The Adventurers*. In 1971 he won the *Coruja de Ouro* and the *Instituto Nacional de Cinema* award for the music for the film *A Casa Assassinada*.[55] His subsequent work included music for the films *Gabriela*, *Santo Módico*, *Para Viver um Grande Amor*, and other documentaries and short television productions. It is also indicative of Jobim's international standing that he was invited to write the music for the film *The Pink Panther*, in 1964, and *Two for the Road*, three years later. He refused both commissions because, at that time, he wanted to concentrate on writing Brazilian music (both commissions were subsequently accepted by Henry Mancini). In the 1970s, he was also asked to write the music for *The Exorcist*, but declined for the same reason.[56]

Bossa nova became a worldwide phenomenon in the early 1960s, but the response to Jobim's songs in Brazil was quite different to their reception in the rest of the world. Commercial success was slow to come in Brazil, until the American release of the 1962 *Jazz Samba* album featuring Stan Getz and Charlie Byrd. Although this album gave bossa nova a voice in the United States, by the time of its release, bossa nova had acquired an 'Americanized' flavour and was seen in Brazil, rightly or wrongly, as having been irrevocably dominated by external forces, just as the image of samba had been distorted by the Hollywood film industry in the early 1940s and sold back to Brazil in the stereotypical guise of Carmen Miranda, Donald Duck and a cartoon Brazilian parrot named Zé Carioca.[57] Jobim was well aware of what had happened to his music in the United States and detested the effect of this tactless and insensitive transformation on its reception in Brazil.

Despite Jobim's successes in the popular-music world, there is little critical commentary in English about his orchestral work, as it is virtually unknown outside Brazil. A live recording of some of his orchestral music, entitled *Jobim Sinfônico*, was released in 2003.[58] It was initiated via a research project from the Instituto Antônio Carlos Jobim and featured an orchestra of over 70 musicians and guest artists.[59] Generally, however, Jobim's desire to write more orchestral music remained a dream unfulfilled throughout his life, constantly interrupted by the result of the popular musical revolution that he had brought about. Because of the limited number of performances and recordings, the reception of his orchestral works overall can best be judged indirectly by his continued collaborations with high-profile and respected artists and musicians, his many commissions for film scores and the honours bestowed upon him by cultural, government and academic institutions.

Critical acceptance of Jobim's work is hampered by many things, not the least of which is language. Translations of his song lyrics into English are especially problematic. They remained a source of much aggravation for Jobim, particularly in the early 1960s when his songs started to become famous internationally. 'I learned English in school, and from Westerns, and then these Americans would write these unbelievable lyrics for my songs, all about coffee and bananas and coconuts'.[60] Apart from unsympathetic translations, song lyrics in Portuguese, no matter how poetic, passionate or profound, will have little effect if they cannot be understood by a non-Portuguese-speaking audience. This is one of the most significant reasons for his lack of worldwide recognition and the meagre dissemination of the greater part of his music. Other impediments to the recognition of Jobim's music were the unfortunate but all too common misappropriation of the bossa nova musical genre, lack of exposure outside Brazil (with the exception of his bossa nova classics), an emotional response to his music formed with little cultural connection or subsequent shared support outside Brazil and the lack of a critical framework (in popular music especially) in which to discuss, analyse, contextualize and validate his work.

Brazil presents a difficult problem for sociological and cultural analysis, as the French sociologist Roger Bastide recognized:

> The sociologist who studies Brazil does not know what conceptual system to use. None of the notions taught in Europe and North America are valid here, where old and new mix together and historical epochs become entangled. [...] It would be necessary to discover in place of rigid concepts, ones that are somewhat liquid and able to describe phenomena characterised by fusion, ebullition, and interpenetration – notions modeled on a living reality in perpetual transformation. The sociologist who wants to understand Brazil must often become a poet.[61]

It is clear that Jobim's music means different things to different people and can be interpreted in many different ways. One can develop strong feelings either for or against it. It is diverse and spans both the popular and art-music worlds. It demonstrates Jobim's command of many different musical aspects: melody, rhythm, harmony and orchestration as well as lyrical poetry and language. An important and substantial reason for its success (and for the polarization of views about it) is Jobim's eclecticism. As is true for most composers with a large body of work, Jobim's musical expertise was in a large part due to his assimilation and incorporation of many different musical styles and ideas ranging from classical or art music to folk and popular music.

Many of Jobim's bossa nova songs are well-known worldwide, but despite this, most audiences outside Brazil do not readily associate Jobim's name with his famous compositions. In his native country, however, he is so well-known that the major international airport in Rio de Janeiro bears his name. It is also surprising that very little has been written in English about such a prolific and successful composer. A second intention of this book, therefore, is to help redress the lack of awareness outside Brazil of the scale, importance and diversity of Jobim's work.

One of the fortunate aspects of any study of Jobim's music is that he was musically literate and able to produce scores of his work as well as sound recordings. He certainly wanted his music to be highly valued and accurately documented. In an interview with Almir Chediak, Jobim expressed his gratitude at having his music 'registered accurately with the right musical notation'.[62] Not only did he ensure that his work was comprehensively documented but he also paid very strict attention to harmonic construction and form, considering them integral to the arrangement of many of his songs. Many of his songs (such as 'Luiza' and 'Sabiá') are through-composed or follow a rigorous structure (such as 'Águas de março') and do not contain free improvisatory sections, as do most jazz standards.

In 2001, Jobim Music in Rio de Janeiro published a five-volume set of scores for piano and voice of the complete works of Antônio Carlos Jobim entitled *Cancioneiro Jobim: Obras Completas* with an additional compilation of some of Jobim's more famous compositions presented as a large hard-bound book, *Cancioneiro Jobim: Obras Escolhidas*. These volumes have proved an invaluable resource for most of the examples presented in this book. The scores in *Cancioneiro Jobim* series were compiled by Jobim and his son, Paulo, and furnished much more musical information than the more straightforward notation of the melody with guitar accompaniment as presented in the earlier *Tom Jobim Songbooks*.[63]

As the primary reason for the presentation of examples in this book is for musicological examination, not for performance, the appearance of an entire score for any single piece is avoided. Instead, comments on selected relevant sections are made with reference to their function within the piece as a whole. There are, however, some cases where presentation of a complete score is vital for the appreciation and understanding of the overall structure of the piece as a whole and for contextual continuity.

Although many recordings feature improvised samba accompaniments, Jobim made accurate transcriptions only of his melodies and their harmonic accompaniment. Jobim's son, Paulo, who began to help him write out his scores in the early 1970s, recounts:

We found, for instance, that in the case of 'Chega de saudade' if we attempted to include in the score all the subtleties of the samba beat in the guitar accompaniment for piano, in addition to the melody, it would make the parts almost impossible to read. This led to our decision to simplify the rhythm, assuming that the pianist would intuitively supply the samba beat.[64]

Publications of Jobim's music therefore do not accurately specify samba rhythmic (usually guitar) accompaniment; consequently, it is rarely, if ever, seen in written score form. This highlights one of the major problems in writing for an instrument that requires a certain rhythmic nuance in its performance. Most of Jobim's bossa nova recordings contain contextual rhythmic nuance evident in consistent beat placement either slightly before or slightly after expected beats. While these beat-timing offsets are small in comparison to the interval between beats, they have been shown in similar cases to be quite noticeable, not so much as individual timing discrepancies but as an overall feeling that the music is somehow imbued with life and possesses characteristics which may be interpreted by words such as 'active', 'infectious' or 'laid back'. These small beat-timing offsets have a profound effect on audience perception of a performance. They also represent a major part of the attraction of Jobim's compositions, but are evident only in live performance and recordings, not the written score. It is to Jobim's credit that he understood the subtleties of rhythm and was able to specify enough essential musical information in his scores (conceived within the framework of a conventional western written medium) to enable acceptable realizations of them by musicians who knew how to interpret them idiomatically. The rhythms he embraced were those from the popular music that surrounded him – *maracatu*, *choro*, *baião* and, most importantly, samba. This aspect of his eclecticism is difficult to quantify in traditional musicological terms, but it remains an extremely important aspect of his collective work.

As outlined by Moore, Middleton, Brackett and others, the musicological analysis of popular music is problematic because it must reconcile disparate analytical/interpretive, anthropological and historical approaches to the discipline that require different methodologies and approaches.[65] In a review of Allen Forte's *Listening to Classic American Popular Songs*, Kopplin points out that few authors have attempted musical analysis of popular works, with the possible exception of such academics as Robert Walser, Susan McClary at UCLA, John Covach at the University of North Carolina and David Brackett at Binghamton University.[66] Kopplin also mentions Forte's 1995 publication *The American Popular Ballad of the Golden Era: 1924 to 1950*, which refers to the 'elegant popular ballads' of this era as having 'a special sonic aura that emanates from the individual harmonies and their combinations'.[67] While Forte's adapted nomenclature system appears relatively well-suited for popular music that exists in conventional written form as well as in recorded form (such as Jobim's), problems with nomenclature for extended harmonies proves problematic.[68] For instance, Forte does not designate any chord extension beyond a 9th. In his system an 11th is expressed as a 4th and a 13th as a 6th. He also uses the nomenclature ♭3 to indicate minor rather than the more conventional 'm' or lower case Roman numerals.

It was, therefore, decided that the analytical system to be used in this book would closely follow the more widely used jazz chord nomenclature as presented in well-known publications such as *The Real Book* series. A shortcoming of this nomenclature is that it does not accurately define chord inversion. Thus, in any score reduction bass notes must always be specified in situations where the root of a chord is not in the bass. Generally this problem is overcome in jazz chord notation by indicating the bass note using '/' after the chord description. For example; Am/C, means 'play an appropriate voicing of an A minor chord with the note C in the bass', or 'play an A minor chord in first inversion'.

Jobim used alphabetic harmonic nomenclature for chord changes as one would find written for a popular song chart (i.e. the system that names chords C6/9 or Fm6 or G♭7(#11)) as is evident from his manuscripts and in the *Cancioneiro Jobim* series. This is not to say that specific chord inversions and voicings can be ignored, however. In fact, prior to the publication of the *Cancioneiro Jobim* scores, Jobim went to great pains to accurately specify guitar chord voicings, particularly in the *Tom Jobim Songbooks*, where, for instance, the bass notes for a succession of chords formed part of a chromatic line.

Discussion of Sources

The earliest series of scores of Jobim's music, the *Tom Jobim Songbooks*, were written predominantly for guitar accompaniment.[69] In these songbooks, guitar chords are defined in tablature so that chord voicing is well-defined. In addition to guitar tablature, the songbooks also include jazz chord notations (chord changes) for each notated guitar chord, for example, A7(♭13), Dm6, E♭7(9) etc. The *Cancioneiro Jobim* series presents most of its scores for piano and voice including jazz chord changes. In some instances, piano reductions of orchestral pieces such as *Saudade do Brasil* are too complex to be played on a single instrument. In these cases, some melodic lines and instrumental accompaniment have been printed in grey in addition to the existing piano reduction.

The system of registral pitch designations is taken from the *Harvard Dictionary of Music* and is also the same as that used by Forte (Ex. 1.1).[70]

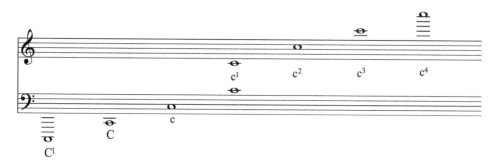

Ex. 1.1. System of registral designations.

One of the unfortunate aspects of any serious study of Jobim and his music is the lack of research material and informed comment written in English. Certainly, the five-volume *Cancioneiro Jobim* series of texts sub-titled *Obras Completas* (Complete Works) contain detailed piano reductions of most of Jobim's work (including his orchestral pieces), yet do not contain any more than superficial musicological comments.[71] Almir Chediak's three *Tom Jobim Songbooks* contain the melodies, guitar tablature, chord changes and the Portuguese and English lyrics for about one hundred of Jobim's songs and much useful historical information in Portuguese and English, but musical analysis of any depth is not included.[72] In 1990 Chediak published a series of five songbooks entitled the *Bossa Nova Songbooks* that complement (and in many instances replicate) songs in the *Tom Jobim Songbook* series. The scores in the *Bossa Nova Songbooks* provide a context for Jobim's work and make possible enlightening stylistic comparisons with music by his contemporaries.

Two comprehensive biographies, Sérgio Cabral's *Antônio Carlos Jobim* (1997) and Helena Jobim's *Antônio Carlos Jobim: Um Homem Iluminado* (1996), both written in Portuguese, contain broad historical information and observations from different viewpoints about Jobim's musical philosophies and motivations, but contain few direct musicological comments. A useful historical text concerning the history of bossa nova is Ruy Castro's *Bossa Nova: The Story of the Brazilian Music That Seduced the World* (2000), a translation of his original 1990 Portuguese publication *Chega de Saudade: A História e as Histórias da Bossa Nova*. Reflecting Castro's background, this account is written from the point of view of a reporter and staff writer rather than a musically informed specialist.

Jean-Paul Delfino's *Brasil Bossa Nova* (1988) (published in French) contains not only a history of the style and its artists, but also more pertinent musical observations, particularly concerning the lyrical content of bossa nova songs. This is to be expected as Delfino is a musician as well as a journalist. Walter Garcia's *Bim Bom: A Contradição Sem Conflitos de João Gilberto* (1999), offers an in-depth analysis (in Portuguese) of some of the early bossa nova songs, including several by Jobim. A useful text containing interviews with Jobim and his contemporaries is *Tons Sobre Tom* (1995) (eds. Cezimbra, Callado and de Souza).[73] Published in Portuguese, this collection of interviews was selected and published in an attempt to answer such questions as 'Who was Tom Jobim?', 'From where did his inspiration and creativity come?' and 'What was life like with him?' Some revealing conversations, particularly regarding Jobim's perception of the techniques of the classical composers, are contained in its pages. Less directed specifically at Jobim (but nevertheless informative) are many texts on Brazilian music and culture available in English.[74] These typically have chapters or sections on Jobim and his music and collectively enable Jobim's life and work to be placed in perspective in relation to other historically important Brazilian musical styles and cultural trends.

Gerard Béhague has written texts on Latin American music, the music of Brazil and Heitor Villa-Lobos, and has also produced numerous articles on Brazilian music, some of which mention Jobim and his music. The entry on Antônio Carlos Jobim in the *New Grove Dictionary of Music and Musicians* was written by Béhague; however, his most comprehensive article on bossa nova, 'Bossa and Bossas: Recent Changes in Brazilian Urban Popular Music', was written in 1973. An excellent article entitled 'Tom Jobim and the Bossa Nova Era' was published by Suzel Ana Reily in 1996.[75] This is one of the few refereed periodical articles (of which the author is aware) that contains significant in-depth musicological analysis of Jobim's music.[76]

A more recent addition to the literature is *Historias de Cançoes: Tom Jobim*.[77]

Notes

1 As David Treece notes, 'It is unarguably the case that the music's technical sophistication and rationality in many ways reflected the self-conscious modernism of a new technocracy' (Treece 11).

2 Ulhôa 210.

3 Ulhôa 210.

4 Ulhôa also identifies important qualities of this search in Rádames Gnattali (an arranger/orchestrator and close friend to Jobim), Rogério Duprat and Alóysio de Oliveira (producer of many bossa nova records) (Ulhôa 210).

5 Reily 2.

6 Araújo 53.

7 Cabral, 'Tom: Revolution with Beauty' 17.

8 Quoted in Cezimbra, Callado, de Souza 10.

9 Béhague, 'Jobim, Antônio Carlos [Tom] (Brasileiro de Almeida)'.

10 *Bossa Nova*. Dir. Walter Salles.

11   Jobim and Jobim, *Cancioneiro Jobim: Obras Escolhidas* 148.
12   Jobim and Jobim, *Cancioneiro Jobim: Obras Escolhidas* 186.
13   Cezimbra, Callado, de Souza 188.
14   Quoted in Jobim 221.
15   Dassin 118.
16   Jobim 221.
17   Hodel, 'Concerts in Review' 35.
18   Hodel, 'Concerts in Review' 35.
19   Holden 32.
20   Jobim and Jobim, *Cancioneiro Jobim: Obras Escolhidas* 207.
21   Jobim and Jobim, *Cancioneiro Jobim: Obras Escolhidas* 208.
22   de Ulhôa Carvalho, 346.
23   Stroud, 89.
24   Jobim and Jobim, *Cancioneiro Jobim: Obras Escolhidas* 121.
25   Tinhorão 25–28.
26   José Ramos Tinhorão quoted in Béhague, 'Bossa and Bossas' 211.
27   Béhague, 'Bossa and Bossas' 211.
28   Béhague, 'Bossa and Bossas' 211.
29   Borim, 'Pride and Prejudice' 1–4.
30   Borim, 'Pride and Prejudice'.
31   Perrone and Dunn 35.
32   Perrone and Dunn 35.
33   Gilberto Freyre quoted in Vianna 61.
34   Perrone and Dunn 18.
35   Lanza 131.
36   Lanza 131.
37   Cabral, 'The Bossa Nova' 20.
38   Cabral, 'The Bossa Nova' 20.
39   Grasse 301.
40   Cabral, 'The Bossa Nova' 21.
41   Cabral, *Antônio Carlos Jobim: Uma Biografia* 205.
42   Translation by Luciana Bordin.
43   Wagner Tiso quoted in de Souza, 'O Arquiteto Da Utopia' 152.
44   Fletcher 512.
45   Fletcher 513.
46   Flanagan.
47   Jobim and Jobim, *Cancioneiro Jobim: Obras Completas, 1959–1965*, vol. 2, 43.
48   Quoted in Chediak, *Tom Jobim Songbook*, vol. 2, 22.
49   de Souza, 'The Tides of a Modernist Maestro' 14.
50   Quoted in *Bossa Nova*.
51   Reily 12.
52   Chediak, *Bossa Nova Songbook*, vol. 1, 18.
53   Chediak, *Bossa Nova Songbook*, vol. 1, 21.

54 Moreno 132.
55 Chediak, *Tom Jobim Songbook,* vol.1, 45.
56 Jobim and Jobim, *Cancioneiro Jobim: Obras Escolhidas* 164.
57 Perrone and Dunn 13–14.
58 Jobim *Sinfônico.*
59 The Antônio Carlos Jobim Institute was initiated to preserve and make available to the Brazilian public, especially for students and researchers, his musical and poetic works, and beyond that, his thoughts, admiration and preoccupation with the natural wonders of Brazil.
60 Jobim and Jobim, *Cancioneiro Jobim: Obras Escolhidas* 101.
61 Roger Bastide quoted in Vianna 117.
62 Chediak, *Tom Jobim Songbook,* vol. 2, 22.
63 Cabral, 'The Bossa Nova'.
64 Jobim and Jobim, *Cancioneiro Jobim: Obras Completas, 1971–1982,* vol. 4, 30.
65 Moore 3; Middleton 177; Brackett15.
66 Kopplin
67 Forte 6.
68 A survey of systems of analysis of popular music reveals highly individual methods, usually adapted to suit individual examples. Moore outlines many of the problems of 'popular musicology' in *Analyzing Popular Music.*
69 There are, however, several pieces scored for piano and voice only.
70 Apel. Forte 5.
71 The five texts are organized chronologically into the time periods 1947–58, 1959–65, 1966–70, 1971–82 and 1983–94 and are published as separate volumes.
72 There are, however, some short, interesting comments, musical observations and tributes by some of Jobim's colleagues – Almir Chediak, Chico Buarque, Sérgio Cabral, Dorival Caymmi, Gal Costa and Tárik de Sousa.
73 Cezimbra, Callado, de Souza.
74 Some of the more comprehensive and erudite publications include McGowan and Pessanha's *The Brazilian Sound: Samba, Bossa Nova and the Popular Music of Brazil* (1998), Vianna's *The Mystery of Samba: Popular Music and National Identity in Brazil* (1999), Schreiner's *Musica Brasileira: A History of Popular Music and the People of Brazil* (1993) and Faria's *The Brazilian Guitar Book* (1995).
75 Reily 1–16..
76 Other comprehensive articles include Fisk 1–7; Lees, 'Um Abraço No Tom Antônio Carlos Jobim' 217–51; Moreno 129–41; Wheaton 136–44.
77 Homem and Oliveira.

Chapter 2

Influences

Historical Background and Development

The diverse influences in Jobim's musical make-up and development began to be felt from the earliest stages of his life. Born in 1927 into a middle-class family in Rio de Janeiro, he began his musical education by learning the guitar from his two uncles. One played popular music and the other classical guitar, in particular transcriptions of Bach. At 14, Jobim began piano lessons with the German composer and musicologist Hans Joachim Koellreutter. Koellreutter, a fugitive from Nazi Germany, had originally studied composition with Paul Hindemith, and later attained great esteem in Brazil's musical establishment by introducing twelve-tone (dodecaphonic) music to the country and by founding the Música Nova movement.[1] Despite his classical background, Koellreutter's attitude to music education was eclectic. He had accommodated popular styles with his own music – indeed, he had studied saxophone in order to play in a cabaret band in Lapa – and encouraged the young Jobim to look for new scales, harmonies and polyrhythms. As Paulo Jobim pointed out: 'It was Koellreutter, together with Villa-Lobos, who showed Jobim that there were no sharp boundaries between the classical and the popular'.[2]

It was in these early lessons with Koellreutter that Jobim discovered Chopin, Debussy and Ravel, composers whose music had an exceptionally strong influence on his own work. As this book will show, Jobim assimilated certain of their techniques into his own compositions, such as the use of unresolved dissonances, coloured or altered chords and the use of modes. Even though Jobim studied Schoenberg's twelve-tone technique, he rarely used it in his recorded music. He was, however, strongly influenced by the Brazilian composer Heitor Villa-Lobos, and, through Villa-Lobos' example, devised a way to create distinctly Brazilian-sounding music using European compositional procedures.

In his late twenties Jobim was working as a nightclub pianist when he was hired by the Continental Recording Company in Rio de Janeiro as musical assistant to the company's chief arranger, conductor and composer Radamés Gnattali.[3] Jobim soon began writing music ranging from instrumental sound tracks, songs and orchestral arrangements for popular recording artists to large-scale compositions for voice and orchestra. His *Sinfonia do Rio de Janeiro*, with its collection of eleven songs written with the lyricist Billy Blanco, was completed and recorded in 1954. In 1997 it was re-released on an album entitled *Meus Primeiros Passos e Compassos* (My first steps and measures) together with many of Jobim's early songs. The first tangible manifestation of Jobim's musical eclecticism, it synthesized popular and symphonic influences and was subtitled 'a popular symphony in samba time'.[4] The *Sinfonia* was essentially a collection of songs about Rio's unique attractions and panoramic views, unified by a recurring theme, or leitmotiv, performed variously by choir, xylophone, oboe, strings, whistle, baritone and orchestra. It demonstrated Jobim's ability to assimilate such popular music forms as *samba canção* and *dobrado* into a large-scale composition while developing thematic and lyrical material as a unified whole. As Thompson elaborates, it is 'filled with carioca tidbits like the cafezinho habit, gafieiras, football games, the beach, and focusing on the contrast between the Zona Sul and the morro. The pre-bossa nova music and arrangements owed a heavy debt to Broadway'.[5]

The Birth of Bossa Nova

As pianist and composer, Jobim later worked with the singer Silvia Telles on her 1957 album *Caricia*. This album included recordings of several of Jobim's songs with orchestral arrangements for his own orchestra. The following year Jobim, together with the lyricist Vinicius de Moraes, worked for the singer Elizete Cardoso as an orchestral composer/arranger on her album *Canção do Amor Demais*, writing almost all the compositions. It was on this album that the guitar playing of João Gilberto was heard for the first time in the song 'Chega de saudade'. Later, this song was eagerly embraced by leading jazz musicians in the United States and heralded the dawn of bossa nova to the world.

In his writings about the early history of *modinha*, a popular Brazilian sentimental song with Portuguese origins,[6] Vianna inadvertently pre-empts the circumstances surrounding Jobim's early musical development in Rio de Janeiro by suggesting that 'the phenomenon that most contributed to the renewal of the *modinha* at mid-century was the interaction of popular-class musicians with young intellectuals and romantic writers'.[7] The parallel here is striking. Jobim's work at the Continental Recording Company in the early 1950s allowed him to meet many of the popular musicians of the time – Pixinguinha, Assis Valente, Ary Barroso, Dorival Caymmi, Jacob do Bandolim, Antônio Maria, Ismael Neto, Evaldo Ruy, and on the ground floor of the Continental Recording Company building there was a bar appropriately named *A Grande Interrogação* (The great question).[8] Jobim's first historic meeting with his future musical collaborator and lyricist for many of his most famous songs, the poet and diplomat Vinicius de Moraes, was at a bar in Rio called the *Villarino*, which was patronized by newspapermen, intellectuals and artists.[9]

In 1955, after a change of position to artistic director for Odeon, the largest studio in the country at that time, Jobim worked on the opera *Orfeu da Conceição* in collaboration with Vinicius de Moraes. This opera was an adaption of the classical Greek myth of Orpheus, set in a carnival environment. Both realized that even though the music was written to fit the text, the main character in the opera, Orpheus, was a musician and there would be occasions in the plot when his creations would have to have a life of their own. This gave Jobim a certain interpretive licence to create music that would have appeal outside the context of the opera while remaining faithful to the idea behind it. In commenting on the variety of influences that shaped the opera, Jobim said: 'The Greek modes, the plagal cadences, our European heritage, our Brazilian manner, all have been freely used, just as they are used in our own music, which is heir to various different cultures and cannot aspire to any sort of "purity".[10]

With the orchestra under Jobim's direction, *Orfeu da Conceição* premiered in Rio de Janeiro's Municipal Theatre on 25 September 1956, and was such a success that an extended season was organized a week later in a different venue, the Theatre Republic. Soon after, Jobim, Moraes and the guitarist Luís Bonfá collaborated on the music for the Marcel Camus film *Black Orpheus*, which was based on the same Greek myth. *Black Orpheus* (or *Orpheo Negro* as this film was known in Brazil) was enormously influential in introducing the early sounds of bossa nova to a worldwide audience. It attracted immense international attention, not only to Jobim's music but also to the percussive sounds of Brazilian musical instruments and the infectious dance rhythms and sambas of the Rio Carnival.

In 1959, the new musical style known as bossa nova was introduced to the world in João Gilberto's album *Chega de saudade*.[11] The album included three songs by Jobim – 'Chega de saudade', 'Brigas, nunca mais' and 'Desafinado' – and embraced the Brazilian samba as a source of melodic, harmonic and especially rhythmic inspiration. The lyric of 'Desafinado' specifically mentions the term 'bossa nova' but, more than that, it was the sophisticated complexity of the melody and harmony that made the song distinctive. The lyrics refer directly to the difficult melodic line in the song that contains an awkward augmented 5th interval. The song began with the line 'If you say my singing is off key my love', with the augmented 5th falling immediately after the words 'off key'. Other lines such as 'You insist my music goes against the rules' also refer directly to the unorthodox approach within the song. They hint at an individual compositional style – a style that embraces complexity and harmonic and rhythmic intricacies and yet packages its complexity attractively to its audience. As Gerard Béhague pointed out:

One of the features of the new style, affecting popular music in general, and the samba in particular, was a deliberate avoidance of the predominance of any single musical parameter. Before bossa nova the melody was generally strongly emphasised, to satisfy the basic requirement of an easily singable tune; bossa nova, however, integrates melody, harmony and rhythm. The performer has a vital role in this integration, but heavy emphasis on the singer's personality is altogether avoided. Strongly contrasting effects, loudness of voice, fermatas or scream-like high pitches are generally excluded from a proper bossa nova singing style; the singing should flow in a subdued tone almost like the normal spoken language.[12]

Even at this stage of Jobim's career, influences are apparent from theatre, local culture (especially carnival), film music and popular instrumental sounds (particularly guitar). Underlying these influences was a thorough musical foundation gained from formal musical training and an intense interest in the music of such composers as Bach, Chopin, Liszt, Debussy, Ravel, Stravinsky and Villa-Lobos.

Instrumental Pieces and Film Music

Bossa nova soon became a worldwide phenomenon with the release of a second album by Gilberto in 1960, which included six new songs by Jobim. Among them were songs such as 'Samba de uma nota só' (One note samba), 'Meditação' (Meditation) and 'Corcovado' – all of which have since become well-known standards in the jazz repertoire. In the same year Jobim was commissioned by then President Juscelino Kubitschek to compose a symphonic piece to be performed at the opening of the country's new capital, Brasília. This work, entitled *Brasília: Sinfonia da Alvorada*, revealed Jobim's ability to compose in a more structured manner and to develop a unifying theme throughout an entire composition. The symphony is in five parts: 'O Planalto Deserto' (The desert plateaus), 'O Homem' (Mankind), 'A Chegada dos Candangos' (The arrival of the workers who participated in the construction of Brasilia), 'O Trabalho e a Construção' (The work and the construction) and 'Coral' (chorale). *Brasília* was based on a wider variety of stylistic resources than *Sinfonia do Rio de Janeiro*. These resources included birdsong, leitmotiv, folksong, fugato, plainsong, recitative and propulsive *marcato* rhythms.[13] In the commentary about the first section of *Brasília*, Jobim described the music and the source of its inspiration:

> At the end of the day the grasslands resounded with the cries of the rufous tinamou, answered by the melancholy chirps of the banded tinamou. Sometimes on the waterside, a vegetable mesh of branches and lianas is seen. The orchestra now reaches for a darker timbre. The measureless horizon is filled with the colours of twilight, and once again the plateau motif is heard.[14]

Unfortunately, the symphony was not played at the inauguration of Brasília because of poor planning and cost overruns, but was subsequently performed on several occasions, the first being in 1966 for a television broadcast and later in 1985 for the first performance in its originally planned setting, in the Praça dos Três Poderes in Brasília.

In the early 1960s the bossa nova boom in the United States was largely fuelled by the songs of Antônio Carlos Jobim. Songs such as 'Desafinado', 'Corcovado', 'Garota de Ipanema' (Girl from Ipanema) and 'Samba de uma nota só' became famous in the United States. Jobim's songs were performed and recorded by such well-known jazz musicians as Stan Getz, Dizzy Gillespie, Charlie Byrd, Coleman Hawkins, Zoot Sims and Herbie Mann. In 1962 Jobim was invited to perform his songs at Carnegie Hall. While he was in New York, he was voted best musical arranger by the National Academy of Recording Arts and Sciences.[15] Such was the success and attraction of Jobim's songs and bossa nova that in 1966 Frank Sinatra recorded an entire album dedicated to his music.[16] Entitled *Francis Albert Sinatra and Antonio Carlos Jobim*, the album was enormously successful and in 1967 it ran second in sales only to the Beatles' *Sgt. Pepper's Lonely Hearts Club Band*.[17] On the strength of this achievement, Sinatra recorded another album *Sinatra and Company* in 1969, which contained seven Jobim songs.

The late 1960s and early 1970s marked a time of great artistic experimentation for Jobim. He continued writing songs and music for the films *The Adventurers* (1970) and *A Casa Assassinada* (1971). Many of his instrumental compositions during this period retained the short song form. The album *Stone Flower*, for instance, contained three instrumental pieces originally composed for the film *The Adventurers*. It highlighted not only Jobim's ability to write very effectively for film, but also, in other tracks, revealed a love of the rich musical heritage of his native country, demonstrated by the inclusion of the traditional Brazilian *choro* form, use of *maracatu* rhythms and the inclusion of two interpretations of the song 'Brazil' by Brazilian composer Ary Barroso.[18] In 1974 Jobim combined classical music influences and local Brazilian rhythms with his own idiosyncratic harmonic progressions to create one of his most sophisticated and widely acclaimed songs, 'Águas de março' (Waters of March). After its release, the critic Leonard Feather proclaimed it to be among the ten best songs of all time.[19] The song was unusual, in that it was harmonically complex yet it featured a simple melody based on two notes. It was spontaneous and accessible and contained an evocative lyric written by Jobim in both Portuguese and English.[20]

Another important album, *Urubu*, which also contains instrumental compositions, was recorded in 1975. From that album, the impressionistic tone poem *Saudade do Brasil* demonstrates, among other things, Jobim's ability to develop a theme over an extended period of time. Jobim's command of orchestral timbres and dynamics, the influence of Brazilian regional music and rhythms, the timbral use of a female choir and the incorporation of unusual playing techniques – such as glissandi played with multiple strings to simulate forest bird calls – confirms an inventive, eclectic and masterful approach to orchestral composition.

Jobim continued writing songs, instrumental pieces and film music throughout the 1970s and 1980s. During this time his status as a Brazilian popular-music composer rose to an unprecedented level, to the extent that he was able to record in the world's best studios with the most talented musicians and conductors and release his music on the most prestigious record labels. He received several Grammy awards and toured around the world with his Banda Nova. Some of his more erudite later compositions included the score for the film *Gabriela* (1983) and the introductory music for the television series *O Tempo e o Vento* (1985). Even before his death in 1994, Antônio Carlos Jobim was proclaimed 'the biggest name ever in Brazilian popular music'.[21]

Rhythmic Influences: *Samba, Maracatu, Baião, Frevo*

Although Jobim borrowed rhythms from many Brazilian folk music styles such as Afro-Brazilian *baião* (dance), *marcha, bolero* and *maracatu*, one particular style provided the foundation for most of his music – samba.[22] Samba is both a festive dance made popular in the cities and country areas of Brazil, and a popular musical form featuring percussion-dominated polyrhythms. It is recognized today as distinctly Brazilian primarily because of the exposure that Rio de Janeiro's samba schools enjoy during Rio's carnival street parades in February every year. Ranks of percussionists known as *bateria* provide energetic performances in street marches creating multiple layers of rhythms as accompaniment for the elaborately costumed dancers and performers. Jobim commented extensively about local musical influences, particularly samba, as it provided the basis for the development of bossa nova in the late 1950s. For instance:

> People say that bossa nova is a drum beat used in the samba schools. It is a beat, one of the beats of samba. Samba is a polyrhythmic dance. It comprises a whole sea of rhythms. All space, all silence is occupied by beats, by rhythms, until it becomes like the sea, like a storm at sea. You don't have just rhythm, you have a continuous sound. João Gilberto knew so well how to refine all that.[23]

There are many styles of samba, each highlighting specific musical aspects or occasions. For instance, *samba de morro* is played by people of the *favelas* (hillside slums) of Rio de Janeiro; *samba de breque* features spoken words interjected at cadences; *samba de enredo* is created specifically for performance at the annual carnival parade; *samba canção*, *samba choro* and *samba fox* are hybrid forms whose lyrics often deal with love and unhappiness; *samba reggae* highlights the offbeat rhythms of reggae; and *samba pagode* represents a response to the overly touristic and commercialized sambas associated with the samba schools.[24]

An enlightened perspective on bossa nova rhythm is given by Jean-Paul Delfino who describes bossa nova as 'the daughter of samba'.[25] He identifies two types of samba rhythms as being especially important in the formation of bossa nova – *samba canção* (samba chanson) and *samba marcado* (or *rascardo*, meaning very energetic and loud). *Samba canção* is characterized by a 2/4 rhythmic character and is often associated with feelings of melancholy, sentimentality and nostalgia. Jobim's songs 'Incerteza' (Uncertainty), 'Corcovado', 'A Felicidade' (Happiness), 'Por causa de você' (Because of you), 'Vem viver ao meu lado' (Come and live by my side), 'Se todos fossem iguais a você' (If everyone were to be like you) and 'Manhã de Carnaval' (Morning of the carnival) are examples of songs that exhibit the romantic and sentimental characteristics commonly connected with *samba canção*. In Jobim's *Sinfonia do Rio de Janeiro* (1954), for instance, he included six *samba canção* – 'Hino ao sol' (Hymn to the sun), 'Arpoador' (Spear thrower), 'Noites do Rio' (Rio nights), 'Copacabana', 'A montanha' (The mountain) and 'O morro' (The hill). By contrast, *samba marcado* reflects its origins in the carnival. It is happy, buoyant and energetic and is performed at a faster tempo than *samba canção*. Jobim's songs 'Samba de uma nota só' and 'So danço samba' (I only dance samba) are influenced by *samba marcado*. Other Jobim songs exhibiting the *samba marcado* rhythm are 'O morro não tem vez' (The hill doesn't have time),[26] 'Samba do avião' (Song of the jet), 'Você vai ver' (You'll see), 'Agua de beber' (Water to drink) and 'Samba torto' (Crooked samba).

Nationalism in Brazilian music has a history traceable back to the late 1800s, when Alexandre Levy (1864–92), a composer who studied for some time in Milan and Paris, composed a piano piece entitled 'Tango Brasileiro'. Now recognized by Béhague as the 'first known Brazilian nationalist work written by a professional musician', this piece highlighted Levy's awareness of urban popular music.[27] In 1890, before the advent of accessible sound recordings, Levy also wrote an orchestral suite, 'Suite Brésilienne', the last movement of which was entitled 'Samba'. It was performed with great success in Rio de Janeiro in 1890 and 'became during the early twentieth century one of the most acclaimed pieces of the symphonic repertoire in Brazil'.[28] Levy's 'Samba' was based on two traditional urban tunes 'Balaio, meu bem, Balaio'[29] and 'Se eu te amei' (If I loved you), and the piano reduction of this piece includes a description of a dance that is assumed to be a rural samba, suggesting that this early samba was developed from a combination of rural dance and urban song.[30]

In the early part of the twentieth century, urban samba developed from African dance forms, primarily in the two major cities, Rio de Janeiro and São Paulo. The first recognized samba to be recorded was 'Pelo telefone' by Ernesto dos Santos (Donga) in 1917.[31] Urban samba displayed many of the characteristics of certain round dances from Angola and the Congo and incorporated rhythms from other musical dance forms such as the *lundú* and *maxixe*. The *lundú* was derived from the rhythm of the *batuque*, the dance of African slaves, but its erotic choreography 'largely imitated the Spanish dance called Fandango'.[32] The *maxixe* emerged in the 1870s and was an urban dance in moderate duple metre created from a fusion of tango, habanera and polka.[33] In describing the development of urban samba in Brazil, Gerard Béhague states:

> The classic urban samba of the 1930s and 40s eventually acquired the character of the ball-room type of sung dance, with the rhythm of the accompaniment often extended to the vocal line, and with the backing of a fairly colourful orchestra, whose percussion section was substantially reduced in comparison with the concurrent carnival samba. Typically, ball-room samba lyrics dealt with love, unhappiness, quite often pathologically melodramatic.[34]

Vianna also points out that in the 1930s samba rose from low-class status to become a national music primarily because of its enforced acceptance by the bourgeoisie. Samba was originally considered 'the stuff of lowlife rascals' and 'the carol of vagabonds', but with the growing importance of carnival and the search for a Brazilian cultural identity by writers and intellectuals such as Gilberto Freyre, samba was elevated to a position where it was embraced by the entire Brazilian population and became a unique symbol of Brazilian culture.[35]

Samba has since become indelibly associated with Brazilian national identity. It is, as Chasteen says, 'Brazil's "national rhythm", its prime symbol of cultural nationalism'.[36] As such, it is an element of unity to which all Brazilians, black or white, can relate and thus has a role in mediating and reducing racial conflict. 'Samba has been implicated historically in making hegemonic the ideology (or myth) of racial democracy in both official and popular discourses. The effect of that myth is to deflect race-conscious dissent'.[37] Its historically varied constituents are also a testimony to its intrinsically eclectic nature. Just as, for instance, Giacomo Meyerbeer and Charles Ives employed eclecticism as a means for reconciling the cultural friction between an elitist art and the vernacular, so too did Jobim's adoption of samba provide, even if inadvertently, an alternative means of cultural reconciliation. In so doing it also ensured a wide acceptance for his individual musical style, bossa nova, as an identifiably Brazilian music.

Although Jobim's use of rhythm in bossa nova was based largely on samba, he was certainly inspired by other musical precedents in Brazilian folk music and its ubiquitous use of polyrhythms. For instance, the *maracatu*, a carnival dance-procession from Recife, in Pernambuco, abounds with polyrhythms. Participants in the procession each play their own percussion instrument and are free to add to the rhythm established by other instrumentalists. The added percussion sounds are highly syncopated and produce complex layers of rhythm. *Maracatu* and samba employ the same cumulative rhythmic principle and exhibit independent, multi-layered syncopated lines. They differ mostly in the instruments used, in tempo and balance. *Maracatu* often includes brass instruments such as trombone, as well as call-and-response singing. Indeed, Jobim's album *Stone Flower* (1970) featured two compositions influenced by *maracatu* rhythms – 'Deus e Diablo na terra do sol' (God and the Devil in the land of the sun) and 'Quebra-pedra' (Stone flower).[38]

Jobim also embraced other rhythms in styles such as *baião* ('Praia branca'),[39] *bolero* ('Anos dourados'),[40] and *frevo* ('Frevo de Orfeu').[41] Together with his singer/guitarist colleague, João Gilberto, Jobim was able to capture the essence of these rhythms and use them as a rich resource to create bossa nova, and with it a rhythm that was less cluttered than its multi-layered rhythmic source but maintained an essential 'drive' and 'life'. *Baião* began as an adaption of a north-eastern Brazilian dance genre known as *baiano*. Traditionally led by the *rabeca*, a fiddle of Portuguese origin, *baiano* combined with other regional genres and was adapted for accordion by Luiz Gonzaga. In the 1940s it became known as *baião*, and later as *forró*.[42] There seems to be little connection between the Spanish-derived *bolero*, as exemplified by Ravel's famous 'Bolero', and the Latin American form of *bolero* that probably originated in Cuba. Early literary sources indicate that it was a 'slow-tempo, duple meter ballroom song-and-dance genre of great popularity'.[43] The Latin American *bolero* spread first to Mexico, and reached Brazil via the Mexican artist Agustin Lara in 1941, whereupon it became popular as a dance genre and as a sentimental song type. *Frevo* began in Recife, Pernambuco in the early twentieth century as a carnival dance that filled the streets of the city. Its name came from the word *frever*, a corruption of fever, and, as its name suggests, it is characterized by a syncopated march-like rhythm of an intense and frenetic nature.

The Portuguese colonization of Brazil in the early 1500s, and the subsequent arrival of slaves from Africa, had a profound effect on not only the folk music of Brazil, but its whole cultural identity. The slaves brought with them their own music and dances, such as the *maracatu, lundu, cateretê* and *jongo* as well as their own musical instruments, such as the *surdo, tamborim, agogô* and *cuica*. After 500 years of acculturation, the African influence manifests itself in today's Brazilian music in many ways: through a wide range of rhythmic devices – particularly polyrhythms and syncopation – the ubiquitous use of percussion instruments, altered melodic modes, call-and-response vocal structures, repetition, melodic structures often built on sequences, improvisation, two-four time in most dance music, a strong emphasis on the down beat, and a basic extended rhythm for many melodies built on the rhythmic cell shown in Ex. 2.1.

Ex. 2.1. Basic rhythmic cell of many
Brazilian melodies of African origin.

This rhythm forms the very basis of the classical samba rhythm.[44] Jobim, of course, was quite accustomed to incorporating this rhythm in the accompaniments to many recorded songs. Strangely, written examples of this specific rhythm are difficult to find in his music, although it is used explicitly in sections of 'Matita Perê' and 'Samba do avião'. The African influence can also be heard in many of the rhythms of Brazilian folk music as a subtle duple-triple ambivalence and characteristically African hemiola.[45] Beyond any stylistic peculiarities, however, the critical ingredient for Brazil's rich musical maturity was the overall acceptance of music as an integral part of daily life and, in time, its recognition as an integral part of Brazilian national culture.[46]

Jobim called bossa nova a 'distillation of samba rhythms', but samba itself was created from other indigenous rhythms and is an excellent manifestation of the generally accepted principle that, culturally, nothing comes from nothing. Compared to some aspects of the western art-music tradition, samba and South American music in general do not tend to use musical innovations that radically extend beyond traditionally accepted practice,[47] but rather absorb them to be reused in a multitude of ways and circumstances. According to the musicologist Carlos Vega:

> One typical feature of South American music is that, whereas in Europe different styles, such as baroque, preclassicism, classicism, romanticism, and so on, succeed one another, in South America they are all used concurrently in their musical traditions. Therefore, the logical linearly progressing history of European art does not correspond to Latin American reality.[48]

It is this inclusive principle of musical eclecticism that characterizes the work of not only Antônio Carlos Jobim, but also the artists who surrounded him. His greatest musical inspiration and role model was, of course, his fellow countryman, Heitor Villa-Lobos, yet he also drew inspiration from local, popular music artists, particularly João Gilberto.

Jobim's song 'Chega de saudade', first released in 1958, was the model that led to the acceptance of bossa nova as a recognized musical style. With the release of this song,

João Gilberto introduced a pioneering guitar rhythm that became known as *violão gago* (stammering guitar) and an inventive, syncopated singing style that was very subdued and quiet.[49] Gilberto also played with the rhythm and phrasing of the lyric, often anticipating the beat. In a statement to the producer Almir Chediak for his *Tom Jobim Songbooks*, Jobim said:

> If it weren't for João Gilberto's influence, bossa nova never would have existed. In the 1950s great changes were happening in Brazilian popular music: harmony, lyrics, melody etc., but Gilberto was the fuse which detonated bossa nova.[50]

Gilberto derived his guitar playing style from the rhythms of the tamborims of the samba schools, emphasizing rhythm and harmony while singing the melody. The influence of samba can be interpreted in his playing of the regular rhythm of the *surdo* (bass drum) with his thumb on the bass strings while playing block chords in a syncopated (*tamborim*) rhythm with his fingers. Gilberto's vocal phrasing added another dimension.

> The bossa nova's great contribution is that, when João sang, there would be a rhythmic interplay between the guitar, the voice and the drums. It wasn't a standardised beat which was consistently repeated. It wasn't a cliché. [...] Each case was different. The melody combined rhythmically with the harmony. I mean the harmony would be in one rhythm and the melody in another. Often they would fall together with a difference of semiquavers. In 'Bim-bom' (written by Gilberto), for example, you see the disassociation between the accompaniment he plays on the guitar and what he sings [...]. [51]

The combination of these eclectic rhythmic borrowings from samba and Jobim's melodic and harmonic sophistication formed the unique admixture that was a substantial part of the appeal of this new popular style.

There were other less ostensible elements that were just as important to bossa nova's acceptance, at least for a Brazilian audience. Race mixture had been seen by authors such as Sílvio Romero as a mark of Brazilian uniqueness. Romero had affirmed that 'each Brazilian is a mestiço [a person of mixed race], if not in blood, in his ideas' and that race mixture was a guarantee of creating non-imitative art.[52] Just as samba had become recognized as a unique Brazilian national music through acceptance and assimilation of music of different races, Jobim's further incorporation of samba with other musical styles led to the no-less significant, widespread acceptance of bossa nova and its recognition as a fundamentally Brazilian musical style.[53] Implied in this acknowledgement was, of course, a related and important aspect that indicated an acceptance of different cultural elements due to race. As Béhague points out:

> In Brazil, the general acceptance of what constitutes, culturally and ethically, an Afro-American is not as unequivocal as in the U.S. Race alone cannot, therefore, be considered a valid criterion in discussing Brazilian popular music. It would appear utterly inaccurate,

from a Brazilian viewpoint, to regard the repertoire under consideration here as that of Afro- or white Brazilians, in spite of the fact that many stylistic features of the *bossa nova* samba, for example, derive from Afro-Brazilian musical traditions. Thus, it should be borne in mind that popular music in Brazil cuts across ethnic lines.[54]

As well, samba's open acceptance and widespread cultural compulsion towards unrestrained music and dance participation is something that is not generally accepted in Western European and Northern American cultures, where performer and audience are usually physically separated. This pervasive and uninhibited attitude towards music participation provided a natural, but nevertheless compelling justification for Jobim to adopt an inclusive compositional philosophy that allowed cooperative musical expression. This form of musical expression, where no particular performer or musical aspect is privileged to any great extent, was a fundamental characteristic of bossa nova.

The extent of bossa nova in Jobim's work is not as predominant as its worldwide success might indicate. Although Jobim's name is inextricably linked with bossa nova and some of his most famous songs are bossa nova classics, his music reveals much broader and eclectic musical influences. Jobim had once said:

Bossa nova became so prestigious that everyone remembers 'Desafinado' and thinks of me as the guy who started the movement. In fact ninety percent of my songs cannot be considered part of bossa nova. This is one of the dangers of pigeonholing musicians.[55]

Jobim's eclecticism, therefore, goes beyond what is commonly acknowledged into areas that embrace folk, popular and art music.

Folk and Popular Music Influences: *Modinha, Choro*

The inclusion of folk melodies, provincial rhythms or regional modes of expression in musical compositions is often associated by default with the concept of musical nationalism. In the late nineteenth and early twentieth centuries, nationalism became an important aesthetic characteristic of European romantic and post-romantic music. The nationalist philosophy was often most strongly taken up by composers from countries other than those considered central to the western art-music tradition (i.e. Germany, France and Italy). National folk music idioms are often said to be evident in the music of such composers as Dvořák, Smetana and Janáček (Bohemia); Grieg (Norway); Musorgsky, Rimsky-Korsakov, Borodin, Glinka, Balakirev and Stravinsky (Russia); Albéniz, Falla and Granados (Spain); Elgar, Holst and Vaughan Williams (England); Bartók and Kodály (Hungary); Ives, Gershwin and Copland (United States) and Sibelius (Finland).

The start of musical nationalism in Brazil also coincided with its worldwide trend. According to Béhague, among the earliest examples is a composition for piano entitled

'A Sertaneja' (The backwoodsman), first published in 1869 by Brasilio Itiberê da Cunha (1846–1913), a diplomat and amateur musician from São Paulo.[56] 'A Sertaneja' is remarkable because it contains Brazilian elements from popular music forms such as the *maxixe*, the Brazilian *tango* and the *modinha*. These elements are evident in Jobim's music, a fact that suggests Jobim was following a nationalistic musical precedent set nearly one hundred years before his time.

Art music in Brazil began to take on a genuinely identifiable national characteristic with the works of Alberto Nepomuceno (1864–1920). His early works included 'Dança de Negros' (Negro dance), a work that served as an indication of his later eclecticism in producing music in many different forms and genres such as 'As Uyaras', based on an Amazonian legend, and his three Suites for orchestra that drew directly upon folk and popular music. Nepomuceno also actively promoted Brazilian music and composers, including the young Villa-Lobos, whose Cello Concerto he presented in 1919.[57] These early Brazilian nationalist composers were inspired by both folk and urban popular music but wrote in conventional art-music forms. Most importantly, however, they created a musical environment favourable to an inclusive and eclectic nationalist musical philosophy, one which their successors, particularly Villa-Lobos and later Jobim, were to assume almost as second nature in their musical endeavours.

When Portuguese settlers arrived in Brazil there were in excess of two million indigenous Brazilian Indians.[58] There are conflicting theories, however, as to the degree of influence the native Indians had on later Brazilian music. McGowan and Pessanha dismiss the local Indian influence on Brazilian music by saying that the Indians that survived the Portuguese invaders were so devastated by the invasion that they lost their cultural traditions when they were forced to leave their native homes to live in the cities and towns.[59] As well, Vianna's interpretation of the writings of the literary critic Sílvio Romero affirm that the mestiço (person of mixed race) was the 'primary symbol of Brazilian originality', rather than the indigenous Indian. By dismissing poetry in Tupi (the indigenous language most important in Brazilian history) as simply Tupi poetry and not Brazilian poetry, Romero adds weight to his biased argument that Brazilian culture really began with race mixing, with no contribution from the indigenous element.[60]

Contrary to this attitude is the theory proposed by Alves that the rhythms of the samba are not of African origin, nor did they originate in Rio de Janeiro, but instead come from North-Eastern Brazil.[61] Alves compares a samba from 1925 with descriptions of indigenous dances done between 1587 and 1618 and finds on this evidence all the indigenous dances in the samba. His research highlights similarities in instruments, verse construction and choreography between long-standing samba and indigenous Brazilian musical and dance types. Alves points out that the Fulniôs Indians have the *samba de coco* as part of their tradition, the Chocós Indians have *coco-sambado*, and in the Tupi language samba means a kind of round dance *dança de roda*. Additionally, Silvio Salema, a researcher in the music of Brazilian native Americans, could not identify any samba elements in any of the 100-year-old African songs he had acquired from his family.

Although Jobim's music shows little direct inspiration from indigenous Brazilian music, there is nevertheless a parallel that can be drawn between Jobim's music and the music of the Brazilian Indians. This parallel, which cannot be confused with an imported Afro-Brazilian influence, is Jobim's musical incorporation of bird song. A genre common among many Indian groups is bird song imitation. These imitations were used to attract birds while hunting, or sometimes to acquire their powers.[62]

Jobim was infatuated with the multiplicity of sounds and melodic invention provided by Brazilian bird life and used bird songs in several of his works. For instance, he used recorded bird calls and many musical references to birds (parrots, parakeets, tinamou) in 'Boto', a piece included on the album *Urubu*. 'In the lyrics, the animals talk about men, and the arrangement includes the actual calls of different birds – the great gray tinamou, male and female, the small-billed tinamou and the potoo'.[63] The album itself was also named after a bird, the *urubu*, or black vulture. Jobim's ecological concern for not only birdlife but also the plight of the Amazon rainforest and its native Indians is highlighted in the song 'Passarim', which tells the story of a defenceless bird who has lost its natural habitat and home through man's destruction by fire of the forest. Jobim made more direct reference to birds in 'Andorinha' (Swallow) and 'Sabiá' (Song-thrush) and included bird song imitations of the *tico-tico* (Crown sparrow) and the *sabia* in 'Chovendo na roseira'.[64] Indeed, Jobim once said that 'Music is improved birdsong, computerised and arranged'.[65]

The music critic Mario de Andrade suggests that among Brazilian popular songs the *modinha* represents the purest European strain and that the early *modinhas* bear a close relationship with Italian operatic arias. In his *Ensaio Sobre Musica Brasileira* (Essay on Brazilian Music), Andrade identifies the multiple influences that helped to create Brazilian music in general, while also highlighting the Brazilian *modinha's* particularly European characteristics:

> Although Brazilian music has attained an original ethical expression, its sources are of foreign derivation. It is Amerindian in a small percentage, African to a much greater degree, and Portuguese in an overwhelmingly large proportion. Besides, there is a Spanish influence, mainly in its Hispano-American aspect [...] The European influence is revealed not only through parlor dances such as the Waltz, Polka, Mazurka, and the Schottische, but also in the structure of the *modinha*.[66]

A general definition of the *modinha* might describe it as a popular sentimental song of Portuguese origins. Slonimsky outlined the characteristics of mid-twentieth-century *modinhas* as being largely sentimental, written mostly in minor keys and often ornamented with appoggiaturas. The harmonic scheme often incorporates modulation into the minor subdominant.[67] The lyrical subject matter of the *modinha* is generally of a romantic and introspective nature and melodies often contain wide arpeggiated leaps.

The history of the *modinha* can be traced back to the mid-eighteenth century when people of mixed race in the Portuguese colonies of Brazil invented interpretations of

Portuguese lyric songs called *modas*. Domingos Caldas Barbosa, a mixed-race priest from Rio de Janeiro, popularized the *modinha* in Portugal during his stay in Lisbon in 1775, and in so doing became Brazil's first historically recognized composer of this form.[68] Like much subsequent Brazilian folk music, the early *modinha* contained influences from Portugal, Africa and Italy, and characterized the willingness of Brazilians to accept a variety of musical sources from different social classes, both popular and elite.

Vianna outlines an important aspect of the *modinha* that became apparent in its early history. Revealing the *modinha*'s 'cultural permeability not only of international frontiers but also of those between classical and popular music', Vianna intimates that it became a classless musical style.[69] Classical composers such as Sigismund Neukomm (a student of Haydn) and Carlos Gomes (a nineteenth-century operatic and orchestral composer) wrote *modinhas*, while they were also performed by poor musicians such as Laurindo Rabelo (a musician and poet of gypsy ancestry) and Alexandre Trovador (a creolinho[70] musician and hairdresser).[71] Freyre also states:

> The modinha [...] was a musical agent of Brazilian unification sung, as it was during the reign of the second emperor, by some to the sound of pianos inside bourgeois and noble houses, by others to the sound of guitars in the night air at the door of even humble shacks.[72]

As an agent of unification the *modinha* brought together people from different social classes. The interactions of popular musicians with upper class intellectuals and writers enabled a sharing of artistic ideas and perceptions in turn fostering an environment of mutual cooperation and a collective creative attitude that embraced musical eclecticism. Not only were such interactions necessary for the continued existence of the *modinha*, but they proved a critical ingredient in Jobim's early musical career and they also had parallels in the history of the samba. Jobim's tribute to this style is his 'Modinha', written for his 1980 album *Terra Brasilis*.[73]

Choro refers to instrumental music of nineteenth-century origin from Rio de Janeiro, noted for its virtuosity, improvisation and counterpoint. In its broadest definition the term *choro* means 'crying', which may relate to the particularly Brazilian way of interpreting *choro* music – with much emotion. It has also come to mean 'a popular musical recital executed by a small orchestra' and at the same time 'the tunes played at such a recital'.[74] Hodel describes *choro* as 'characterised by a bouncy mood contributed to by elaborate melodies, frequent harmonic changes, and an active bassline in counterpoint to the melody'.[75] In the 1870s in the cities of Brazil, particularly Rio de Janeiro, the mixture of Portuguese salon music and African rhythms developed into the style of popular urban music that eventually became known as *choro*. The music was commonly performed by an ensemble of virtuoso musicians who played instrumental music with usually one member as a soloist. These early ensembles generally included flute, clarinet, ophicleide,[76] trombone, cavaquinho (a type of ukelele with four metal strings), guitar and a few percussion instruments. Virtuosity and improvisation were an important characteristic. The early *choro* ensembles performed for dances and popular festivals and would occasionally accompany a solo singer who may have sung several sentimental songs in the *modinha* style. Several musical influences are predominant in *choro*, especially the waltz, samba and *maxixe*.[77]

The early history of the *choro* involves two composers in particular – Chiquinha Gonzaga (1847–1935) and Ernesto Nazaré (1863–1934), both of whom produced music of unique rhythmic structure and phrasing interspersed with improvisatory passages. Important later *choro* composers were the guitarist João Pernambuco (João Teixeira Guimarães, 1883–1947), a prolific and popular composer from whom Villa-Lobos transcribed many pieces; the flutist/ saxophonist Pixinguinha (Alfredo da Rocha Viana Filho, 1898–1973), whose conducting and arranging abilities transformed *choro* into a popular, commercial and professional musical style in the 1920s and 1930s; and Garôto (Aníbal Augusto Sardinha, 1915–55), an exceptionally talented guitarist who greatly extended the conventions of *choro* by use of unexpected chords, key changes, rhythmic punctuations, deceptive phrases and syncopations.[78]

Choro has played a prominent part in both the popular and classical music of Brazil. Many of Villa-Lobos' compositions, for instance, were based on the *choro*. In the foreword to *Choros No. 3*, one of a series of fourteen *choros* that Villa-Lobos composed for various instrumental ensembles from solo guitar to wind ensemble, Villa-Lobos characterizes the musical elements of *choro* and alludes to an indigenous Indian influence, although he does not elaborate on that influence:[79]

> The Choros represent a new form of musical composition in which different modalities of the Brazilian Indian and popular music are synthesised, having as its principal elements rhythm and some typical melody of a popular nature, which appears in the work every now and then, always modified according to the personality of the composer. The harmonic procedures, too, are almost a complete stylisation of the original. The word 'serenade' can give an approximate idea of what 'Choros' means.[80]

Despite its widespread acceptance in Brazilian musical culture, it would seem that there is no reliable description of one single characteristic that actually defines *choro*, or, indeed, its form. Tarasti suggests that the name *choro* was merely used by Villa-Lobos as a term that would identify his compositions as distinctly Brazilian.[81] Indeed, Villa-Lobos denied that *choro* had any absolutely strict form.[82] However, even though there are some well-known exceptions, many of the early *choros* followed the form A-B-A-C-A. One of these exceptions is Pixinguinha's magnificent 'Carinhoso', which appears on Jobim's 1970 album *Tide*. It is generally regarded as a *choro* even though it consists of only two parts. By way of example, Tarasti defines the following generative rules for Villa-Lobos' works for winds with a *choro*-form:

> Discrete motives, often without any clearly defined key, are presented in the introduction followed by a markedly *rhythmico-motoric* section with sforzato-syncopations in changing meters. A singing, sentimental, *melodic* section follows with references either to *modinha*

or *valsa-choro*. Virtuoso solos for different instruments can be found throughout e.g. as transitions between various sections. At the end, a section based on a rhythmic-melodic ostinato gradually accelerating and intensifying in volume climaxes the whole work.[83]

Sève identifies two loosely defined forms of *choro*: chamber *choro*, consisting of guitars, cavaquinho, pandeiro and a soloist, and orchestral, or big band *choro*.[84] He continues:

> Traditionally, this music has been kept alive through choro jam sessions – 'rodas de choro' in Portuguese – which have continuously launched new instrumentalists and composers. [...] The Choro, like other musical genres, has its own codes – responsible for its personality – which, through time, has created an equally unique 'vocabulary'. However, little is known on this subject due to the absence of published material on the subject, since the predominant method of learning is through (increasingly rare) choro circles.[85]

Many of these characteristics can be found in Jobim's work. For instance, one of Jobim's earliest songs, 'Chega de saudade' (No more blues) written in 1958, is in *choro* form and contains virtually all of Tarasti's criteria for the *choro*.[86] Jobim's 1970 album *Stone Flower* contains an instrumental track simply entitled 'Choro', which is in a form close to that outlined above but with a repeated first section.[87] As previously mentioned, Jobim included Pixinguinha's *choro* 'Carinhoso' on the album *Tide*, and, as a tribute to the great pianist, conductor and composer Radamés Gnattali, wrote two *choros* entitled 'Meu Amigo Radamés' and 'Radamés y Pelé', including them on the album *Antonio Brasileiro*.[88] 'Falando de amor' (Speaking of love) is Jobim's tribute to the sentimental *choro* style for flute, two guitars and percussion and 'Choro de nada' (Choro of nothing), although not written by Jobim, was included on his 1977 album *Miucha and Antônio Carlos Jobim*.

Integral to Jobim and Villa-Lobos' oeuvre, *choro* was also one of the most prominent popular music styles that both composers used to convey a sense of nationalism.

> Taking the serenading choro as his point of departure, Villa-Lobos ended up constructing the apotheotic vision of the Brazilian reality of his day, by articulating a number of signs indicative of the Brazilian diversity, while contributing to the forging of the myth of a unified national culture. And here is the essential explanation of the eclecticism of Villa-Lobos and of subsequent Brazilian composers: the need to be nonexclusive and comprehensive concurrently in the attempt to disclose the various cultural vibrations of Brazil.[89]

Both composers found in *choro* a truly representative style that contained sufficient musical subtleties to make it attractive. The rhythmic independence of melody and accompaniment had always been an important attribute of Brazilian *choro*, a fact that prompted Villa-Lobos to comment:

38

What is most interesting in this *Choro* are the rhythmic and melodic cadences, irregular within a quadruple meter, giving the disguised impression of rubato, or of a delayed melodic execution, which is precisely the most interesting characteristic of the serenaders.[90]

The song 'Chega de saudade' refers directly to the Portuguese word *saudade*, an intangible but nevertheless important characteristic of not only Jobim's music, but also of much Brazilian folk and popular music, particularly *choros*, *modinhas* and classical music. When strictly translated *saudade* means 'longing, yearning, homesickness or nostalgia'. The word appears, for instance, in the title of Jobim's song 'Só saudade', his orchestral tone poem *Saudade do Brasil* and in other composers' *choros* such as Pixinguinha's 'Saudade do Cavaquinho' and 'Oscarina (Saudades do Monteiro)' and also in Villa-Lobos' 'Saudades das Selvas Brasileiras'. This intrinsically Brazilian sense of sadness has been documented in Brazilian music since 1869 when Brasilio Itiberê da Cunha wrote his piano piece 'A Sertaneja'. Béhauge comments that the introduction to this piece contains arpeggios alternating between A♭ major and A♭ minor, contrasting with 'a sorrowful phrase characteristic of the melancholy of our race'.[91] Although it can be highly subjective and context-sensitive, another mechanism for engendering a feeling of *saudade* is by the use of a descending (often chromatic) melodic line. Jobim's music abounds with descending chromatic lines, often found in successive chords (especially in the bass) as well as in the melody. Descending chromatic lines are also a common feature of *modinhas* and *choros*.

The *choro*, 'Chega de saudade', is the song that is widely recognized as having started the bossa nova musical revolution in the late 1950s, first in Brazil then later in the United States. Bossa nova, like many of its predecessors, had a musically inclusive and eclectic ethos that ignored cultural barriers and encompassed many elements of folk and popular musical styles. Although samba was the most observable influence in its creation, it was by no means the only influence. As one of the prominent bossa nova artists, Carlos Lyra, said: 'With regard to bossa nova, there's an old misconception that it was solely an outgrowth of samba. That's not true, bossa nova is also modinha, baião, samba canção, all these. Bossa nova is the spirit of the music'.[92]

Western Art-Music Influences: Villa-Lobos, Chopin, Debussy, Ravel, Stravinsky, Gnattali, Gershwin

As mentioned at the beginning of this chapter, Jobim had a comprehensive classical musical training in his early years and was taught the fundamentals of classical tonal harmony, counterpoint and twentieth-century techniques by Koellreuter and others. It was in these formative years that Jobim developed a deep respect for classical music and endeavoured to emulate this body of work throughout his life. Indeed, Jobim claimed that Chopin, Debussy,

Stravinsky and Villa-Lobos were his masters. 'They have given me musical and spiritual sustenance', he said.[93] For Jobim, however, the most influential of these composers was undoubtedly Villa-Lobos.[94] Fisk states that Jobim met Villa-Lobos in Rio when he was working on 'A Floresta do Amazonas' (Forests of the Amazon), the music for the MGM film *Green Mansions*. 'This contact with Villa-Lobos while creating a soundtrack affected Jobim's own approach the following year when he began co-writing the music for the award-winning French film, *Black Orpheus*, with guitarist Luiz Bonfá'.[95]

Through his unique assimilation of folk song and local rhythms within an essentially European idiom, Villa-Lobos became Brazil's most important composer and the first to become internationally recognized. European music traditions underpin his musical language, but the strongest musical influences are predominantly Brazilian. *Bachianas Brasileiras*, for instance, evokes the music of Bach while using idiosyncratic Brazilian musical expressions based on the Brazilian tradition of *choros* or serenades. While Jobim admired Villa-Lobos, Jobim's compositions contain surprisingly few specific points of reference to Villa-Lobos' music. Instead, it is predominantly Villa-Lobos' musical philosophy that Jobim took to heart, above all, his strong nationalism. Villa-Lobos believed that 'art must be national in character but universal in its groundwork and must reach the majority of the people'.[96]

The parallels between Jobim's eclectic compositional philosophy and that of Villa-Lobos are very strong. Villa-Lobos was, as Jobim acknowledged, a great source of inspiration. Tarasti says of Villa-Lobos that he 'expressed himself in a style borrowed from Brahms, Wagner, Debussy or Franck' and that 'the Brazilian flavour was quite obvious in folk music, in the carnival songs and rhythms, as well as in the works of Ernesto Nazareth, a composer whose fluent, indefinable and sad playing helped [him] to better understand the Brazilian soul'.[97] Villa-Lobos was able to portray in music the spirit of Brazil because he had the ability to create 'his own individual symbols of identity and make them acceptable to his country as uniquely national symbols'.[98]

> In many ways, his personality, his career and his production reflect typical Brazilian traits such as grandeur, flamboyance, restlessness, lack of organic unity, disparity, and gaudiness, along with others such as individuality, spontaneity, allurement and sophistication. [...] Throughout his career he avoided conformity, in his life as well as his musical style. His nonconformity helped him in achieving strength, originality and success.[99]

It can be said that Jobim similarly developed a nationalist aesthetic by means of an attitude of cultural eclecticism in his music. He was also able to capture the fluidity and sense of sadness, or *saudade*, that characterizes much of Brazilian folk music and transform it into his own 'symbol of identity' – the bossa nova style of popular music.

In many respects Jobim's eclecticism can be regarded as even broader than that of Villa-Lobos. In particular, his attraction to the multi-layered rhythms of samba, *maracatu*, *batucada* and *baião* are much more apparent. Moreover, Jobim's adoption of the popular song as the major vehicle for his work, together with his compositions in orchestral art music, meant he was able to employ a much wider range of musical styles. Both composers had the first-hand experience of playing popular music for small audiences: Villa-Lobos played guitar and clarinet as a *choro* musician in the suburbs of Rio, and Jobim played piano in bars and nightclubs around Rio in the 1950s, playing 'as many songs as possible in order to please the clientele'.[100] Both realized that the inclusion of popular music in their work was an effective way to achieve an authentic nationalist Brazilian expression. Chediak refers to Villa-Lobos as '[...] the planetary Brazilian Villa-Lobos, to whom Jobim can be called a kind of successor'.[101] Indeed, Jobim also recalled a conversation between Villa-Lobos and the composer Cláudio Santoro: 'Olha, eu estou partindo, mas os dois que podem me seguir, um é você, o outro é Tom Jobim. (Look, I am going, but the two that must follow me, one is you, the other is Tom Jobim.)'[102] In a dedication to Antônio Carlos Jobim, Gal Costa, one of Brazil's most famous popular music singers, declared:

> He writes melodies at the same time simple and difficult, that sort of Villa-Lobos thing that he has, those harmonies, sometimes classical, sometimes rather grandiose – and, in the end, all of it beautiful. I am proud to have worked with him, both in Brazil and in Los Angeles and New York.[103]

The political situation that developed in Brazil during the populist Vargas dictatorship (1930–45) was helpful to Villa-Lobos. It encouraged nationalism in the arts, supported the formation of orchestras and music institutions, established networks within popular music circles and offered a means of international promotion. With the leadership and encouragement of Getúlio Vargas, samba rose in status to become the premier genre of Brazilian popular music, eventually leading in 1939 to the acclamation of Ary Barroso's samba 'Aquarela do Brasil' as 'one of the nation's trademark compositions'.[104] This song was also responsible for the creation of the 'sub-genre *samba-exaltação* (samba-exultation), characterized politically by romantic patriotism and musically by long, involved melodies and grandiose arrangements'.[105] The nationalist fervour that enveloped the country in the 1940s was not only favourable to Villa-Lobos' musical endeavours but was also integral to the development of a supportive artistic environment, an environment that set the scene for the eventual development of bossa nova and later nationalist-inspired musical movements such as Tropicalia in the 1960s and 1970s.

Villa-Lobos experimented early in his career with novel timbres and rhythms. 'Nonetto' (1923) for flute, oboe, clarinet, saxophone, bassoon, harp, piano, mixed chorus and (Brazilian) percussion was also influenced by urban popular music of the time.

> Actually, the 'Nonetto' is one of the earliest examples of Villa-Lobos' daring experiments with timbres and medium and is at times reminiscent of Debussy and early Stravinsky. The harmonies are very Impressionistic also, with altered chords, formations by fourths and fifths, frequent pedal points, and parallelism; the use of tone clusters, however, reveals Villa-Lobos's search for new sonorous combinations.[106]

One particularly sonorous combination can be found in the *Bachianas Brasileiras, No. 5*, where Villa-Lobos uses the human voice as an instrument for the melody of the Aria (cantilena). The wordless melody is sung by a solo soprano with eight celli playing pizzicato as harmonic support. Béhague describes Villa-Lobos' treatment of this melody:

> Cantabile melodies of the modinha type abound in his works, but none as emotionally expressive and powerfully engaging as the famous soprano line of the Aria-Cantilena of *Bachianas Brasileiras no. 5*, the deservedly best-known and most popular work of Villa-Lobos. This 'chanting' line, which the composer referred to as a 'languid, lyric and neo-Classic melody' (Museu Villa-Lobos 1972: 191), is performed as a vocalise on the 'a' vowel. The improvisatory character of this long, wide phrase is created by its contour, which stresses its never-ending quality by means of pitch, harmonic, and rhythmic factors causing unpredictability and surprise.[107]

This vocal technique, which Jobim also embraced and used frequently, had become indelibly associated with Villa-Lobos due to the success of *Bachianas Brasileiras No. 5*, Obviously fascinated by the instrumental effect of female voices singing in unison, Jobim used this texture as an orchestral section in recordings such as 'Águas de março' (*Tom Jobim Inedito*), 'A felicidade' (*Tom Jobim Inedito*), 'Samba de uma nota só' (*Antônio Carlos Jobim*) and in the tone poem 'Saudade do Brasil'.

As with Villa-Lobos, the similarities between the music of Jobim and Debussy are mostly implied since they shared a common musical philosophy rather than specific compositional techniques. Both composers created music that is intricately crafted, sublimely subtle and yet intensely expressive. Their form of musical expression was an audacious and exploratory departure from the conventions of accepted musical theory – a discovery of new sonorities and rhythms. Debussy, for instance, felt restricted by the rules of conventional harmony as taught by the academy, and in 1902 commented about the training in harmony at the Paris Conservatoire:

> There is nothing one could more sincerely desire for French music than the suppression of the study of harmony as practised at school – which is indeed the most pompously ridiculous method of assembling sounds. It has in addition this grave fault, that it standardises composition to such a point that all musicians, with but few exceptions, harmonise in the same manner.[108]

Jobim likewise was disappointed with one of his more fastidious teachers, Paulo Silva. 'He was too systematic, full of tyrannical rules, he wouldn't let me do fourths or fifths, I felt quite restrained'.[109] In many respects Jobim, inspired by Villa-Lobos (who was also influenced by Debussy), continued Debussy's harmonic explorations within a tonal framework. In contrast to the European approach to new music composition, which embraced such techniques as dodecaphonic and aleatoric composition, Jobim favoured a more accessible and eclectic approach that embraced Debussy's experimental harmonic philosophy and enabled sonority to be placed above functional context.

Debussy and Jobim focused on the use of an innovative harmonic language and both possessed an ability to paint sensuous, impressionistic musical landscapes woven throughout with the refined threads of carefully selected melody. They delighted in the discovery of new chord constructions and often used them to evoke subtle sensuality. Debussy praised César Franck's harmonic adventurism by saying: 'In this Franck is at one with the great musicians for whom sounds have a definite meaning in their sonorous acceptation. They employ them just for what they are, without ever asking of them more than they contain'.[110] Debussy said of his own music: 'I myself love music passionately; and because I love it, I try to free it from barren traditions that stifle it'.[111] Much of Debussy's music uses progressions of isolated chords with individual and distinctive tonal colours and complex harmonic structure to conceal tonal centres. Jobim also used this approach in much of his orchestral work, and it is evident particularly in 'Sabiá' and 'Passarim'.[112]

Debussy's love and exploitation of instrumental timbre is evident in virtually all his music for piano that explores abstract harmonic sonorities peculiar to this instrument in a comprehensive manner. Villa-Lobos followed this example in the *Etudes* for guitar in which the multitude of chordal sonorities available for guitar are thoroughly investigated and documented. Jobim was able to take advantage of these 'sonic experiments', for piano and guitar, and found in them an inspirational aural resource and point of departure for his own stylistic invention.[113] Other similarities between Debussy and Jobim include the juxtaposition of static and shifting harmonic and melodic material (as shown in Debussy's 'La Cathédral Engloutie' and Jobim's 'Se todos fossem iguais a você'), a tendency for the use of downward-moving phrases,[114] the use of pedals as a contrast to other rhythms[115] and an attraction to sequences of thirds.

One of the greatest collections of Jobim's orchestral works appears in the aesthetically adventurous 1976 album *Urubu*. These mainly instrumental compositions are modern impressionistic tone poems that show evidence of diverse musical influences – *baião*, classical music, Brazilian regional music (especially heard in the *capoeira* rhythms) and the sounds of nature, including simulated bird calls. In particular, Jobim explores instrumental timbres and complex harmonic structures in *Saudade do Brasil*, an orchestral piece in which distinct sections outlining characteristics of Brazilian life can be heard. The French composer Darius Milhaud had previously set a precedent for this work with his *Saudades do Brasil*, a suite of orchestral pieces written in 1921, comprising a collection of twelve 'tangos', each named after a different district in Rio de Janeiro and highlighting a different dance rhythm. Milhaud had enjoyed a short sojourn in Rio de Janeiro from 1917 to 1919, when he was attaché to the minister of the French legation, the poet Paul Claudel. It was through Claudel that Milhaud met Villa-Lobos, who in turn introduced Milhaud to Rio's *choro* string bands and carnival festivities. Milhaud recalls in his autobiographical *Notes sans musique* (1945):

I was intrigued and fascinated by the rhythms of this popular music. There was an imperceptible pause in the syncopation, a careless catch in the breath, a slight hiatus which I found very difficult to grasp. So I bought a lot of maxixes and tangoes, and tried to play them with their syncopated rhythms that run from one hand to the other. At last my efforts were rewarded and I could both play and analyse this typically Brazilian subtlety. One of the best composers of this kind of music, Nazareth, used to play piano at the door of a cinema in the Avenida Rio Branco. His elusive, mournful, liquid way of playing also gave me deeper insight into the Brazilian soul.[116]

Milhaud realized there was something other than mere notation in score necessary to capture the essence of this music. This realization and his receptive attitude towards popular music and its practitioners reflected the same values that were fundamental to Jobim's approach to musical composition. The recognition that all musical styles had something to offer, regardless of their origins, was at the core of both Milhaud's and Jobim's attitude to music.

The influence exerted on Milhaud by Brazilian popular music (and later blues and jazz) underscores the eclectic and participatory attitude towards his own compositions. As indicated by Mawer, 'Milhaud's travels to Brazil and the United States, from 1917 onwards, were of critical importance, enabling him to experience such styles at first hand, and thus facilitating his assimilation and subsequent reinterpretation, or reworking, of them within his own musical language.'[117] 'Le Boeuf sur le Toit', for instance, is loosely based on a popular Brazilian song entitled 'O Boi no Telhado', and, in *Deux Poèms Tupis, Op. 52* two songs entitled 'Caïné' and 'Catiti' were inspired by the music of the native Indians of Brazil and Paraguay.[118] In his autobiographical *Ma Vie Heureuse*, Milhaud describes how he '[...] enjoyed bringing together popular tunes, tangos, maxixes, sambas, and even a Portuguese fado, and transcribing them with a theme recurring between each tune like a rondo'.[119] While not the first to embrace the musical culture surrounding him, Milhaud showed that the artistic rewards in doing so were immense.

In the early part of the twentieth century, polytonality – the simultaneous, superimposed presence of two or more distinct tonalities – had begun to attract the interest of composers in Europe and America. Ives experimented with its dissonances in *Psalm 67* (c 1900), Stravinsky in *Petrushka* (1910),[120] Prokofiev in *Sarcasmes, Op. 17 No. 3* (1912–14) and Bartók in his *Bagatelles* for piano (1908), but it was Darius Milhaud who became the most important figure in the extensive espousal and exploration of the technique. He used it frequently, but it is particularly evident in the 'Copacabana' and 'Botafogo' sections of his *Saudades do Brasil*. Milhaud's approach to polytonality may have influenced Jobim as there is distinct similarity in harmonic thought evident in each composer's music. Anxious to indicate the bitonal derivation of his harmonies, Jobim went so far as to designate superimposed chords in *Arquitetura de morar* and 'Trem para Cordisburgo'.[121]

Ravel was another early twentieth-century composer whose harmonic idiom influenced Jobim. Jobim studied Ravel's music with Lucia Branco in the 1940s, when he would have become familiar with Ravel's use of extended harmonies, 9ths and major 7th chords in particular, and the use of parallel harmonic progressions. Ravel's early piano work, 'Jeux d'eau', for instance, has many examples of consecutive progressions. Jobim showed a similar disposition towards extended-chord, parallel harmonic progressions and extended harmonies in, for example, his 'Você vai ver', 'O morro não tem vez' and 'Chora coração'. Debussy also had used a similar procedure in pieces such as 'Poissons d'Or', 'La Cathédral Engloutie' and 'La Soirée dans Grenade' and others.

Another aspect of Ravel's music is the eclectic use of rhythms, including folk dance rhythms from Spain, France and Central Europe.

> Ravel had a lasting preoccupation with the dance, which he considered significant not only from a structural point of view, but also as an important source of rhythmic invention. He paid homage to numerous dance traditions, both Western and non-Western, including French (pavane and forlane), Central European (minuet, waltz and passacaglia), Spanish (habañera, bolero and malagueña), and Malay (pantoum).[122]

Jobim found in Ravel a composer whom he greatly admired, a model of austerity and craftmanship, someone who could absorb local folk culture and who could also act as a role model for the successful assimilation of different musical styles such as jazz, modernism and bitonality. He also recognized that Ravel's compositional style was formed by an assimilation of the music of his predecessors. Ravel, for instance, made a practice of studying other composers' scores in preparation for particular projects.

Ravel's attention to proportion and classical form is evident in 'Pavane pour une Infante Défunte', for instance, which is in rondo (sonata) form (A-B-A-C-A), and the Sonatine, which is in three movements, with the middle movement fulfilling the dual function of slow movement and scherzo.[123] Jobim was likewise conscious of aspects of musical design, evident in the rondo form of his *choros*, the chaconne-like form of 'Águas de março', 'Matita Perê' that traverses all but one of twelve keys, the structural melodic sequence in *Saudades do Brasil*, and in the appropriately named *Arquitetura de morar* (Architecture to live) with its repeated sections of alternating minor 9th/suspended 4th harmonies.

One of Jobim's earliest pieces, the waltz 'Imagina', which he wrote when he was 18, was inspired, as he said, by Chopin.[124] Jobim also maintained that his 'One Note Samba' was inspired by Chopin's *Prelude in D flat*[125] and the similarity between Jobim's 'Insensatez' and Chopin's *Prelude in E minor, Op. 28 No. 4* is so strong that it has given rise to accusations of plagiarism.[126] The similarity of both the harmonic and melodic construction in these two pieces makes Jobim's 'Insensatez' the most obvious example of Chopin's direct influence. Jobim's friends often joked about the supposed derivation of 'Insensatez', the similarity between the two pieces not being lost on the jazz saxophonist Gerry Mulligan who subsequently recorded a samba version of the *Prelude*.[127]

Certain aspects of the harmonic vocabulary used in Jobim's songs – suspended 4ths, augmented 5ths, added 6ths, major 7ths and flat 9ths – are also evident in Chopin's music that often makes a feature of repeated chordal suspensions and delayed resolutions. Jobim delighted in the sonorities of these 'passing' harmonies and suspensions and retained them in their own right without subjecting them to conventional resolution. Chopin's music thus became a great source of harmonic inspiration and invention for Jobim. Other similarities can be seen in the use of repeated melodic motives that span a few semitones, similarities in harmonic progressions and a propensity for including descending chromatic relationships in the inner voices and the bass.

Igor Stravinsky was one of the twentieth century's most influential and eclectic composers, who incorporated styles from neo-nationalism through neo-classicism to serialism. That Jobim admired Stravinsky's work, particularly his rhythmic innovations, is undeniable. As Jobim recounted, 'Stravinsky says that music is a chronic art because it relies on the past and unfolds in time'.[128] Indeed, Stravinsky's rhythmic inventions and juxtapositions underlie much of Jobim's music – from his early work in the 1960s to his later creations in the 1980s.

Born in Porto Alegre, Rio Grande do Sul in 1906, Radamés Gnattali is considered one of the most significant Brazilian nationalist composers.[129] Initially self-taught, Gnattali began his musical career as a pianist, then as a viola player in a string quartet, and eventually acquired the position of official conductor for the Radio National Orchestra. He developed a reputation for skilful arrangements of fashionable popular tunes and dance rhythms and was able to incorporate popular aspects into his compositions and arrangements providing a strong foundation for nationalist expression. This ability was to have a profound effect on Jobim. In 1945 Radamés Gnattali was elected a founding member of the Academia Brasileira de Música and in the 1950s underwent a style change more towards neo-romantic and neo-classic composition. During the 1950s, while at the Continental recording company, Gnattali worked with Jobim on *Rio de Janeiro, a montanha, o sol, o mar* – a 'popular symphony in samba beat'.[130] Later Gnattali incorporated the rhythms of the bossa nova in his work, particularly in his *Second Violin Concerto* (1962), while maintaining a populist compositional style with such works as the *Concêrto Romântico* (three guitar concertos), *Sinfonia Popular, Concertos Cariocas, Sonatina Coreográfica* and the *Quarteto Popular*.[131] There had always been much mutual admiration between the two composers, and in the early 1990s Jobim wrote a choro entitled 'Meu Amigo Radamés' as a tribute to Gnattali.

Although Jobim denied that he was influenced by American jazz, he was nevertheless influenced by George Gershwin. Paulo Jobim describes the *Sinfonia do Rio de Janeiro* as 'a piece similar to George and Ira Gershwin's musical *An American in Paris*' and Jobim's 'Chansong' as 'Gershwinian'.[132] However, apart from specific works, it is the similarity of the professional lives of Gershwin and Jobim that is remarkable. Both began playing the piano after their family bought an instrument for another member of the family – in Gershwin's case for his older brother Ira, and in Jobim's for his sister Helena. Both showed enormous enthusiasm for music when they were young, and avidly took to studies of harmony and theory. Jobim spent many hours at the piano playing and sifting through the music of Bach,

Beethoven, Chopin, Debussy, Ravel and Villa-Lobos and was particularly fascinated when he discovered the Russian composers Rachmaninoff, Prokofiev and Stravinsky.[133]

Gershwin's musical tastes were also broad. He listened to classical music and to the popular music of the day, in particular the music of black Americans, which was then gaining widespread appeal. After becoming a professional musician in 1912, he played the piano at holiday resorts in upstate New York and worked as a song plugger for the renowned Remick Music Company.[134] As well as having similar broad musical tastes, Jobim also played piano in bars around Rio de Janeiro in the early 1950s and later worked as an arranger for the Continental Record Company. Both composers came to prominence soon after working in stage productions. Gershwin was hired in 1917 as a rehearsal pianist for the Jerome Kern/Victor Herbert Broadway show *Miss 1917*. Shortly afterwards Gershwin had his first 'hit' with the song 'Swanee' sung by Al Jolson for the musical *Sinbad* in 1919. Jobim came to worldwide prominence with his 'Chega de saudade', the song that introduced bossa nova to the world in 1959. The song was written with lyricist Vinicius de Moraes who had worked with Jobim on the music for the play *Orfeu de Conceição* (*Black Orpheus*) several years before.

Gershwin's influence on Jobim was based on the persuasion of precedent, a demonstration that the integration of a popular idiom (jazz in Gershwin's case) and classical form was possible. Both wrote in classical forms – Gershwin wrote 'Rhapsody in Blue', his *Concerto in F*, the tone poem 'An American in Paris' and his folk opera *Porgy and Bess*, while Jobim wrote for the opera *Orfeu da Conceição*, the government-commissioned *Brasilia, Sinfonia da Alvorada*, and later his orchestral tone poem *Saudade do Brasil*. The integrity of their popular songs was enhanced, in turn, by their integration of classical and popular idioms. Both composers have had songbooks produced of their music – *The George and Ira Gershwin Song Book* (1960), designed by Milton Glaser – provided a model for the *Tom Jobim Songbook* series produced by Almir Chediak (1990) and led to the more extensive *Cancioneiro Jobim* series (2001). At the end of the twenty-first century both composers' songs formed the heart of the standard jazz repertoire and are still played worldwide. Of all popular songs there would be relatively few people who have not heard either Gershwin's 'Summertime' or Jobim's 'Girl from Ipanema'.

Jobim's Aesthetics and Philosophy

There are several events in Jobim's life that, while seemingly unimportant in themselves, tell much about his artistic motivation and his personal sense of values. Even though he became one of the world's most successful popular music composers, Jobim almost certainly regarded serious (orchestral) or art music as the ultimate means of his musical expression – a musical art form above all others. In his early years, under the guidance of Koellreutter, Jobim 'played scales and learned to read music, sometimes practicing as much as ten hours a day. By then he had already decided what he wanted to be when he grew up: a great concert pianist'.[135] Several years later another of Jobim's teachers, Lucia Branco, pointed out that the span of his hand was too narrow to play even an octave comfortably, and subsequently encouraged him to concentrate on composition rather than pursue a career as a performer.[136] Jobim had a desire from the start to become a recognized art-music performer, but, as it became clear that this was unlikely to be fulfilled, a career as a composer offered itself as a course that would at least retain a sense of credibility and acknowledgement from educated and respected commentators. The decision for Jobim to become a popular music composer, as distinct from a serious art-music composer, may not have been a difficult one. If nothing else, he could earn a living playing, arranging and composing popular music. More than that, however, Jobim had the examples of Koellreuter and Villa-Lobos, both of whom had played in popular music groups, as an encouraging precedent. Their example at least enhanced the perception of popular and art music as expressions of more or less equal cultural and artistic value.

Another indication of Jobim's desire for recognition and acceptance was the planning and recording of his own albums using his own money. Jobim's explanation for this undertaking showed that in his estimation the pursuit of art and one's own creative inclinations had a much higher value than monetary success:

> In the '60s I began to finance my own records. This ensures you freedom of choice. You invite the musicians you want, the ones with the exact attributes you need for the kind of music you are making. When you work with a producer the first thing he thinks of is the commercial side; the artistic side, which is most important, is forgotten.[137]

In retrospect, this decision enabled Jobim to produce two of his most critically acclaimed albums in the 1970s. Paulo Jobim recalls:

> In Jobim's career, this phase seems to me to be the richest from a musical viewpoint. *Matita Perê* and *Urubu* were produced by Jobim and Claus Ogerman, with Jobim's own money and without the involvement of any recording company. On these albums his music follows a freer, more abstract path, and he and Claus make use of every nuance of the orchestra. They worked without any commercial concerns, and Ogerman chose the best musicians for the recordings, the New York Philharmonic Strings.[138]

The range of influences that Jobim embraced in his music was unquestionably extensive and without prejudice. His philosophy was to integrate those musical influences that had demonstrably influenced others, especially local folk idioms, and undertook his work as seriously as did his predecessors who provided a model for it – Villa-Lobos, Chopin, Debussy, Ravel, Stravinsky and Gershwin.[139] These diverse musical influences will be explored in more detail in the following chapters.

Notes

1 Cabral, *Antônio Carlos Jobim: Uma Biografia* 44.
2 Jobim and Jobim, *Cancioneiro Jobim: Obras Completas, 1947–1958*, vol. 1, 31.
3 Chediak, *Tom Jobim Songbook*, vol. 2 19.
4 Jobim and Jobim, *Cancioneiro Jobim: Obras Completas, 1947–1958*, vol. 1, 33.
5 Thompson, 'Let's Hear It for Jobim' 1.
6 The *modinha* is discussed more fully on pages 33–34 of this text.
7 Vianna 20.
8 Jobim and Jobim, *Cancioneiro Jobim: Obras Completas, 1947–1958*, vol. 1, 32.
9 Jobim and Jobim, *Cancioneiro Jobim: Obras Escolhidas* 56–57.
10 Jobim and Jobim, *Cancioneiro Jobim: Obras Completas, 1947–1958*, vol. 1, 34.
11 The musical features of bossa nova are discussed in more detail on pages 30–33.
12 Béhague, 'Bossa Nova'.
13 *Marcato* means 'marked' and implies here a strong, accentuated beat.
14 Jobim and Jobim, *Cancioneiro Jobim: Obras Completas, 1959–1965*, vol. 2, 45.
15 Chediak, *Tom Jobim Songbook*, vol. 1, 44.
16 With the exception of three songs – 'Change Partners' (Irving Berlin), 'I Concentrate on You' (Cole Porter) and 'Baubles, Bangles and Beads' (Wright-Forrest) – all songs on the album were by Jobim.
17 Chediak, *Tom Jobim Songbook*, vol. 1, 45.
18 See page 171 for an explanation of *choro* form and page 30 for an explanation of *maracatu* rhythmic style.
19 Cezimbra 168.
20 A detailed analysis of 'Águas de março' is given on pages 152–165.
21 Cabral, 'The Pathway of the Master' 45.
22 McGowan and Pessanha 58.
23 Antônio Carlos Jobim, interview, *Bossa Nova*.
24 Béhague, 'Samba'.
25 Delfino 95.
26 Also known as 'Favela'.
27 Béhague, *Music in Latin America* 118.
28 Béhague, *Music in Latin America* 119.
29 Literally 'Basket, my darling, Basket' referring to the singer wishing to be a basket hanging at the side of his lady friend.
30 Béhague, *Music in Latin America* 119.
31 Béhague, 'Samba'.
32 Vianna 27.
33 Apel.
34 Béhague, 'Bossa and Bossas: Recent Changes in Brazilian Urban Popular Music' 211.
35 Vianna 12.
36 John Charles Chasteen, quoted in Vianna xviii.
37 Perrone and Dunn 26.

38 Jobim and Jobim, *Cancioneiro Jobim: Obras Completas, 1966–1970,* vol. 3, 22; also Jobim, *Stone Flower.*

39 Chediak, *Tom Jobim Songbook,* vol. 3, 18.

40 Chediak, *Tom Jobim Songbook,* vol. 3, 18.

41 Chediak, *Tom Jobim Songbook,* vol. 2, 64.

42 Murphy 247.

43 Araújo 44.

44 This particular rhythm is noted in Appleby, *The Music of Brazil* 112, and Slonimsky 109. Samba rhythms are examined in more detail on pages 109–112.

45 Béhague, 'Brazil'.

46 Perrone and Dunn 1.

47 Such as in the case of atonal or aleatoric music for instance.

48 Quoted in Tarasti 7.

49 Grasse 294.

50 Jobim, quoted in Chediak, *Tom Jobim Songbook,* vol. 1 125.

51 Chediak, *Bossa Nova Songbook,* vol. 2, 16.

52 Vianna 47.

53 It is useful to note, however, that the rider to Romero's theory was that Brazilian culture was a result of race mixing and that the indigenous Brazilians were not part of that culture. 'Poetry in Tupi (the indigenous language most important in Brazilian history) was [just that] Tupi poetry', according to Romero, and not Brazilian poetry at all. The extension of this argument was that Brazilian culture began with race mixing, not with indigenous art.

54 Béhague, 'Bossa and Bossas' 209.

55 Jobim and Jobim, *Cancioneiro Jobim: Obras Escolhidas* 100.

56 Béhague, *The Beginnings of Musical Nationalism in Brazil* 11.

57 Béhague, *The Beginnings of Musical Nationalism in Brazil* 28.

58 McGowan and Pessanha 9.

59 McGowan and Pessanha 9.

60 Vianna 48.

61 Navegador, rev. of *A Pré-História do Samba,* by Bernado Alves, trans. James Sera, *Discos Raros,* (Jan 2001), http://www.historiasamba.hpg.ig.com.br/text.htm.

62 Béhague, 'Latin America' 510.

63 These bird calls were identified by the ornithologist, Helmut Sick in his book *Ornitologia Brasileira.* Quoted in Jobim and Jobim, *Cancioneiro Jobim: Obras Completas, 1971–1982,* vol. 4, 25.

64 Jobim and Jobim, *Cancioneiro Jobim: Obras Escolhidas* 123.

65 Jobim and Jobim, *Cancioneiro Jobim: Obras Completas, 1947–1958,* vol. 1, 31.

66 Quoted in Slonimsky 110.

67 Slonimsky 110.

68 Vianna 18.

69 Vianna 19.

70 A mixed-race man of small stature.

71 Vianna 20–22.

72 Gilberto Freyre, quoted in Vianna 19.

73 This piece's musical characteristics are shown on page 168.

74 'Chôro', *Michaelis Dicionário Ilustrado*, vol. 2.

75 Hodel, 'The Choro' 31.

76 Modern ensembles often include cornet as a substitute for the ophicleide.

77 'Maxixe', *Harvard Dictionary of Music*.

78 Hodel, 'The Choro' 33.

79 According to Eero Tarasti, Villa-Lobos' *Choros Nos. 13* and *14* have been lost. See Tarasti 89.

80 Quoted in Tarasti 87.

81 Tarasti 87.

82 Tarasti 130.

83 Tarasti 117.

84 Sève 5.

85 Sève 6.

86 'Chega de saudade' is examined in more detail on page 56.

87 Also known as 'Garoto'. The melody and form of this *choro* is discussed on page 171.

88 Jobim and Jobim, *Cancioneiro Jobim: Obras Escolhidas* 207.

89 Béhague, *Heitor Villa-Lobos* 157.

90 Heitor Villa-Lobos, quoted in Béhague, *Heitor Villa-Lobos* 84.

91 Béhague, *The Beginnings of Musical Nationalism in Brazil* 19.

92 Carlos Lyra, quoted in Chediak, *Bossa Nova Songbook*, vol. 2, 147.

93 Jobim 212.

94 Jobim occasionally visited Villa-Lobos in the late 1950s as an assistant to Leo Perachi who had been hired to help write his scores. Cezimbra 67 and 73.

95 Fisk 2.

96 Quoted in Béhague, *Music in Latin America* 130.

97 Tarasti, *Heitor Villa-Lobos* 42.

98 Béhague, *Heitor Villa-Lobos* 154.

99 Béhague, *Music in Latin America* 183.

100 Chediak, *Tom Jobim Songbook*, vol. 2, 18.

101 Chediak, *Tom Jobim Songbook*, vol. 3, 14.

102 Cezimbra 73.

103 Chediak, *Tom Jobim Songbook*, vol. 3, 6.

104 Perrone and Dunn 13.

105 Perrone and Dunn 13.

106 Béhague, *Music in Latin America* 186.

107 Béhague, *Heitor Villa-Lobos* 114.

108 Quoted in Vallas 26.

109 Jobim and Jobim, *Cancioneiro Jobim: Obras Completas, 1947–1958*, vol. 1, 31.

110 Vallas 45.

111 Vallas 10.

112 This harmonic approach is discussed on page 73.

113 See pages 80–81 for examples of particular guitar sonorities used by both Jobim and Villa-Lobos.

114 Lockspeiser discusses this downward-moving tendency in Debussy's *Syrinx* and *Le Faune* (*Fêtes galantes,* second series) in Lockspeiser 237.

115 Lockspeiser 234.

116 Milhaud, *Notes without Music* 64.

117 Mawer 116.

118 Mawer 115.

119 Mawer 116.

120 'Bitonality, polytonality', *Harvard Dictionary of Music.*

121 See pages 84–87 for a discussion of bitonal similarities in both composers' music.

122 Kelly, 'Maurice Ravel'.

123 Shera 51.

124 Jobim and Jobim, *Cancioneiro Jobim: Obras Escolhidas* 34.

125 Reily 10.

126 See pages 141–148 for a discussion of the similarities and differences between the two pieces.

127 Gene Lees, *Antonio Carlos Jobim: Jazz Masters 13*, CD, Los Angeles: Verve, 1993.

128 Jobim and Jobim, *Cancioneiro Jobim: Obras Completas, 1947–1958*, vol. 1, 32.

129 Béhague, *Music in Latin America* 209.

130 Jobim and Jobim, *Cancioneiro Jobim: Obras Completas, 1947–1958*, vol. 1, 30.

131 Béhague, *Music in Latin America* 211.

132 Jobim and Jobim, *Cancioneiro Jobim: Obras Escolhidas* 185.

133 Cabral, *Antônio Carlos Jobim: Uma Biografia* 60.

134 Larkin 516.

135 Jobim and Jobim, *Cancioneiro Jobim: Obras Escolhidas* 33.

136 Jobim and Jobim, *Cancioneiro Jobim: Obras Escolhidas* 34.

137 Jobim and Jobim, *Cancioneiro Jobim: Obras Escolhidas* 163.

138 Jobim and Jobim, *Cancioneiro Jobim: Obras Completas, 1971–1982*, vol. 4, 24.

139 Jobim's attitude towards his music was revealed in a seemingly innocuous event, on the night of a gala benefit concert for the Rain Forest Foundation, 'emceed by Sting and starring Jobim himself, there was a rumour backstage that when Jobim and his band played the Ipanema song, Elton John would appear dressed like Carmen Miranda, or at least wearing one of those turbans full of bananas or umbrellas'. Fortunately, nothing happened mainly because of Jobim's anticipated negative reaction. Jobim regarded his music too seriously for it to be associated so flippantly with the crass commercialism and cliché that Carmen Miranda had endured. Perrone and Dunn 42.

Chapter 3

Harmonic Language

Introduction

One of the difficulties in an analysis of a composer's music is the prioritizing of the characteristics that constitute his style. The order in which these stylistic characteristics are discussed here should not be taken as a measure of their importance, nor should it be taken to indicate the frequency of their occurrence in Jobim's music. Bearing these considerations in mind, the following chapters will examine the most fundamental aspects of Jobim's style and in most cases will indicate not only a probable source of inspiration for specific characteristics but also how he used diverse sources and influences to construct a language identifiable as his own. In order to demonstrate the extent of Jobim's musical style, six representative pieces that contain many of the techniques and stylistic characteristics contributing to Jobim's eclectic style are considered in full. The complete scores of these pieces are presented online and will thus make possible a thorough inter-contextual understanding.[1] These pieces will be used as points of departure to discuss other examples of Jobim's music that contain stylistic characteristics similar to those under consideration. The following chapters are arranged to cover the broad stylistic areas of harmonic, rhythmic and melodic and structural techniques. In the discussion of complete pieces, however, there may be specific characteristics presented that do not necessarily fall into the immediate area of interest, but, as far as possible, in all examples, the emphasis will be on the area under discussion.[2]

This book attempts to demonstrate that the success of Jobim's music was in a large part due to his eclecticism and openness to a diverse range of musical styles. It attempts to explain how Jobim incorporated different musical influences into his own work to create a language identifiable as his own. Many of these influences can be attributed to specific composers or local folk and popular styles, but Jobim also used conventional art-music techniques not directly attributable to any individual composer. These compositional techniques are notable not so much for their departure from normal compositional practice, but for their collective definition of Jobim's style. It will be necessary, therefore, to identify these techniques, by analysis of appropriate pieces in their entirety and also of specific extracts taken from the body of his work. Examination of these techniques will reveal the extent of Jobim's wide-ranging absorption of influences from the broadly stylistic to the technically specific. It will become evident that Jobim's musical language evolved from the individual way in which these compositional techniques and styles were synthesized.

Harmonic Techniques: 'Chega de saudade'

'My music is essentially harmonic. I've always sought harmony. It's as if I tried to harmonise the world.'[3]

In many respects 'Chega de saudade' is typical of Jobim's popular music style yet borrows much of its inspiration, overall structure and melodic characteristics from the *choro* musical form. Specifically, it contains a lyrical, sentimental melody with irregular modulations, harmonically complex chords and, in the original recording, featured João Gilberto's distinctive syncopated acoustic guitar-playing, a style that eventually became permanently associated with bossa nova. The title 'Chega de saudade' literally means 'that's enough yearning', but it is often translated in English as 'No more blues'. The harmonic complexity in this song was an attraction to West-Coast American jazz musicians who took to it avidly and found its simple yet elegant melody and exotic harmonic constructions particularly innovative and appealing. It soon became a jazz standard, helped by the release of the 'definitive' version of the song by Gilberto in 1959, and became one of the first songs to be included in the 'Latin' repertoire of jazz standards, a category that was until the late 1950s virtually non-existent.

It is Jobim's extensive use of harmonically complex chords throughout the song that characterizes it as being representative of his particular style. Not only is it distinguished by the idiosyncratic harmonic construction of these individual chords but also by Jobim's distinctive choice of chord progression. Almost all chords are built using extended harmonies – added 7ths, 9ths, flat 9ths, 6ths, sharp 5ths, suspended 4ths and major 7ths predominate. There are no unadorned major triads, while in the few instances where the harmony consists of simple minor triads, extended harmonies are re-introduced within the space of (at most) one measure. There is also a propensity for chromatic relationships between successive chords to be emphasized, particularly evident in the bass. In general, harmonic change occurs from measure to measure, unlike many jazz styles, for instance, which lend themselves to changes occurring for each beat.[4] As suggested by Reily, Jobim created tonal ambiguities in various ways: by using major chords with supertonic functions and minor chords with dominant functions.[5] In 'Chega de saudade', this major/minor vacillation also extends to chords of tonic, subdominant, mediant and submediant degree. This is typical of *choro* style where diatonic and non-diatonic chords can appear with equal regularity. However, unlike traditional *choro*, in which there is only occasional use of extended harmonies, Jobim's use of complex harmonies not only extends to most chords, but his particular use of the major 7th chord in prominent locations at the start and end of melodic phrases marks a significant characteristic of his style.[6]

Sève points out that in *choro* the use of an instrumental introduction is common, particularly in compositions with lyrics.[7] 'Chega de saudade', typically, opens with an energetic eight-measure introduction (played by flute in the original recording) that is separated from the body of the song with a richly harmonized accented chord in measure 8 (see Ex. 3.1). This is one of several highly coloured chords used in exposed positions throughout the song and is reminiscent of the complex dissonant harmonies that were the result of Milhaud's chordal superimpositions and Villa-Lobos' use of complex chords in exposed positions.[8] The last chord in the subsequent eight-measure passage at measure 16 (see Ex. 3.2) is also a virtual repeat of this complex chord and highlights the sense of expectation at the end of this passage, as does the final A7(♭9) chord at measure 24 (see Ex. 3.8) where the last melody note (upper voice) is the suspended (flat 9th) note.[9]

Ex. 3.1. Antônio Carlos Jobim, 'Chega de saudade', introduction, measures 1–8.[10]

Melodic Sequence with Non-Sequential Altered Harmonies

Another significant aspect of the introduction is the sequential, transposed repetition of a melodic phrase with non-sequential, altered harmony. While this technique is not unique to Jobim, he took it to a very sophisticated level, to the extent that it can be found frequently in many of his songs and also in his orchestral works, as will be demonstrated in the following examples. It is one of the most significant characteristics of Jobim's musical style.

In the introduction (Ex. 3.1) the melodic phrase spans measures 1–2 and is repeated a step lower through measures 3–4, while the supporting harmony moves through the non-sequential progression Gm7–A7 to Dm(add9)–Dm/C. Jobim used melodic sequences in the body of this song as a means of extending the song's structure. For instance, much of the first section of the song, after the introduction, is constructed from a simple, sequential, two-measure, melodic phrase that contrasts with its complex harmonic accompaniment. The opening theme is stated in measures 9–16, but, unlike the introduction, the melody merely outlines the constituent notes of the accompanying chords.[11] The shape and rhythm of the melodic phrase in the first two measures (9–10) is duplicated in measures 11–12 and again in measures 13–14.

Ex. 3.2. Antônio Carlos Jobim, 'Chega de saudade', main theme (upper voice), measures 9–16.[12]

An early indication of the technique of melodic phrase repetition with altered harmony can be seen in the elegantly simple 'Não devo sonhar' (I must not dream), a piece that Jobim wrote with his sister Helena in 1956 (Ex. 3.3). The main theme, stated in measures 5–6 (upper voice), is sequenced in measures 7–8 and measures 9–10, a step lower at each repeat, but is set with non-sequential harmony.

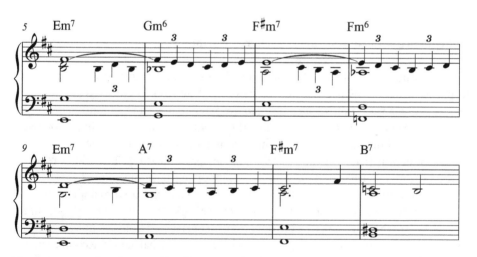

Ex. 3.3. Antônio Carlos Jobim, 'Não devo sonhar', measures 5–12.[13]

Some of Jobim's better-known pieces are composed using this technique of motive sequence against non-sequential harmonic motion as a means of extension. Songs such as 'Corcovado', 'Garota de Ipanema', 'Zingaro' (Gypsy), 'Outra vez' (Another time), 'Andam dizendo' (They are saying), 'Tereza meu amor' (Tereza my love), 'O que tinha de ser' (What had to be), as well as orchestral pieces such as 'O planalto deserto' (Deserted plain), the 'Coral' (Chorale) from *Brasilia Sinfonia da Alvorada* and the opening measures of the orchestral *Saudade do Brasil*, employ this technique, sometimes as the basis of composition for the entire piece. Jobim's command and development of this technique to extend a composition indicates that the musical and inventive focus is no longer on melody, but is instead on harmonic progression. Harmonic progression consequently becomes a surrogate means of musical 'identity' for a piece, in addition to melody. Indeed, because it remains relatively static, the significance of melody in some of Jobim's compositions becomes somewhat secondary. Melody is often highlighted as the most innovative and characteristic aspect of Jobim's work and his most significant contribution to popular music.[14] However, it was his structural and innovative control of harmony that was a definitive factor in the creation of his musical style. The key was the contrast of simplicity and sophistication created by the juxtaposition of simple melodies and complex, often chromatic, harmony.

Another noteworthy example that demonstrates this principle is 'Engano', in which the rhythm and melodic shape of a simple motive (occupying one measure) is used as a building block for the development of virtually the entire song (Ex. 3.4). Here, altered and extended chords are used in the harmony as well as major/minor fluctuations in tonic and dominant harmonies. This is clearly an exploration through harmony of the contrast set-up between simple motivic repetition and sophisticated chromatic harmonizations.[15] It is the harmony, more than the melody, that drives the piece.

The technique of melodic motive (or phrase) sequence is commonly found in many Brazilian *choros*. For instance, the melodic phrase in the first two measures of Pixinguinha's choro 'Ainda me recordo' (Ex. 3.5) is repeated (a tone lower) in the following two measures, as is the melodic phrase in the first measure of José Maria de Albreu's 'Tomando sereno' (Ex. 3.6).[17]

In both above examples 3.5 and 3.6, the chord progression is sequential as the melody is transposed by the same interval as the harmonic root of successive chords. Although Jobim was obviously influenced by this form of song construction, his innovation was to underscore the independence of harmonic and melodic development by using non-sequential harmony that was unrelated to melodic motive/phrase transposition. This non-sequential technique was also used by Villa-Lobos. The famous *Choros No. 1* for guitar (Ex. 3.7) is based on a one-measure melodic phrase that is the fundamental building block of the entire piece. Its rhythm is repeated for the first eight measures and, with subtle changes in intervallic content, reappears frequently throughout the piece.

Ex. 3.4. Antônio Carlos Jobim, 'Engano', measures 1–16.[16]

Ex. 3.5. Pixinguinha, 'Ainda me recordo' (*choro*), opening measures.[18]

Ex. 3.6. José Maria de Albreu, 'Tomando sereno' (*choro*), opening measures.[19]

Ex. 3.7. Heitor Villa-Lobos, *Choros No. 1*, measures 1–8.[20]

Major-Minor Mode Changes

Also of note in the above example is the introduction of the major subdominant (in a minor key) at measure 7, which is typical of major-minor modal changes found in *choro*. As seen in 'Engano' (Ex. 3.4), Jobim was also not averse to using modal changes.[21] This also occurs in 'Chega de saudade', for example, in measures 19–20 where the melody moves to c1, giving a minor colour to the dominant harmony (Ex. 3.8).[22]

The dominant harmony subsequently alternates between major and minor – it is found in major at measures 23, 38 and 70 and minor at measures 36 and 64. This is typical of the modal ambiguity in *choro* style, where chords of every diatonic scale degree can change frequently between major and minor. For instance, in 'Chega de saudade' after the modal change to D major at measure 41, there are examples of submediant major chords (measures 42, 68, 72 and 80), supertonic major (measures 43, 53, 59, 69, 73, 81), mediant major (measures 61 and 71) and subdominant minor (measures 55 and 66). A typical example of this localized modal ambiguity is seen in the opening measures of the *choro* 'Aguenta o leme' by José Maria de Abreu (Ex. 3.9).[24] Here the dominant fluctuates between minor and major in the space of two measures (measures 6 and 8) and the tonic temporarily changes from minor to major at measure 12.

Ex. 3.8. Antônio Carlos Jobim, 'Chega de saudade', measures 17–24.[23]

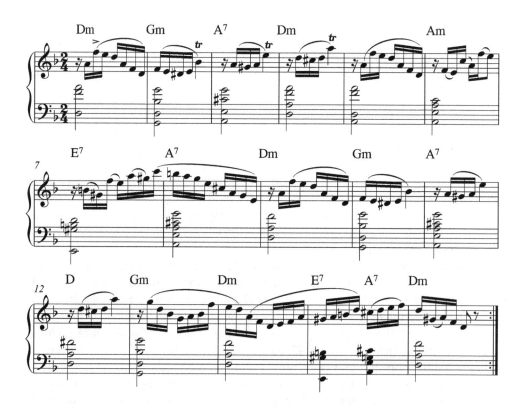

Ex. 3.9. José Maria de Abreu, 'Aguenta o leme' (*choro*), measures 1–16.[25]

Jobim effects a similar tonic minor-major-minor change in 'Chega de saudade' at measure 31. Again, this is typical of *choro* style, where modal differences are created in a manner that does not draw attention to itself but contributes seamlessly to the essential character of the style.

In Jobim's 'Oficina' (Ex. 3.10) for instance, minor-major changes occur frequently:

D minor to D major (measures 16–17), G major to G minor (measures 18–19), and A major to A minor (measures 23–24).

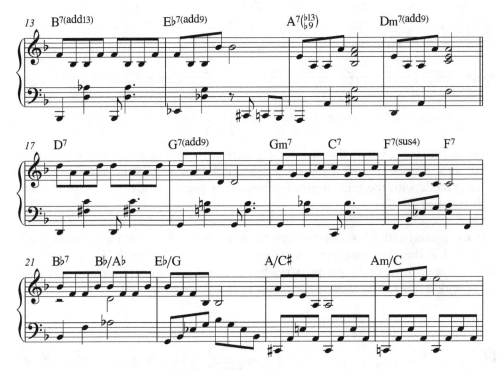

Ex. 3.10. Antônio Carlos Jobim, 'Oficina', measures 13–24.[26]

In other songs Jobim used minor dominants in his own idiosyncratic manner distinct from traditional *choro* style. Another example of Jobim's individualistic use of minor-major modal fluctuation is shown in Ex. 3.11. In this example, the minor dominant is used in a manner that is more functionally independent of the tonic with a dominant harmony prolonged over measures 15–20.

These particular modal changes are also found in traditional *modinhas*. Béhague points out that these modulations occur in what he calls 'the *modinha* of the Second Empire', and quotes Mário de Andrade:

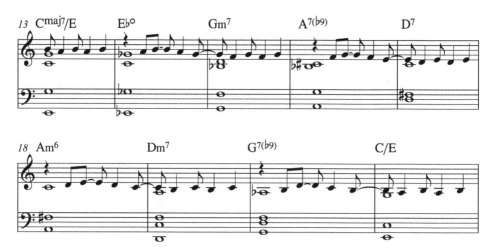

Ex. 3.11a. Antônio Carlos Jobim, 'Discussão', measures 13–21.[27]

The impression given is that those composers of *modinhas* had a sixteenth-century harmonic sensibility, conceiving the minor mode, not as another mode, but as the major mode with the third degree lowered. They used it to give variety to the tonal physiognomy.[28]

Neto also points out that 'switches between major and minor modes in the same key' can be traced back to Brazilian popular music from the early 1800s. He cites the *lundu* 'a sensuous and syncopated dance brought from Africa by slaves and performed in the courtyards after a day's work' as possessing these major/minor modal characteristics.[29]

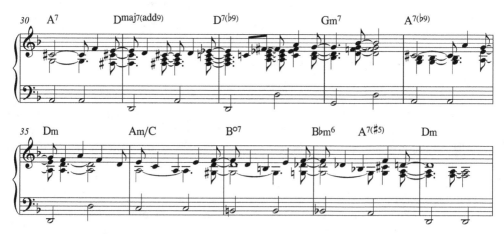

Ex. 3.11b. Antônio Carlos Jobim, 'Chega de saudade', measures 30–39.[31]

As would be expected, the use of major/minor modal variation allows a greater flexibility in melodic progression and choice of notes than in a situation where only one mode is used. As exemplified in 'Chega de saudade', this flexibility is particularly obvious in the passage from measures 30–39.[30] Here the melody becomes rather circuitous and, because of the change in modality, virtually every semitone within the octave b^{b1}– b^b is sounded – indicative of the melodic flexibility that can be gained by the use of minor/major mode changes.

Table 3.1 shows the overall harmonic structure of 'Chega de saudade' and the modal changes of the different sections. Measure 41 is the mid-point of the song, with a double measure line marking what may be construed as the division between a verse and chorus and a D major modality firmly established by a change of key signature. The mode change from tonic minor to major (or the reverse) is another example of typical mode changes that occur at section boundaries in *choro* style.[32]

Table 3.1: Antônio Carlos Jobim, 'Chega de saudade', overall harmonic structure showing key changes.

Intro	A	B	A	C	D	A'	E (coda)
mm 1–8	9–16	17–24	25–32	33–40	41–56	57–64	65–85
D minor	D minor	D minor	D min/maj	D maj/min	D major	D major	D major

Descending Linear Chromatic Harmonic Relationships

As has been discussed previously, the element of *saudade* is one of the most ubiquitous characteristics in Brazilian music, but it is very difficult to define musically. One of Jobim's most identifiable characteristics, and one which also helps to engender the spirit of *saudade*, is his propensity for retaining chromatic, descending linear relationships in the accompaniment of his songs and orchestral works. For instance, he frequently constructed chords that had constituent notes as part of a descending chromatic line, often in the bass. This characteristic is an inimitable aspect of Jobim's style, and appears to be a major determining factor in the construction of the harmony to many of his compositions.

Two examples in 'Chega de saudade' of descending chromatic relationships (evident in the bass) can be seen in measures 10–14 and 36–38. In both instances, the bass descends chromatically c–B–Bb–A.[33] A descending, extended chromatic relationship in the inner voices of successive chords is also evident in measures 79 to 83, where the descending chromatic sequence b–bb–a–g#–g♮–f# is discernible in the lower notes of the right-hand accompaniment (Ex. 3.12). It would seem that the maintenance of this chromatic line in the inner voices plays a large part in the construction of the accompanying chords for this section.

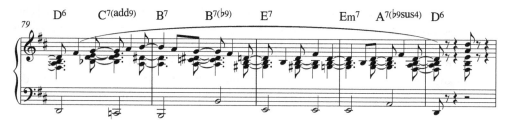

Ex. 3.12. Antônio Carlos Jobim, 'Chega de saudade', measures 79–83.[34]

In Ex. 3.13, 'Samba de uma nota só', descending chromatic lines can be found in the bass: B–B♭–A–A♭ (measures 6–9) and D–D♭–C (measures 10–12), and also in the inner voices: a–a♭–g–g♭–f♮–e–e♭ (measures 6–13).

Ex. 3.13. Antônio Carlos Jobim, 'Samba de uma nota só', measures 6–13.[35]

In another example, 'Corcovado' (Ex. 3.14), the instances of descending chromatic lines in the bass and inner voices are particularly apparent.

In this section there is a chromatic line c^1–b– b♭–a♮–a♭ (g#)–g♮–f# in the inner voices of measures 13–26. The bass descends chromatically A–G#–G♮–G♭–F–E throughout measures 13–23.[37] Of particular interest here is the chromatic line formed by the notes $c\#^2$, $c♮^2$, b^1, $b♭^1$ added above the chords in measures 23 and 24. These notes are not always heard in non-orchestral arrangements of this song and are marked in grey in the original *Cancioneiro Jobim* score, indicating that they have been added as 'additional' harmony

Ex. 3.14. Antônio Carlos Jobim, 'Corcovado', measures 13–28.[36]

above the melody.[38] Their inclusion, nevertheless, says much about Jobim's approach to harmonic construction by revealing his predilection for highlighting descending chromatic relationships between chords.

The result of this tendency to develop linear chromatic chordal relationships helped to create not only smooth chord transitions but also idiosyncratic, non-standard chord progressions that defined the sound of Jobim's music as much as his melodies. 'Diálogo' is a prime example of a piece designed almost entirely with harmonic progression in mind rather than melody. Indeed, the melody here is essentially defined by the chord progression. At the outset, the melody consists essentially of a one-measure repeated motive having a rhythmic pattern of a minim followed by four quavers (Ex. 3.15). This rhythmic motive is repeated for almost every measure in the piece. In the first five measures the melody sounds the constituent notes of the accompanying chord in ascending order, so that the last quaver sounds the root. Jobim made a point of arranging the harmonic progression so that the roots of consecutive chords descend chromatically from D to A. Ex. 3.15 shows the first eight measures (after a four-measure introduction).

The following eight measures (13–21) (Ex. 3.16) are based on measures 5–12, except that now the chromatic line (D–A) is interrupted by an Ab diminished and an F# diminished chord in measures 14 and 16 respectively. There is also a modal change from D major to D minor in measures 13–18 and the quavers in the melodic motive descend chromatically. The harmonic progression now consists of chords with roots that progress D–A–C–F#–B–A–D. This is certainly not a chord progression likely to be encountered in most popular music, and yet it sounds entirely natural, partly because of its chromatic derivation in the previous measures and partly because of the simplicity of the melodic motive 'sewing' the whole construction together.

Ex. 3.15. Antônio Carlos Jobim, 'Diálogo', measures 5–12.[39]

Ex. 3.16. Antônio Carlos Jobim, 'Diálogo', measures 13–20.[40]

Although the harmonic chromaticism in Jobim's style (particularly his use of a chromatic descending bassline) is one of his music's major features, it is not, of course, unique to Jobim. It is prevalent in *choro* and *modinha* and is also a frequent feature of the classical music Jobim admired, such as that by Chopin, Debussy and Ravel.

Ex. 3.17 shows one instance of Debussy's many treatments of the chromatic descending bassline – a technique that in this instance successfully enhances the programmatic imagery of the piece by alluding to the descending motion of falling rain. There are other striking correspondences between the music of both composers that indicate that Jobim had at least been captivated by the sonic effect of the chromatic descending bassline.[41] It should be noted that in this example the chromatic bass notes are not of course all chordal roots.

Jobim became quite enamoured with the sound of successive chords with roots forming a chromatic descending bassline. For instance, in 'Eu te amo' (I love you) (Ex. 3.18), Jobim creates a sequence of chords almost all of which have roots that run from D♭ to F.[43]

Ex. 3.17. Claude Debussy, 'Jardins sous la pluie' (Gardens in the rain), measures 90–95.[42]

Other examples of Jobim's use of chromatic descending basslines can be found in 'Ana Luiza', 'Flor do mato' (Bush flower), 'Pra dizer adeus' (To say goodbye), 'Soneto de separação' (Separation sonnet) and 'Chovendo na roseira' (Rain in the rose garden).[45] All these songs contain basslines that descend chromatically over at least five semitones.

Jobim's propensity for use of the chromatic descending bass is well shown in 'Corcovado' (Ex. 3.14). After a 12-measure introduction, the song begins in the key of C major with a chord designated as Am6, but that chord functions as a secondary dominant.[46] According to Lees (who wrote the English lyric for the song), Jobim called this opening chord 'D9/A', thus

Ex. 3.18. Antônio Carlos Jobim, 'Eu te amo', measures 9–18.[44]

indicating its function, but the note D is never included as a constituent note of the chord.[47] The chord's function is at odds with its designation, but its particular inversion enables the formation of the chromatic bassline A–G#–G–F#–F–E as a distinctive harmonic statement at the beginning of the song.

Contextual Use of Extended Harmony

Another important characteristic of Jobim's compositional style that is consistent throughout most of his music is his use of major 7th chords as a replacement for (or an extension of) a simple tonic triad in major keys. In fact, the vast majority of Jobim's compositions in major keys feature the major 7th chord in the first appearance (and often in all subsequent appearances) of the tonic chord. Major 7th chords are common in jazz and some popular music, but it is the consistency and prominence of their use in Jobim's music that indicates his ostensible infatuation with their sonority.

Jobim acknowledged his indebtedness to composers such as Chopin, Debussy and Ravel for his appreciation and understanding of extended harmony. A composition such as Ravel's 'Jeux d'eau', for instance, which exploits the chord of the major 7th, would have provided Jobim with much insight into the mechanisms of extended harmonies and a sense of legitimacy in its use. The piece begins and ends with a tonic major 7th chord and there are numerous examples of it within the piece itself.[48]

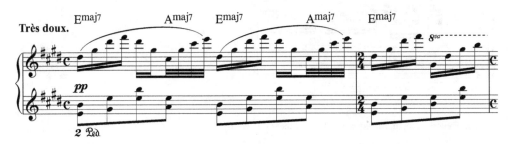

Ex. 3.19. Maurice Ravel, 'Jeux d'eau', introduction, measures 1 and 2.

Jobim's infatuation with the sonority of not only major 7th chords but chords built by extension and augmentation is evident in all of his music. He rarely wrote unembellished major chords and would invariably use, if not major 7th, then 6th or 9th chords in their place. He would often transform minor chords into minor 7th or minor 6th chords, in much the same way as jazz performers embellish basic chords with coloured or 'added' notes. Although the extent of jazz influence on Jobim's work is debatable, his appreciation of the sonic characteristics and contextual use of harmonically complex chords must have been enhanced by his exposure to jazz.[49] His use of harmonically complex chords may also have been influenced by an adoption and expansion of the popular style introduced by Dorival Caymmi and the *choro* guitarist Garoto, both of whom used four-note extended chords as a distinctive element of their sound.

Jobim had also been fascinated by the music of Chopin since he was 17, studying with Lúcia Branco. 'When I began to listen to Chopin seriously I thought, my God, what is this? How is it that a person who was born a 'thousand' years ago already knew all that I know now?'[50] Jobim's enchantment with the sonic discoveries revealed in Chopin's music is shared with Gerard Abraham, who, in his observations of two Chopin *Nocturnes, Op. 15 No. 1* and *Op. 27 No. 1*, refers to the 'innumerable beautiful or powerful transition chords (or pseudo chords) produced by suspensions or passing notes'.[51] Abraham delights in the 'faint clash of the suspended C and A natural' in measure 30 of the *Nocturne, Op. 15 No. 1* (Ex. 3.20), and the 'delicious' G♭ passing notes in the following measure 31.

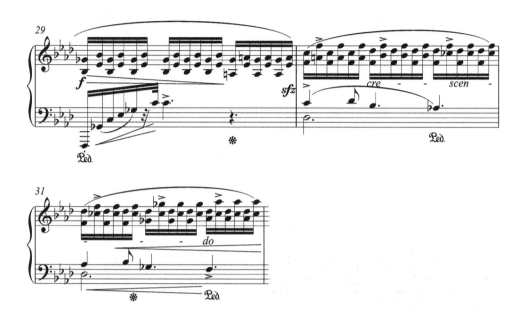

Ex. 3.20. Frédéric Chopin, *Nocturne, Op. 15 No. 1* measures 29–31.

Abraham also admires Chopin's creation of a 'pseudo-chord of great intensity' from the chromatic passing note in Ex. 3.21.

Ex. 3.21. Frédéric Chopin, *Nocturne,*
Op. 15 No. 1 measures 64–65.

It is easy to imagine that these complex 'passing' harmonies could be retained in their own right and not be subjected to conventional resolution. This practice, as Abraham points out, 'led nineteenth-century harmony through *Tristan* to the Schönberg of the *Klavierstücke* op. 11, and ultimately to the abandonment of tonality'.[52] Jobim, on the other hand, found in this procedure an extraordinary wealth of sonic colours that became fundamental to his compositions, but he nevertheless maintained a strong sense of tonality and harmonic context. Although supposedly working independently from jazz (in which similar complex harmonic developments were occurring), he was able to take this procedure to an exceptional level of complexity for popular music.[53]

In the decades surrounding the turn of the twentieth century, an era that was more favourable to 'dissonant' harmonic exploitation than that of Chopin, Debussy's employment of 'dissonant' chordal sonorities became an important part of his musical personality. This was especially evident in situations where a chord was presented in an exposed position that was not part of a logical harmonic progression or cadential harmony, as is illustrated in Ex. 3.22. The first chord of the second measure of this example bears no obvious functional relationship to the previous measure or the following measure, but exists purely as a colourful interjection between a temporally distorted repeat of a rather angular musical phrase.[54] The chord is there for sonic effect.

Also, the final chord in this passage is an excellent example of Debussy's blurring of both a sense of tonal centre and a sense of resolution in having reached an ultimate destination.[55] Jobim also ends his 'Passarim' in a similarly tonally nebulous manner, as illustrated in Ex. 3.23, by including the note D in the bass, subverting an F# major tonality implied by the previous chord.

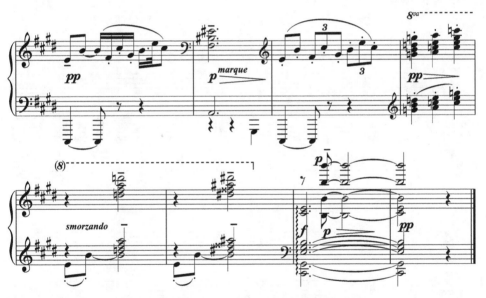

Ex. 3.22. Claude Debussy, 'Pour les Sonorités Opposées' from *Douze Études*, last eight measures.

The adventurous nature of Jobim's harmonic craft can also be seen in Jobim's instrumental piece 'Surfboard', written in 1964.[57] Jobim was not averse to using unusual harmonic techniques to enhance a sense of anticipation or to give a piece a particular harmonic twist. The harmonic surprise in this piece appears in the middle section, where Jobim's use of

Ex. 3.23. Antônio Carlos Jobim, 'Passarim', final measures.[56]

Ex. 3.24. Antônio Carlos Jobim, 'Surfboard', measures 17–32.[58]

repeated notes played by the strings at the interval of a diminished-5th (f1 natural and b) over 16 measures is quite striking.

This passage can be regarded as a four-measure alternation of G7 and D♭7(add9) (tritone substitution) chords that ends (in the second repeat) with a rather elaborate E7♭13♭9 chord (as outlined in Ex. 3.25). Here the extended g#^{1} horn note functions as the 3rd of the E major triad.[59] The highly coloured E7♭13♭9 'punctuation chord' occurs in the transition between this and the succeeding section and is another example of Jobim's love of complex chord construction for sonic effect, with little regard for traditional voice-leading principles or harmonic resolution.

In Ex. 3.25 the chord that appears at measure 51 has a secondary function. Despite its elaborate construction, it is heard as a natural resolution to rising g^1 – g#^{1} figure of the horns accompanied by the repeated diminished 5th interval played by the strings.

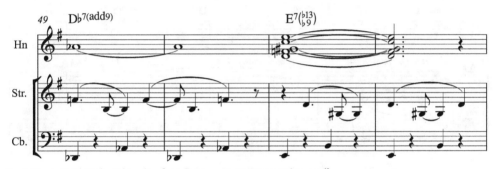

Ex. 3.25. Antônio Carlos Jobim, 'Surfboard', measures 49–52, second repeat.[60]

Jobim's love of rich and sonorous harmonies is particularly evident in the orchestration for the opening of his song 'Sabiá'.[61] The orchestral harmonies that introduce 'Sabiá' are of majestic proportions and work particularly well to enhance the song's sentiment. The lyric of the song talks of the futility of returning to a past life that no longer exists.[62] At the outset an illusion of overwhelming disorientation and despair is achieved by the use of sustained complex harmonies, which function independently to disrupt any sense of tonal centre. Eventually, these resolve to support a simple melody and the opening lyrical sentiment that is a determination to go back to a past life (Ex. 3.26).

'Sabiá' is an excellent example of Jobim's use of 'dissonant' or 'complex' chords for sonic effect. The arresting sonority of the first chord, for instance, is sustained over three measures while the complexity of the following chords helps to blur any sense of tonal centre. Taking the root of the opening chord as B♭, the chord in fact contains an augmented 4th (#11), a flat 9th, a dominant 7th and a 6th (13) note.

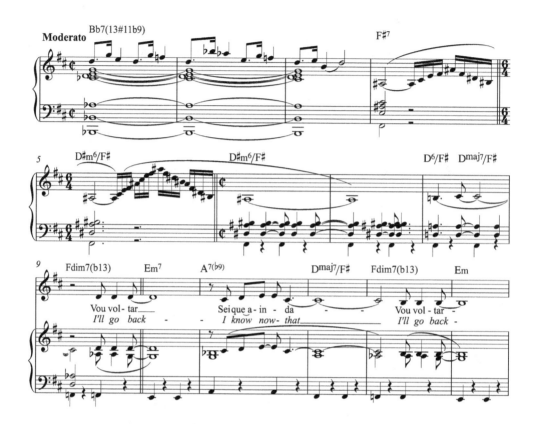

Ex. 3.26. Antônio Carlos Jobim, 'Sabiá', opening measures (piano reduction).[63]

Adding to the sense of tonal disorientation, the harmonic progression throughout the first nine measures is also highly unusual with a transition from the highly coloured B♭ chord, through F#7, to a first inversion D#m6 chord, followed by a transition to D major. In this respect these opening measures reflect a similar impressionistic technique to that heard in, for example, Debussy's 'Hommage à Rameau', measures 65–70, where sustained (mostly major) chords are presented in a detached manner as part of an unusual harmonic progression (Ex. 3.27).

Although most chords in this passage are built on straightforward major (or minor) triads, the G# suspended-4th bass note of the D# minor (last) chord in measures 69 and 70 adds unexpected colour and enhances the disorienting effect of the atypical chord progression. Its unusual sonority is enhanced by its juxtaposition with more familiar chord voicings.

Ex. 3.27. Claude Debussy, 'Hommage à Rameau', measures 65–70.[64]

Parallel Harmonic Progression

Maurice Ravel, along with his contemporaries, Debussy and Satie, often used coloured and extended chords, 9ths, 11ths and 13ths in his compositions. In the passage presented in Ex. 3.28, from one of Ravel's earliest pieces 'Pavane pour une infante défunte', several harmonic idiosyncrasies are evident. The succession of parallel and accented (9th) chords in measures 26 and 27 appears as a noticeable characteristic of not only this passage but the piece overall. Their repetition, accent and exposed position are a manifestation of Ravel's sheer delight in their sonority. Unlike his predecessors, who frowned upon parallel 5ths, 7ths and 9ths, Ravel used this form of parallel harmonic progression frequently in his works.

Jobim shows a similar disposition towards extended-chord parallel harmonic progression in 'Você vai ver' (Ex. 3.29), 'O morro não tem vez' (Ex. 3.30) and 'Chora coração' (Ex. 3.31).

Jobim wrote many other pieces that included parallel harmonic progressions, two of the more notable being 'Rockanalia' (repeated parallel 7th chords throughout) and 'Pois é' (parallel 6ths, 7ths and 9ths, in the opening chords).

Ex. 3.28. Maurice Ravel, 'Pavane pour une infante défunte', measures 24–27.[65]

Ex. 3.29. Antônio Carlos Jobim, 'Você vai ver', measures 21–24.[66]

Ex. 3.30. Antônio Carlos Jobim, 'O morro não tem vez', measures 23 and 24.[67]

Ex. 3.31. Antônio Carlos Jobim, 'Chora coração', measures 36–40.[68]

Tonal Ambiguities

Another aspect of Jobim's harmonic style was his use of complex chord sonorities and the associated promotion of tonal ambiguities similar to that mentioned in the opening of 'Sabia' (Ex. 3.26). Certain attributes of Villa-Lobos' work may have provided Jobim with inspiration for his harmonic experimentation. For instance, the chordal sonorities presented in Villa-Lobos' *Choros No. 5* reveal a propensity to use complex harmonies in exposed places for statement and effect.[69] In Ex. 3.32 the harmonious sonorities and rhythm set-up in measures 26–32 are shattered by the intrusion of the falling triplet arpeggio and the ominous repeated sforzando chords that follow (measures 33 and 34). These repeated chords, with their multiple chromatic extensions in the bass, blur any sense of tonality and herald a completely different militarist feel to the following section.

This approach to harmonic architecture, particularly the use of stacked 3rds, is typical of Jobim's style as can be seen (for example) in the final measures of 'Insensatez' (Ex. 3.33).

Guitar-based Sonorities

Many of Jobim's complex harmonies in his music can be attributed directly to the fact that he composed using guitar as his instrument of choice.[72] For instance, the accompaniment for the introduction to 'Se todos fossem iguais a você' contains an E minor 9th chord with a particularly 'open' structure that would be unlikely to have been developed on piano.

Ex. 3.34 shows the E minor 9th chord in measures 5 and 6. The chord contains the note G which is easily voiced on guitar by playing an open string, but it is quite removed from the grouping of the other higher notes of the chord. The discovery of this chord voicing

Ex. 3.32. Heitor Villa-Lobos, *Choros No. 5*, measures 29–32.[70]

Ex. 3.33. Antônio Carlos Jobim, 'Insensatez', final measures.[71]

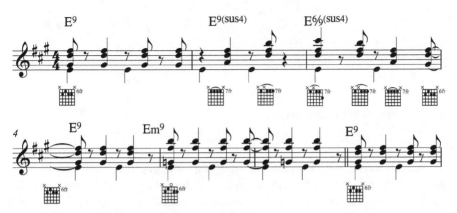

Ex. 3.34. Antônio Carlos Jobim, 'Se todos fossem iguais a você'.[73]

may well have been unintentional. The preceding chords sit comfortably on the 6th and 7th fret of the guitar and are voiced using stopped strings. However, the voicing of the E minor 9th chord, in measures 5 and 6, includes the open G string while using a chord shape that is remarkably similar to the preceding chord. Not only does this indicate a guitar-based compositional approach to harmony, but it also serves to indicate perhaps why a propensity for a vacillation between major/minor tonality may have originated in guitar-based music.

As an accomplished guitar player, Villa-Lobos was aware of the rich and colourful sounds provided by different chord voicings on the guitar and explored many of these voicings in his *Etude No. 4*. Significantly, Béhague draws a link between this *Etude* and the music of the bossa nova composers:

> [Villa-Lobos'] *Etude No. 4*, with its chromatic chord formations, its nonresolved harmonies, and the sudden changes of tonal levels, anticipates for some the harmonic ingenuity of many bossa nova guitar players of the late 1950s and early 1960s.[74]

Villa-Lobos' *Etude No. 4* no doubt provided Jobim with an exceptional insight into the mechanics of polyphony, guitar chord formation and the effect of dissonance in particular voicings. The guitar chord voicings in this piece require a specific playing technique, which involves the sounding of only four of the six strings of the guitar for any given chord. This style of playing can only be performed effectively by using the thumb and three fingers of the right hand in a way that avoids sounding the remaining two strings, not part of the chord.[75] The range of chord voicings is, therefore, much more extensive than those available to the jazz electric (plectrum) guitar player. Plectrum guitar players must avoid the strings that are not part of the specified chord or else find a comfortable finger position for each of the six strings that make up the chord.[76] Plectrum guitar players are therefore limited to chord formations that consist of notes played on adjacent strings. Therefore, chords devised for plectrum guitar have an entirely different set of performance criteria as part of their derivation and have quite

Ex. 3.35. Heitor Villa-Lobos, *Etude No.4*, measures 1–4.[77]

different voicings from chords devised for four-note fingering on acoustic guitar. Jobim and his colleague João Gilberto were able to take advantage of the richer palate of chords available from four-note finger-style chord technique to produce a sound that, when combined with the syncopated rhythms of samba, became one of the most defining features of bossa nova.

In his *Etude No. 4*, Villa-Lobos presents many different guitar sonorities, but each sonority is revealed in a rather isolated, studied manner without obvious harmonic development. Within the first four measures, however, there are three guitar voicings that Jobim used subsequently as the opening chords to three of his most popular songs, 'Insensatez', 'Corcovado' and 'Águas de março' (Ex. 3.35).

Chords for Harmonic Effect

Villa-Lobos' rather pedagogic treatment of the many guitar sonorities in *Etude No. 4* belie his ability to use unusual chordal harmony for effect. For instance, he would occasionally use a complex harmonic structure in the final chord of a piece, almost as a sort of ultimate closing statement. The last chord in his *Choros No. 8*, for instance, has a very unusual, close construction (Ex. 3.36). It would seem that the major reason for its inclusion at the end of the piece was to proclaim its individual sonority, thereby enhancing the final cadence of the piece.

Another example of Villa-Lobos' inclusion of complex harmony for sonic effect is the final chord of the second piece from his *Bendita Sabedoria* (Ex. 3.37). The contrast between the final chord and the preceding A major chord, which fulfils the expected cadential ending, is quite unexpected and stark.

Similarly, Jobim presented some unusual and complex chord structures to embellish the final cadence in a number of his songs (Ex. 3.38).

Ex. 3.36. Heitor Villa-Lobos,
Choros No. 8, final chord.[78]

Ex. 3.37. Heitor Villa-Lobos, *Bendita Sabedoria, No. 2,* Andante, measures 45–46.[79]

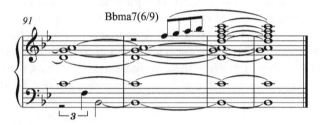

(a) 'Bebel', final measures.[80]

(b) 'Bangzália', final measures.[81]

(c) 'Trem de ferro', final measures.[82]

Ex. 3.38. Antônio Carlos Jobim, complex chord structures in the final cadences of three songs.

Bitonal Influences and Chordal Superimposition

Although any direct acknowledgement of the influence of Milhaud on Jobim's harmonic thinking is not publicized, there are several remarkable coincidences between both composers' writings that indicate that Milhaud did have a significant effect on Jobim's understanding of harmony, and polytonality in particular.

In an article for the *Revue Musicale* of 1 February 1923, Milhaud wrote:

> [...] the analysis of a chord is a conventional and arbitrary matter, and there is no reason, for example, not to consider a major ninth chord on C as the superimposition of a g minor and a C major triad, so that we can further envision the superimposition of two melodies, one in C major, the other in g minor.[83]

The implications of this statement led to Milhaud's thorough exploration of polytonality and its occasional use by such western art-music composers as Bartók, Holst and Villa-Lobos. While not embracing polytonality as a guiding force in his compositions, Jobim was obviously thinking in terms of chordal superimposition when he included the marked section shown in Ex. 3.40 in the orchestral *Arquitetura de morar* (Architecture to live) from the album *Urubu*. This section was clearly designated with superimposed chordal nomenclature written above the score (these designations are Jobim's, not the author's). The similarity between this extract and the Milhaud set of inversions (Ex. 3.39) is remarkable.

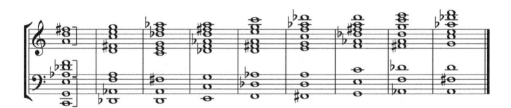

Ex. 3.39. Darius Milhaud, inversions built on (the first eight notes of) a chromatic scale of the chord consisting of three major triads (C, D♭ and D major).[84]

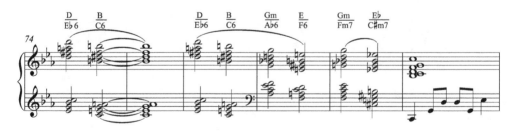

Ex. 3.40. Antônio Carlos Jobim, *Arquitetura de Morar*, measures 74–78, including his superimposed chordal designations (nomenclature) above the staff.[85]

The harmonic design of overlaying triads is obvious, although Jobim's harmonic structures are built using two chords rather than three chords (as in the Milhaud set of inversions in Ex. 3.39).

The set of inversions shown in Ex. 3.39 was presented in Milhaud's *Revue Musicale* article and shows a super-imposition of three tonalities or harmonies. Milhaud demonstrated initially that the chord that includes triads built on C, D♭ and D (shown with square brackets) can be written in eight different ways. Extrapolating from this observation, Milhaud found that if the first position (all major triads) of this chord is inverted and restated on ascending degrees of a chromatic scale, sounds of immense richness are produced. Jobim was aware of this technique and (uncharacteristically) took pains to demonstrate that he was using it. Both the Milhaud and Jobim examples use chords with their roots a semitone (or a tone) apart. The difference here was that Jobim used the technique as an isolated bridging passage, whereas Milhaud saw this more as a basis and a point of departure for further exploration in polytonal composition.

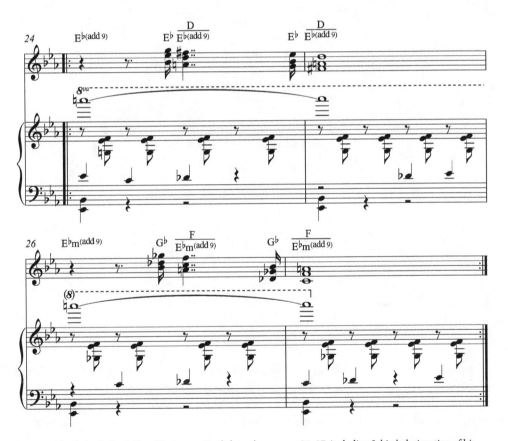

Ex. 3.41a. Antônio Carlos Jobim, 'Trem para Cordisburgo', measures 24–27, including Jobim's designation of his superimposed chordal voicings.[86]

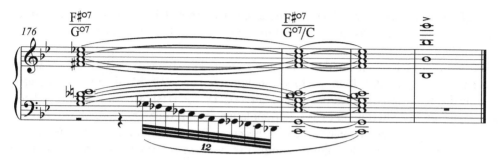

Ex. 3.41b. Antônio Carlos Jobim, 'Borzeguim', final measures.[87]

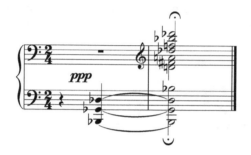

Ex. 3.42. Darius Milhaud, 'Ipanema', *Saudades do Brazil*, vol. 1, no. 5, final chord, measures 84–85.[88]

Ex. 3.43. Antônio Carlos Jobim, 'A correnteza', measures 3–6.

Jobim included another pointedly designated chordal superimposition section in 'Trem para Cordisburgo' (Train to Cordisburgo) (3.41a), one of the orchestral pieces from the score to the film *Cronica da Casa Assassinada* (Chronicle of the murdered house), but again, it constituted a small section and was used for sonic effect, rather than a *raison d'être* or point of departure.

A further example of Jobim's use of this method of harmonic construction can also be seen in the final measures of 'Borzeguim' (Ex. 3.41b), where superimposed diminished chords with their roots a semitone apart are also designated as such in the score.

Both Jobim and Milhaud employed chordal super-imposition for harmonies that functioned as 'exclamations' at the end of certain phrases. For instance, Milhaud's final chord in 'Ipanema' from *Saudades do Brasil* is constructed by the placement of a D major triad between the chords of G♭ major and B♭ minor (Ex. 3.42).

Jobim may have taken a similar approach for the highly coloured chord at the end of the introductory phrase (measure 6) in his 'A correnteza' (Ex. 3.44). The harmony can be considered a result of a chordal superimposition of D♭ major and E (no 3rd) arpeggiated in the bass with a B♭m6 in the treble).[89]

Milhaud performed his bitonal experiments with chords that were generally harmonically unrelated. However, Jobim employed this superimposition technique to chords regardless of their harmonic relationship.[90] For instance, from the appearance in the score, it is likely that Jobim planned a superimposed D minor 7th chord above a G minor triad for the penultimate chord in the introduction to his 'Falando de amor' (Ex. 3.44). Although the outcome is different in affect and the clash of tonalities is less severe compared to Milhaud's 'Ipanema', the conception of two superimposed chords is quite apparent.

An extension of this approach to harmonic architecture is the use of stacked 3rds. Common in jazz, this method of chord construction is typical of Jobim's style as can be seen (for example) in the final measures of 'Insensatez' (Ex. 3.33).

Ravel's harmonic explorations also influenced Jobim, particularly his use of the tonic flat 7th and 9th. Although the tonic flat 7th is not unique to Ravel, the treatment of it in his compositions is distinctive. A good example appears in the third movement of Ravel's *Sonatine*, where he includes the flattened 7th note (G♮) of the tonic chord A major (Ex. 3.45).[92]

In the 'Noites do Rio' section of Sinfonia do Rio de Janeiro, Jobim also uses the tonic flat 7th in a similar extended manner, but here adding the 9th (and 4th) notes as well and a half-measure tonic minor (Ex. 3.46).

Ex. 3.44. Antônio Carlos Jobim, 'Falando de amor', measures 10–11.[91]

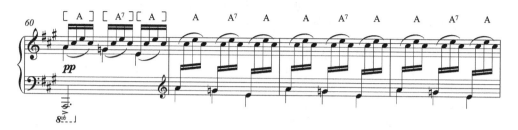

Ex. 3.45. Maurice Ravel, *Sonatine*, third movement, measures 60–63.[93]

Ex. 3.46. Antônio Carlos Jobim, 'Noites do Rio', measures 181–85.[94]

As in the above example, many instances of Jobim's use of the tonic flat 7th are preceded by a minor dominant harmony, the flat 3rd of the dominant harmony becoming the flat 7th of the following tonic.[95]

When he was 18, Jobim composed what he considered his first 'real' composition, a classical waltz that was influenced by Chopin and Liszt.[96] Later, Chico Buarque wrote lyrics for this waltz and the composition became known as 'Imagina', but it was without a title when Jobim first presented it to his teacher. She not only approved of what she heard, but also suggested that he should invest more of his talent writing music instead of practising to become a concert pianist (mainly because the span of his hands was limited). Jobim may have stated that his waltz 'Imagina' was influenced by Chopin and Liszt, and that influence can certainly be heard, but its sonority also reveals an aura strongly reminiscent of Erik Satie's waltz 'Je te veux'. In particular, the use of major 7th and major 9th chords and the structure of the melody in both cases introduced as a two crotchet anacrusis with the next (most exposed) note on beat one being the major 9th note of chord I (Ex. 3.47).[97]

The sound of Jobim's sparse and economic chords in 'Imagina' reveals little of the complexity of their origins. For instance, the first eight measures are essentially an alternation of chords V (D7) and I (G). However, far from voicing these chords conventionally, Jobim omits the 5th note of D7 and instead includes a flat 9th as part of the chord (measures 1 and 3). Also, in measures 2 and 4, chord I (G) is voiced, not as a major triad, but as a major

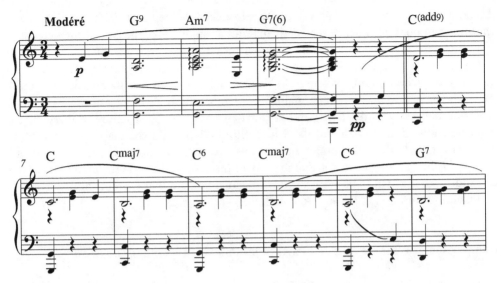

(a) Erik Satie, 'Je te veux', measures 1–9.[98]

(b) Antônio Carlos Jobim, 'Imagina', measures 1–16.[99]

Ex. 3.47. Comparison of harmony and melody between Satie's 'Je te veux' and Jobim's 'Imagina'.

7th chord with an added 9th. This may be thought of as a suspension resolving to the tonic traid on beat three, but Jobim placed this coloured sonority on the accented first beat of the measure and deliberately sustained its sonority, obviously savouring its sound. On the third appearance of chord V (D7) in measure 5, the D major quality defined by f# in the bass clashes temporarily with the minor tonality introduced by the f² natural in the right hand. This major-minor ambivalence is an early manifestation of one of the typical characteristics of Jobim's style and indeed of Brazilian popular music since the early 1800s.

The addition of extended or coloured notes to embellish the harmony can be seen in measure 7 where Jobim's voicing of chord V (D7) includes a sustained flat 9th and a flat 13th, as well as a temporary major/minor tonal clash.[100] In measures 9–16 Jobim alternates between chords III (B) and vi (Em) and extends the structure of these chords with the addition of the 7th and flat 9th to chord III (B) and the major 7th and 9th to chord vi (Em).[101] Jobim also omits the root and 3rd notes of chord III (B) in measures 9 and 11, further adding to the tonal ambiguity of the progression. These opening measures conclude with a VI (E) major 7th chord with added 9th, another example of major/minor vacillation so common in Jobim's later work.

Comparison of Whole Works and Parts of Jobim's Works: *Saudade do Brasil*

Debussy's use of chords for sonic effect not only broke down the rigidity of the principles of conventional tonality but also had a consequent effect on form and thematic development in his work. Debussy realized that thematic development 'in the form of a musical argument ruthlessly pursued, demands a firmer, less ambiguous harmonic structure' than that which used coloured and complex harmonies where the tonal centre was often obscured.[102] His distrust of organic thematic development as a method of composition supported his individual approach of using 'isolated, sensuous chords, varied in intensity' and 'fragmentary themes pursued in an improvisatory fashion'.[103] Jobim also adopted the same compositional philosophy in his *Saudade do Brasil*.[104]

The orchestral tone poem *Saudade do Brasil* is an example of Jobim's nationalistic approach to his more serious music. The title of the piece gives an indication of its content, the various incarnations of the *saudade* aspects of Brazilian life with its sadness and drama, contrasted with periods of light-heartedness and beauty. The piece itself is in three sections – introduction, statement and postlude – the main section consisting of recurring statements of the two themes (shown in Ex. 3.48) separated by short, often dramatic, interludes. These themes are played variously by strings, flute, oboe and bassoon and also sung by a female choir. Underpinning the statement of each theme is a harmonic structure that generally follows a cycle of 5ths. Overall the piece can be thought of as episodic – themes are repeated in an episodic manner – with different surface characteristics appearing on each repeat. Sequences are connected by way of short interludes that also vary dramatically in content and effect. A sense of unity is created by the sequential repetition of related musical material rather than by the continuous development of a theme. The use of a considerable number of double measure lines throughout the piece may reflect Jobim's desire to highlight the delineation between each section by indicating an imminent change of approach and a different interpretation required of each section. The piece shows influences from classical art-music, particularly Debussy, Ravel, Chopin and Villa-Lobos, and local folk music.

Jobim introduces the main theme (a) and the secondary theme (b) (shown in Ex. 3.48) in the middle section of the piece.

The introduction (Ex. 3.48c) begins with a lyrical melody characteristic of the Brazilian *modinha* with a repeated falling motive and fluid melodic line. The orchestration is typical of Jobim – the melody is played by a high solo cello, with flutes playing the upper accompaniment. Jobim often used the sonority of three or more flutes articulating the harmonies in his orchestrations. The two-measure motive is repeated three times before a change of orchestration from cello to cor anglais at measure 8, whereupon the motive is repeated another three times at a different pitch. Also notable is the rhythmic syncopation in the accompaniment, being offset by a quaver rest at the start of each measure and introducing a subtle rhythmic momentum at the outset. The introduction ends at measure 15 after which the main theme is introduced.

(a) Main theme

(b) Secondary theme

Ex. 3.48. Antônio Carlos Jobim, *Saudade do Brasil*, main and secondary themes.

The main theme is introduced at measure 16 in the strings (Ex. 3.48d), and repeated a step lower three times in the succeeding measures. The harmonic accompaniment follows a half-repeated cycle of 5ths F–B♭–E♭–A♭–D♭/F–B♭–(C), which allows the theme to be stated a step lower at each repeat. The fluid, descending motion of this repeated theme contrasts with the static upper pedal in each measure (c, b♭, a♭, g) played in the same measured rhythm, evokes a sense of melancholy throughout this section. In contrast, the following transition at measure 21 is jaunty and buoyant. At measure 24 the secondary theme is introduced, harmonized again using a cycle of 5ths in much the same manner as the main theme, allowing its statement to descend a step lower on each repeat.

Ex. 3.48c. Antônio Carlos Jobim, *Saudade do Brasil*, introduction.[105]

These themes recur in varied guises throughout the middle section and demonstrate Jobim's flexibility of approach to their orchestration. For instance, after the main theme is stated in the strings, on its second repeat (measures 34–37) it is orchestrated using a female choir as a wordless instrumental texture, reminiscent of Debussy's *Nocturnes – Sirenes* and Villa-Lobos' similar use (albeit with a solo voice) in *Bachianas Brasileiras No. 5*. The main theme is again stated at measure 48 in the strings with the choir as harmonic support, and again at measure 58.

The transitions that unite the various statements of themes also highlight Jobim's wide-ranging approach to orchestration and his knowledge of classical techniques. The interlude from measures 42–43, for instance, features a rich layering of strings playing a sextuplet figure contrasted with horns playing a triplet figure against sustained lower strings playing on the beat.

In contrast, at measure 54, the sparse, contrapuntal passage led by a solo cor anglais and answered by bassoon and oboe is reminiscent of a contrapuntal passage by Bach. It again follows a cycle of 5ths, and is a variation of the main theme with each repeat sounded a step lower than in the preceding measure.

A similar passage written for flute and bassoon appears at measures 82 and 83. The main theme is re-introduced at measures 48 and 58 in the strings with the female choir either adding to the harmonic background or providing an answering counter-melody.

Ex. 3.48d. Antônio Carlos Jobim, Saudade do Brasil, measures 16–33.[106]

Ex. 3.48e. Antônio Carlos Jobim, *Saudade do Brasil*, measures 42–43.[107]

Ex. 3.48f. Antônio Carlos Jobim, *Saudade do Brasil*, measures 54–57.[108]

Bird Calls

In the postlude of *Saudade do Brasil* there is a seven-measure section (measures 106–112) that emulates what may be interpreted as the sounds of distant bird calls in the forest. This is achieved by use of a multi-layered orchestral texture that comprises four distinct compositional techniques or ideas. The first is a repetitive figure of alternating diminished chords played by the violins in their upper register doubled by piano. The second is a solo cor anglais playing a dotted quaver countermelody, which is contrasted with the third, that of sustained strings sounding an E7 chord throughout. Finally the horns replace the cor anglais with a descending chromatic semiquaver phrase towards the end of this section.

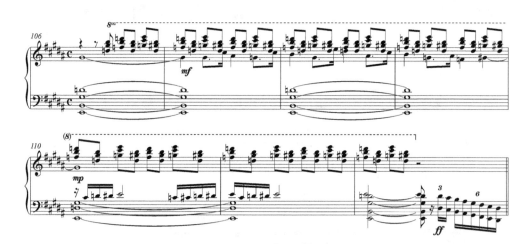

Ex. 3.48g. Antônio Carlos Jobim, *Saudade do Brasil*, measures 106–12.[109]

The result of Jobim's fascination with bird calls was not only their inclusion in many of his recordings (such as 'Boto') and performances (such as his *Sinfonia da Alvorada*)[110] but also his emulation of them (such as the opening to 'Sabiá').

Ravel achieves a similar effect in his *Oiseaux Tristes* (Ex. 3.49).

Jobim's technique is similar to Ravel's, in that both rely on repeated patterns featuring diminished 5th (or augmented 4th) intervals. However Ravel's 'emulation' is more two-dimensional – it relies on a repeated background pattern and isolated, high-pitched and accented chordal punctuations, in contrast to Jobim's multi-layered approach.

In many respects Jobim's imitation of nature in *Saudade do Brasil* is the manifestation of a musical compulsion shared with other classical (art-music) composers, in particular Heitor Villa-Lobos, who included simulated bird calls in *A Floresta do Amazonas*, and Olivier Messiaen, who adapted the melodies of bird calls in many of his compositions.

Ex. 3.49. Maurice Ravel, *Oiseaux Tristes*, measures 13–14.[111]

Female Choir as an Orchestral Instrument

Jobim's use of a female choir in *Saudade do Brasil* echoes Villa-Lobos' use of the human voice as an orchestral timbre in the soprano line of the Aria-Cantilena in *Bachianas Brazilieras* no 5. Part of the melody of Villa-Lobos' piece is outlined in Ex. 3.50 (measures 14–19) where its fluid, cantabile nature can be easily seen.

Jobim uses a similar technique to that used in *Bachianas Brasileiras* in the melody of 'Canta, canta mais'. Both the themes in *Saudade do Brasil* and 'Canta, canta mais' share a similar, repeated, sequential development to the voice in Villa-Lobos' piece (the brackets

Ex. 3.50. Heitor Villa-Lobos, *Bachianas Brasileiras No. 5* (first movement), measures 14–19, soprano melody.

Ex. 3.51. Antônio Carlos Jobim, 'Canta, canta mais', measures 67–74, female vocal melody.[113]

show the repeated theme). In all instances there are no words in the sung sections. The voice is treated purely as an instrument. [112]

Both Jobim and Villa-Lobos may have been influenced by Debussy's use of the human voice in his orchestral arrangements.

> From his youth, Debussy tended to treat the singing voice like an instrument, integrating it into the orchestra, as in Printemps where he wrote, 'the choral part is wordless and treated, rather, as a section of the orchestra,' and then in *Sirènes*, the third of the orchestral *Nocturnes*, in which 16 women's voices vocalize, while trying to blend into the orchestra.[114]

Debussy's attitude towards the use of female voices was that they should not be considered as separate entities – as chorus plus orchestra. He wrote with instructions that the choir for *Sirènes* should be '[...] placed within the orchestra and not in front, which would result in an effect diametrically opposite to that which I am looking for: this vocal group should not be more prominent than any other section of the orchestra. In short they should not stand out, but rather blend in'.[115] Debussy may have been the first to use this musical device with such success, but he was soon followed by Maurice Ravel, who transcribed *Sirènes* for two pianos and employed 'exuberant' orchestral textures in his *Daphnis and Chloé* using Debussy's vocal instrumental concept.

In many respects Jobim's episodic approach to *Saudade do Brasil* is similar to his approach to songwriting. His songs are often characterized by a statement of a short theme or motive that is repeated at a different pitch, or with altered harmony or orchestration. The same could be said about this piece, although here each repetition of the theme is separated by short interludes. Consequently, in this piece there is no focus or sense of arrival at a destination, it is more an unravelling of a series of varied musical vignettes.

Arquitetura de morar

Jobim composed much of his commissioned orchestral music from the mid-1950s to the early 1960s (*Brasilia, Sinfonia da Alvorada, Orfeu da Conceição, Sinfonia do Rio de Janeiro*). However, it was in his later film music (1970s), particularly in the music written for the film *Cronica da Casa Assassinada* (Chronicle of the Murdered House), and the orchestral pieces written for the album *Urubu* that are decidedly impressionistic. Ex. 3.52 shows a piano reduction of a passage from Jobim's orchestral *Arquitetura de morar* with sustained complex harmonies underpinning short melodic phrases – typical of his writing in this period.[116]

The piece begins with a technique that Jobim had incorporated in his earlier work (particularly the song 'Dindi'), that is, the use of an extended pattern of measures that alternate between two chords.[117] The effect of this is to create a prolonged rhythm that extends beyond the measure and repeats every two measures. The chords used for the

Ex. 3.52. Antônio Carlos Jobim, *Arquitetura de morar*, measures 19–30.[119]

Ex. 3.53. Claude Debussy, *Les sons et les parfums tournent dans l'air du soir*, measures 8–10.[120]

Ex. 3.54. Claude Debussy, *Feuilles Mortes*, measures 11–15.

opening 23 measures are also complex harmonically with 9ths and suspended 4ths featuring in most. The opening section is interrupted at measure 12 with a flute arpeggio that changes from minor to major and then re-introduces the opening chromatic phrase (transposed a major 3rd).[118] This minor–major change, and the complex harmonies of the opening chords, adds to the nebulous nature of the tonality that is characteristic of Jobim's style.

The opening section ends at measure 24 with a complete break and a rising (broken chord) figuration that signals a change in ambience. This change is reinforced by the ominous, accented D♭7(#9♭5) chord in measure 25.

The rising broken chord figuration in measure 24 has a similar sonic sense of expectation to that in Debussy's *Les sons et les parfums tournent dans l'air du soir* (Ex. 3.53). While Debussy uses simultaneous minor 3rds in his rising figuration, Jobim uses single notes and includes an upper leading note to each step in the figuration. Either way the effect is similar.

The three sustained and richly coloured monumental chords in measures 28–30 of *Arquitetura de morar* (Ex. 3.52), coming immediately after the fermata in measure 27,

Ex. 3.55. Antônio Carlos Jobim, *Arquitetura de morar*, measures 88–99.[123]

mark not only a reflective pause but also a distinct sectional break and another change of atmosphere. The fact that there are three repeated chords increases the gravity of their suggestion. These chords also mirror a similar tendency for exposed and sustained chordal statements in Debussy's works, as can be seen in *La Cathédrale Engloutie* for instance, or in the passage from *Feuilles Mortes* shown in Ex. 3.54. In this example the complex sonorities of each chord at the beginning of measures 14 and 15 are particularly noticeable, appearing on the first beat of the measure and sustained for the full measure. They are well-grounded harmonically in the bass, imparting to them a strong sense of solidity.[121] All these criteria are present in Jobim's chords mentioned above in measures 28–30 (Ex. 3.52).

The five-measure section in *Arquitetura de morar*, measures 74–78 (Ex. 3.40), constitutes one of the most sonically arresting and conspicuous passages in all Jobim's orchestral music. The section is remarkable because it clearly shows Jobim's use of superimposed chords for harmonic construction.[122] These chords are deliberately devoid of any sense of tonality and are clearly included as complex and isolated harmonic events, not as support for any melodic motive or phrase.

Later, following this rather bleak and isolated interlude, is another flowing section ending with four repeat soundings of a complex and sectionally defining chord in measure 91.

The sense of expectation engendered by the sequence of chords and their arpeggiations throughout measures 88–91 is masterful. At measure 92 a triplet tritone motive is established that continues virtually to the end of the piece.[124] This motive provides support for a *modinha*-like melody introduced at measure 94, which is itself constructed essentially from a transposed sequential repetition of a single-measure motive, typical of Jobim's episodic melodic and harmonic constructions.

Conclusion

Jobim's idiosyncratic approach to harmony (as distinct from melody, rhythm or lyrical content) is a compelling and profound characteristic of his musical style. His harmonic progressions consist for the most part of complex (altered and extended) chords, often chosen to highlight downward chromatic relationships between successive chords built as support to simple sequential melodic motives. A propensity for major-minor mode changes reflects local Brazilian *choro* and *modinha* styles, while his extensive use of the major 7th chord, especially as a replacement for the tonic major triad, is another significant characteristic of his style. The sonorities of complex chords, occasionally built on stacked 3rds or by the superimposition of triads, also held a profound attraction for Jobim. He used complex chords typically in exposed positions to embellish a cadence at the end of a phrase or a section where they did not form part of a chromatic sequence. With all his harmonic experimentation, Jobim nevertheless retained a strong sense of tonality in his work, even though the complexities of his individual harmonic constructions may have indicated otherwise.

Notes

1 Scores presented in full online are 'Chega de saudade', 'Águas de março', 'Insensatez', 'Retrato em branco e preto', 'Dindi' and the orchestral *Saudade do Brasil*. All of these scores are freely available as PDF downloads from http://www2.uol.com.br/tomjobim/download.htm.

2 For instance, *choro* form is mentioned in relation to the song 'Chega de saudade', even though the song is presented, in the first instance, for an examination of its harmonic characteristics.

3 Jobim and Jobim, *Cancioneiro Jobim: Obras Escolhidas* 31.

4 A discussion of the influences of jazz on Jobim's music and vice versa can be found on pages 7 and 11.

5 Reily 10.

6 The major 7th chord in *choro* appears nowhere nearly as frequently as in Jobim's music. An examination of 180 *choros* presented in the series *O Melhor do Choro Brasileiro* (The Best of Brazilian Choro) reveals only eleven *choros* where the major 7th is used at all, and in most of these instances it occurs in a cycle of 5ths, or is not sustained for more than one measure, or does not re-occur.

7 Sève 20.

8 Apart from the unusual harmonic progression from D minor to a chord with an E♭ root, the chord itself can be regarded as a tritone substitution for a dominant V^7 chord, but in this case there is not the II–♭II–I progression normally associated with this type of dominant substitution. See pages 82 and 86 for descriptions of Villa-Lobos' and Milhaud's use of complex chords in exposed positions.

9 For contextual reference, see the complete score of 'Chega de saudade' available online at http://www2.uol.com.br/tomjobim/download.htm.

10 Jobim and Jobim, *Cancioneiro Jobim: Obras Escolhidas* 225.

11 The melody does this at least until measure 14 where an f^1 is sounded against an A7 chord.

12 Jobim and Jobim, *Cancioneiro Jobim: Obras Escolhidas* 225.
   In measure 13 the alternative G half diminished designation for the Bbm6 chord is avoided in favour of the minor 6th, because the bass note Bb is the root note of the chord.

13 Jobim and Jobim, *Cancioneiro Jobim: Obras Completas, 1947–1958*, vol. 1, 132.

14 See, for example, de Ulhoa Carvalho 346.

15 Albeit with motive transposition and small changes to motivic shape.

16 Jobim and Jobim, *Cancioneiro Jobim: Obras Completas, 1947–1958*, vol. 1, 80–81.

17 Although they remain true to the designated chords in the original source, left-hand chord voicings in these two examples are the author's suggested interpretations only.

18 Carrasqueira 16.

19 *O Melhor do Choro Brasileiro: 60 Peças com Melodia e Cifras*, vol. 1, 83. The left-hand chord voicings in these two examples are those of the author. Although they correspond to the names of chords given in the source, the voicings are by no means definitive.

20 Fisk 12.

21 In this case a minor chord with a dominant function (measure 4), major and minor subdominant chords (measures 8, 9, 11, 13, 15 and 16) and major and minor tonic chords (measures 2, 8, 12 and 14).

22 An alternative explanation is to assume a temporary key change to A minor at measure 17. This would be supported by the b natural of the E7 chord in measure 18, but its presence would only be felt for four measures where at measure 21 the B♭ major 7th chord signals a return to the key of D minor.

23 Jobim and Jobim, *Cancioneiro Jobim: Obras Escolhidas* 226.

24 José Maria de Abreu (1911–66).

25 *O Melhor Do Choro Brasileiro*, vol 1, 9. As in Exs. 3.5 and 3.6, the left-hand chord voicings in this example are those of the author.

26 Jobim and Jobim, *Cancioneiro Jobim: Obras Completas, 1971–1982*, vol. 4, 188.

27 Jobim and Jobim, *Cancioneiro Jobim: Obras Completas, 1959–1965*, vol. 2, 135.

28 Quoted in Béhague, *The Beginnings of Musical Nationalism in Brazil* 17.

29 Neto, 'Brazilian Piano Styles' 1.

30 Refer to the complete score of 'Chega de saudade' online at: http://www2.uol.com.br/tomjobim/download.htm.

31 Jobim and Jobim, *Cancioneiro Jobim: Obras Completas, 1959–1965*, vol. 2, 56–57.

32 This type of modulation occurs in, for example, 'Aguenta o leme' (José Maria de Abreu), 'Mulato Anti-metropolitano' (Laurindo de Almeida), 'Alma' and 'Brasileirinho' (Waldyr Azevedo), 'Doce de coco' (Jacob do Bandolim), 'Tico-Tico no fuba' (Zequinha Abreu), 'É do que há' (L. Americano), 'É logo ali' (Dante Santoro) and in many other *choros*.

33 Apart from the E in the unaccented second half of measure 11.

34 Jobim and Jobim, *Cancioneiro Jobim: Obras Escolhidas* 229.

35 Jobim and Jobim, *Cancioneiro Jobim: Obras Completas, 1959–1965*, vol. 2, 123–24.

36 Jobim and Jobim, *Cancioneiro Jobim: Obras Escolhidas* 258–59.

37 With the exception of the C at measure 18, although even here the G continues the chromatic relationship.

38 In the explanatory presentations by Paulo Jobim in each volume of the series *Cancioneiro Jobim*, he writes: 'We have tried to give as much information about the music as possible; for this reason, in some pieces […] the resulting arrangement is too complex to be played on a single piano. In these cases a few details have been printed in gray as additional information, or an extra line of melody has been added for voice or melodic instrument. Sometimes, […] gray has also been used for the harmony when the main melody, printed in black, appears below the accompaniment.'

39 Jobim and Jobim, *Cancioneiro Jobim: Obras Completas, 1966–1970*, vol. 3, 48.

40 Jobim and Jobim, *Cancioneiro Jobim: Obras Completas, 1966–1970*, vol. 3, 48.

41 Other examples found in Debussy's piano works include 'Les tierces alternées', 'Mouvement' (*Images*, Book I) and 'Cloches à travers les feuilles' (*Images*, Book II).

42 Debussy, 'Jardins sous la pluie' 21.

43 The exception appears in measure 16 where the E♭ minor chord is written in first inversion with the flat 3rd note of the triad (G♭) in the bass.

44 Jobim and Jobim, *Cancioneiro Jobim: Obras Completas, 1971–1982*, vol. 4, 178–79.

45 'Chovendo na roseira' literally means 'rain in the rose garden', but the song is also known as 'Double Rainbow' and 'Children's Games' (an obvious reference to Debussy's influence).

46 The designation Am6 appears in *Cancioneiro Jobim*, *Tom Jobim Songbooks* and other pubications such as the *Real Book*.

47 Lees, *Singers and the Song* 213.

48 Shera 57.

49 See the discussion of jazz influence on page 11.

50 Cezimbra 67.

51 Abraham 80.

52 Abraham 81.

53 See discussion of Jobim and jazz on page 11.

54 It could be argued that this chord has a dominant function to the c# minor before and after, but at the outset it contains only the 3rd (b#) and 7th (f#) notes of the dominant chord (G#7), with no root or 5th, while its sonority is muddied by the addition of the flat 9th (A) and major 13th (e#[1]) notes.

55 While it can be argued that the final chord functions as a B major tonic chord, emphasized particularly by the occurrence of the note B in four separate octaves, there is a tendency for the ear to regard the notes e, g#, b in the bass as an E major triad. To add to the tonal

confusion, Debussy includes the notes c# and g# below the triad – hardly a confirmation of B major tonality.

56 Jobim and Jobim, *Cancioneiro Jobim: Obras Completas, 1983–1994*, vol. 5, 83.

57 The contra-rhythmical beat division, which is another feature of this piece, is discussed on page 119.

58 Jobim does not specify instruments in this score, which appears in the *Tom Jobim Songbook* vol. 2. Instead, the score specifies three staves (two treble clef and one bass clef) as appears in this example. The instruments that are specified in this particular arrangement were by Nelson Riddle from the 1964 recording: Jobim, *The Wonderful World of Antonio Carlos Jobim*.

59 It is interesting to note that the sustained g# horn note is spelled a♭ in the *Cancioneiro Jobim* scores. This is a better functional spelling in light of the preceding D♭ harmony, although the spelling of this note changes to g# with the introduction of the E7♭13♭9 chord.

60 Jobim and Jobim, *Cancioneiro Jobim: Obras Completas, 1959–1965*, vol. 2, 257.

61 Jobim and Chico Buarque originally presented 'Sabiá' at the third International Song Festival in Rio de Janeiro in 1968, subsequently winning first prize. 'Sabiá' was also to have been included on the second of Frank Sinatra's albums dedicated to Jobim, entitled *Sinatra and Company*. Two of the songs that Sinatra and Jobim recorded together – 'Sabiá' and 'Bonita' – were not included in the 'official' release of the time. They have since become independently available.

62 In her *Lyrical Brazil* post, https://lyricalbrazil.com/2012/04/10/sabia/, Victoria Broadus says that Sabiá can be classified as a 'song of exile', the lyric evoking a 'sense of nostalgia for a lost Brazil that was a direct blow to the oppressive military regime that had taken power in 1964'.

63 Jobim and Jobim, *Cancioneiro Jobim: Obras Escolhidas* 325.

64 Debussy, *Debussy Piano Works*, vol. 2, 31.

65 Ravel, *Pavane Pour Une Infante Défunte*.

66 Jobim and Jobim, *Cancioneiro Jobim: Obras Completas, 1971–1982*, vol. 4, 164.

67 Jobim and Jobim, *Cancioneiro Jobim: Obras Completas, 1959–1965*, vol. 2, 243.

68 Jobim and Jobim, *Cancioneiro Jobim: Obras Completas, 1971–1982*, vol. 4, 87.

69 See page 82, *Choros No. 8* and page 83 'Bendita Sabedoria' for examples of Villa-Lobos' use of complex harmony for sonic effect.

70 Villa-Lobos, *Choros No. 5*.

71 Jobim and Jobim, *Cancioneiro Jobim: Obras Completas, 1983–1994*, vol. 5, 99.

72 Jobim composed with guitar in the early part of his musical career (1950s to 1970s), but composed using piano almost exclusively from 1980.

73 Author's transcription from 'Se todos fossem iguais a você': Jobim, *Antônio Carlos Jobim: Composer*.

74 Béhague, *Heitor Villa-Lobos* 139.

75 Naturally, *four* fingers and the thumb can be used as well, thereby enhancing the possibilities of chord construction, but most of the chords specified in bossa nova guitar are four-note chords.

76 Accomplished guitarists can use a plectrum to play the bass note of a chord while playing the other three notes with their fingers. This, however, gives a brighter timbre to the bass

note of the chord, and on the whole detracts from the balanced sonic effect obtained by using the fingers and thumb of the right hand exclusively.

77 Villa-Lobos, *Etude No. 4*.

78 Tarasti 123.

79 Villa-Lobos, *Bendita Sabedoria*.

80 Jobim and Jobim, *Cancioneiro Jobim: Obras Completas, 1983–1994*, vol. 5, 89.

81 Jobim and Jobim, *Cancioneiro Jobim: Obras Completas, 1983–1994*, vol. 5, 77.

82 Jobim and Jobim, *Cancioneiro Jobim: Obras Completas, 1983–1994*, vol. 5, 187.

83 Milhaud, 'Polytonalité Et Atonalité' 4.

84 Milhaud 'Polytonalité Et Atonalité' 37.

85 Jobim and Jobim, *Cancioneiro Jobim: Obras Completas, 1971–1982*, vol. 4, 140.

86 Jobim and Jobim, *Cancioneiro Jobim: Obras Completas, 1971–1982*, vol. 4, 83.

87 Jobim and Jobim, *Cancioneiro Jobim: Obras Completas, 1983–1994*, vol. 5, 99.

88 Kelly, *Tradition and Style* 157.

89 The final measures of 'Dindi' also show Jobim's incorporation of superimposed chordal construction. See page 182.

90 This technique was not Jobim's invention. Similar techniques had developed in jazz and classical music. For instance, Stravinsky had used chord superimposition in *Petrushka* and *The Rite of Spring*.

91 Jobim and Jobim, *Cancioneiro Jobim: Obras Escolhidas* 378.

92 An alternative description would be the use of the mixolydian scale on tonic harmony.

93 Ravel, *Sonatine, Pour Le Piano*.

94 Jobim and Jobim, *Cancioneiro Jobim: Obras Completas, 1947–1958*, vol. 1, 66.

95 This can also be construed as a temporary (localized) change of key to the subdominant.

96 Jobim and Jobim, *Cancioneiro Jobim: Obras Escolhidas* 34.

97 The melody in 'Je te veux' is introduced at measure 5.

98 Satie, *Je Te Veux*.

99 Jobim and Jobim, *Cancioneiro Jobim: Obras Completas, 1947–1958*, vol. 1, 42.

100 It is interesting to note that although the chord D7b13b9 clearly acts as a dominant 7th the root note D does not appear anywhere within the measure. The minor tonality introduced by the f^2 natural could be interpreted as a dominant 7 #9, but it is an unusual note extension to add to a chord with a ♭9.

101 This could also be considered as a temporary modulation of the first eight measures to E minor.

102 Lockspeiser 231.

103 Lockspeiser 231.

104 The complete score for *Saudade do Brasil* is available online at: <http://www2.uol.com.br/tomjobim/download.htm> or Jobim and Jobim, *Cancioneiro Jobim: Obras Completas, 1971–1982*, vol. 4, 128.

105 Jobim and Jobim, *Cancioneiro Jobim: Obras Completas, 1971–1982*, vol. 4, 128.

106 Jobim and Jobim, *Cancioneiro Jobim: Obras Completas, 1971–1982*, vol. 4, 128–29.

107 Jobim and Jobim, *Cancioneiro Jobim: Obras Completas, 1971–1982*, vol. 4, 130.

108 Jobim and Jobim, *Cancioneiro Jobim: Obras Completas, 1971–1982*, vol. 4, 130.

109 Jobim and Jobim, *Cancioneiro Jobim: Obras Completas, 1971–1982*, vol. 4, 133.

110 Jobim's 'pio de perdiz' (Partridge peep) instruction is included in the score of 'O planalto deserto' from *Brasilia - Sinfonia da Alvorada* (measures 22 and 23). Jobim and Jobim, *Cancioneiro Jobim: Obras Completas, 1959–1965*, vol. 2, 161.

111 Ravel, *Miroirs*.

112 Although Jobim's melody is sung by a female choir, rather than a solo soprano.

113 Jobim and Jobim, *Cancioneiro Jobim: Obras Completas, 1959–1965*, vol. 2, 84–85.

114 Lesure, 'Debussy, Claude: Orchestration and Timbre'.

115 Debussy, *Sirènes*.

116 The complete score of *Arquitetura de morar* can be found in Jobim and Jobim, *Cancioneiro Jobim: Obras Completas, 1971–1982*, vol. 4, 138–43.

117 See page 174 for a discussion of techniques used in 'Dindi'.

118 Not shown here.

119 Jobim and Jobim, *Cancioneiro Jobim: Obras Completas, 1971–1982*, vol. 4, 139.

120 Debussy, *Debussy: Piano Works*, vol. 3, 15.

121 If the notes C# and G# in the bass are taken as root and 5th then the other notes of the chord constitute the major 3rd, flat 7th and minor 3rd – an unusual combination that obscures any sense of major or minor tonality. Jobim's chords have similar construction being built upon a root and 5th in the bass. In this instance the added right-hand notes are a major 3rd, 6th, major 7th, 9th and augmented 4th.

122 This similarity to Milhaud's polytonal examples has been discussed on pages 84–86 (Ex. 3.39).

123 Jobim and Jobim, *Cancioneiro Jobim: Obras Completas, 1971–1982*, vol. 4, 141.

124 The repeated motive forms a descending chromatic sequence that is in stark contrast to the buoyant lilt of the preceeding section.

Chapter 4

Rhythmic Techniques

Samba

The key to much of the attraction in Jobim's recorded work is to be found in its rhythms, particularly syncopated rhythms. In his introduction to the folk music of Brazil, Béhague makes a general observation that identifies 'the peculiar rhythmic characteristic of [most] Brazilian music [...] either by irregular accentuation or anticipation' as syncopation.[1] Syncopation can be found not only in bossa nova's rhythmic accompaniment but also in the complex rhythm and phrasing of its melodies.[2] Layered syncopation is also at the rhythmic heart of samba, which, as indicated in Chapter 2, was the basis behind the development and expression of the bossa nova rhythm.

Before the effects of syncopation can be examined in samba, it is necessary to be familiar with the different instruments that make up samba ensembles. Some of the most important instruments that can be heard in samba's layered rhythmic performances include the *surdo* (a large bass drum), the *repinique* (a kind of tom tom played with a drum stick and a bare hand), the *caixa* (a tight, shallow drum), the *tamborim* (a small tambourine without rattles often played with a stick or a set of bunched, course, rigid brushes), the *reco-reco* (a kind of scraper) and the *chocalho* (shaken rattles). The *pandeiro* (a shallow tambourine with rattles) is often used to accompany smaller ensembles. Ex 4.1 shows a typical layered samba rhythm as performed with these instruments.[3]

In describing bossa nova's derivation from samba, Béhague outlines two samba rhythms found frequently in bossa nova accompaniment (Ex. 4.2). Rhythm (a) can be seen in the tamborim rhythm of Ex. 4.1. Also, the lower notes in rhythm (b) are typical of the anticipated semiquavers of the surdo rhythm sounding immediately before the measure in Ex. 4.1.

While rarely specifying the rhythmic accompaniment for his recorded songs because of difficulties in adequate notation, Jobim alludes to the rhythm of Ex. 4.2(a) in the orchestral piece, 'Matita Perê' (Ex. 4.3), and, in augmented form, in 'Samba do avião' (Ex. 4.4).[6] Several other written examples of this samba rhythm appear in Jobim's songs 'Acho que sim', 'Vem viver ao meu lado' and 'Velho riacho (Para não sofrer)'.

Ex. 4.1. Typical samba rhythm as played by G.R.E.S. Unidos do Porto da Pedra [4]

Ex. 4.2. Classical samba rhythms. [5]

Ex. 4.3. Antônio Carlos Jobim, 'Matita Perê', measures 92–95. [7]

The melody of 'Samba do avião' also follows the same samba rhythm as shown in Ex. 4.2(a) in an augmented form (Ex. 4.4).

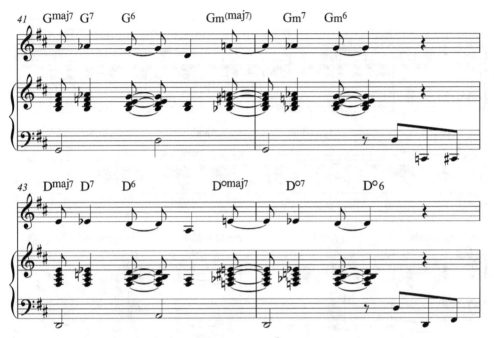

Ex. 4.4. Antônio Carlos Jobim, 'Samba do avião', measures 41–44.[8]

Example 4.5 shows a typical samba bassline that has become almost a cliché bass accompaniment rhythm for bossa nova songs.[9] Its rhythm is clearly derived from the lower voice shown in Ex. 4.2(b).

Ex. 4.5. Typical samba and bossa nova bass accompaniment.[10]

Béhague also specifies another, typical, samba rhythm shown in Ex. 4.6. The left-hand accompaniment in 'Matita Perê' (Ex. 4.3) uses the same samba rhythm as in this example.[11]

Ex. 4.6. Classical samba rhythm.[12]

Another example is the chordal (right-hand) accompaniment to Jobim's 'Samba de uma nota só' that follows this rhythm (in augmented form):

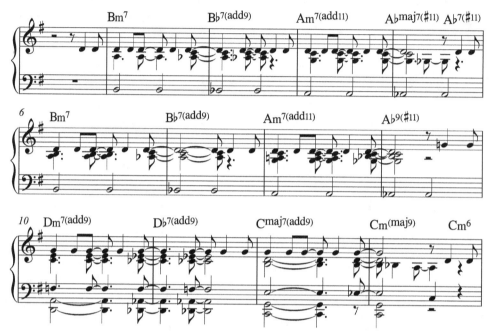

Ex. 4.7.   Antônio Carlos Jobim, 'Samba de uma nota só', measures 1–13.[13]

In Jobim's 'A chegada dos candangos', this rhythm appears throughout the entire piece as a bass accompaniment. It is also found in other pieces such as 'O trabalho e a construção' and in augmented form in 'Pato preto' and 'Gabriela'.

Clave Rhythmic Patterns[14]

The samba rhythm given in Ex. 4.6 is also a form of the bossa nova 'clave' rhythmic pattern found in many bossa nova songs. The clave rhythm is an unchanging basic rhythmic unit repeated throughout a song. It is usually played on an aurally conspicuous percussion instrument such as a snare rim or polished hardwood sticks (i.e. 'clave'). The clave rhythm can be reversed (retrograded) or offset, as shown in Ex. 4.8, while still retaining its fundamental characteristic of syncopation.

Bossa Nova clave rhythm

Retrograde clave rhythm

Ex. 4.8. Bossa nova clave rhythm and its retrograde.[15]

There are many examples of both these clave rhythms in recordings of bossa nova songs. A transcription of João Gilberto's guitar accompaniment for Jobim's song 'Insensatez', for example, shows the use of the retrograde clave rhythmic figure played with the right-hand fingers contrasted with a bass in regular crotchets played with the thumb.

Ex. 4.9. Antônio Carlos Jobim, 'Insensatez' introduction, guitar accompaniment showing a typical bossa nova 'clave' rhythmic figure.[16]

Béhague offers an explanation of what characterizes bossa nova rhythm by finding a 'common trait in the predominance of ternary [sub]divisions against a binary one which occurs only once or not at all'.[17] He offers four examples of bossa nova rhythms in which binary and ternary beat [sub]divisions are designated as numbers above the notes (Ex. 4.10). The binary beat division labelled '4' (Ex. 4.10(c)) occurs over the measure and can be considered as a case where the binary division occurs 'not at all', in which case it can be considered as a combination of 1 and 3 semiquaver beats as indicated. In Exs. 4.10(a), (b) and (d), the binary divisions (marked 4) occur once in every two measures. In Ex. 4.10(c) the binary divisions occur over the measure and can be considered as a combination of 1 and 3 semiquaver beats as indicated.

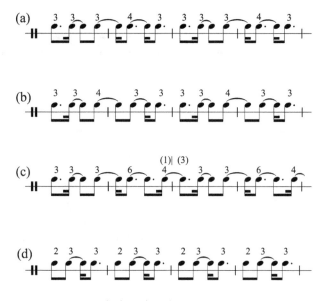

Ex. 4.10. Bossa nova rhythmic formulae.

In many respects Béhague's definition of bossa nova rhythms as ternary divisions against a binary one can be seen to be similar to, and possibly influenced by, the clave rhythms. For instance, the clave rhythm shown in Ex. 4.11 appears in two tracks, 'Samba de uma nota só' and 'Garota de Ipanema', from the album *A Arte de Tom Jobim*.[18]

Ex. 4.11. Clave rhythm from Jobim's 'Samba de uma nota só' and 'Garota de Ipanema'.

Another variation of the clave rhythm can be heard on the track 'Vivo sonhando', from the same album. In this instance (Ex. 4.12), the binary division (crotchet) is longer than the ternary division (dotted quaver) but the rhythmic syncopation is still maintained.

Ex. 4.12. Clave rhythm from Jobim's 'Vivo sonhando', *A Arte de Tom Jobim*.

Polyrhythmic Techniques

One of the few, but nevertheless excellent, examples of scored bossa nova rhythms is the introduction to 'Meninos eu vi'. This example highlights the ternary/binary rhythmic combination quite clearly and is typical of the complex rhythmic foundation of bossa nova.

Ex. 4.13. Antônio Carlos Jobim, 'Meninos eu vi', introduction, measures 8–11.[19]

In Ex. 4.13 the ternary rhythmic divisions, indicated in measure 8, are derived from the duration between note attacks. The rhythmic juxtaposition of the right-hand rhythm playing 3+3+3+3+4 within the measure against the bass playing 4+4+4+4 adds a rhythmic dimension to this passage that sets off the intrinsic syncopation against a regular beat. Both regular and syncopated beats are usually present in bossa nova arrangements – rarely will a syncopated beat occur in isolation.

Jobim's juxtaposition of duple and triple rhythms had counterparts in Villa-Lobos' deceptively simple yet highly idiosyncratic rhythmical craftwork. In Villa-Lobos' 'Abril', for instance, the piece begins with an unevenly accented percussion shaker as an accompaniment to a simple two-measure polyrhythmic figure played on the guitar. In the introduction (Ex. 4.14) the open top 'e' string on the guitar emphasizes an even rhythm (4+4+4+4+4+4), while a triple rhythm is played on the fretted 'b' string ([3+3]+[4+2]+[3+3]+[4+2]). These contrasting duple and triple rhythms are indicated in this example by notes with different stem directions, although both rhythms are played on the same instrument.

Ex. 4.14. Heitor Villa-Lobos, 'Abril', introduction showing two-measure polyrhythmic guitar figure with unevenly accented percussion accompaniment.[20]

Rhythmic Accent

Villa-Lobos' *Choros No. 5* for piano, *Alma Brasileira*, also demonstrates a compositional style that may have provided Jobim with much melodic, harmonic and rhythmic inspiration. The melodic aspects of this piece are discussed on page 151, but its rhythmic accompaniment also reveals Villa-Lobos' particularly resourceful approach. His use of an intricately syncopated left-hand accompaniment (Ex. 4.15) is indicative of the rhythmic interpretation of Brazilian popular music where accents are not placed on the beat according to a strictly even time division. Béhague refers to the 'swaying' quality of this accompaniment, a quality that may be construed as a precursor to the subtle rhythms of bossa nova.[21] The accompaniment rhythm here is in fact the retrograde of the bossa

Ex. 4.15. Heitor Villa-Lobos, *Choros No. 5*, measures 3–8.[22]

nova rhythmic formula presented in Ex. 4.10(d), although in this case one measure of the Villa-Lobos accompaniment occupies two measures of the bossa nova rhythm.

There is also an intentional lack of rhythmic correspondence between the melody and the accompaniment in the above example, with the melody most often anticipating the beat. This tendency to 'pre-phrase' the melody is especially prevalent in Jobim's music.[23] Not only is the melody often written as anticipating the beat in Jobim's music scores (as they appear in the series of *Cancioneiro Jobim* and *Tom Jobim Songbooks*), but also, 'pre-phrasing' of the melody is particularly noticeable in recordings of Jobim's songs by João Gilberto.

João Gilberto's rhythm guitar accompaniment to the opening measures of Jobim's 'Chega de saudade' is shown in Ex. 4.16. The rhythm is derived from samba, and is highlighted by the relationship of the even, 'two-to-the-bar' bass played with the thumb (surdo rhythm) to the syncopated block chords played by the fingers of the right hand. There are many variations of this basic rhythm, but the essential element is a syncopated rhythmic offset. In this example the rhythmic offset is effected by the delayed sounding of beats three and four.

Ex. 4.16. Antônio Carlos Jobim, 'Chega de saudade', introduction measures 1–4.[24]

Hypermetre

However prevalent, vibrant and sophisticated local rhythms might have been, one cannot assume that all Jobim's rhythmic imagination was inspired solely by them. Jobim said, for instance, that Stravinsky had been an inspiration to him, and there are certain similarities in rhythmic design between some of Stravinsky's and Jobim's compositions.[25] Certainly, in Jobim's music there is much syncopation, irregular beat accentuation and irregular metre, just as there is in a work such as Stravinsky's *The Rite of Spring*. However, Jobim's deliberate use of two sustained contrasting rhythms in 'Surfboard' (for instance) mirrors, in a more straightforward way, Stravinsky's similar use of layered rhythmic ostinati in *Petrouchka* or later, *The Rite of Spring*. Ex. 4.17 shows a four-measure passage from the first movement of *Petrouchka*. In contrast to the 5/8 metre in this passage (which is emphasized by the strings playing on the first beat of each measure), the winds play an alternating melodic figure that has a decided duple character. This dichotomy sets up a polyrhythmic tension between the winds and strings.

Ex. 4.17. Igor Stravinsky, *Petrouchka*, first movement, measures 81–85.

In Ex. 4.18, Jobim's 'Surfboard' shows similar sustained contrast in metre(s), although in this instance it involves a triple metre with quaver subdivisions against a common time background – the horns playing the repeated triple-beat figure against the even-beat bass.

The superimposition of two contrasting metres in 'Surfboard' creates a meta-rhythmic pattern or cell. In the Stravinsky example, the meta-rhythmic pattern lasts for four measures and is not repeated, whereas in the Jobim example the meta-rhythmic pattern is one-and-a-half measures in length and is repeated. This adds an extra structural dimension to the music – a 'hypermeter' – created by the interaction of smaller rhythmic elements.

Ex. 4.18. Antônio Carlos Jobim, 'Surfboard', opening measures.[26]

Another example of Jobim's use of rhythmical contrast in beat division can be seen in the introduction to 'Vivo sonhando' (Ex. 4.19).

Here the melody has a triple rhythmic grouping for the first four notes of each successive two-measure section starting on measures 1, 3, 5 and 7. At the end of each two-measure rhythmic pattern or cell, Jobim adds two crotchet notes as a simple but effective rhythmic contrast to the triple beat grouping. As found in many Jobim compositions, the musical construction here appears as a kind of playful rhythmic/melodic game. It certainly engenders

Ex. 4.19. Antônio Carlos Jobim, 'Vivo sonhando', introduction.[27]

a feeling of displacement, and leaves the listener unsure of the placement of the beat.[28] This is entirely appropriate for this song – 'Vivo sonhando' is entitled 'Dreamer' in its English version.

Examples of writing using (relatively sustained) contrasting rhythmic beat division can also be found in Debussy's work. His 'Passepied' from the *Suite Bergamasque* for instance has a three-measure section in which triple and duple beat divisions are contrasted (Ex. 4.20).

Ex. 4.20. Claude Debussy, 'Passepied', measures 24–29.[29]

Other examples of writing using contra-rhythmic beat subdivision such as seen in 'Surfboard' and 'Vivo sonhando' are quite frequent in Jobim's work, the most common being a melody in triple time set against a regular (duple) beat accompaniment, such as the triplet figure (upper voice) set against the duple beat accompaniment in Jobim's 'Remember' (Ex. 4.21).

Ex. 4.21. Antônio Carlos Jobim, 'Remember', measures 23–34.[30]

In his 'Deus e o Diablo na terra do sol' (God and the Devil in the land of the sun), Jobim constructs a passage with two dissimilar beat subdivisions by setting up a duple repetition within a sextuplet[31] figure and setting that against a dotted duple rhythm (baião) in the bass (Ex. 4.22).

Ex. 4.22. Antônio Carlos Jobim, 'Deus e o Diablo na terra do sol', measures 24–27.[32]

Jobim's predisposition for rhythmic ambiguity and contrasting metrical groupings is well shown in his onomatopoeic composition 'Trem de ferro' (Train of iron). Here triplet minims are superimposed over a repeated common-time motive that has been constructed to simulate the repetitive cycle of the sounds of a moving train.

Ex. 4.23. Antônio Carlos Jobim, 'Trem de Ferro', measures 40–42.[33]

Pedal Tones

While the use of pedal tones is certainly not unique to either Jobim or Villa-Lobos, the frequent use of this technique is a significant feature of both composers' music. Pedal tones were used by both composers in several ways – as a contrast to other rhythms, as a means of rhythmic propulsion and, in a more conventional manner, as harmonic grounding. A typical example of pedal tone use can be found in Villa-Lobos' *Suite Populaire Brésilienne No. 5*, 'Chorinho' for guitar (Ex. 4.24). Here a repeated pattern of chords is built over a static repeated pedal A in the bass, imparting a sense of unity and drive to an otherwise independent succession of chords.

Ex. 4.24. Heitor Villa-Lobos, *Suite Populaire Bresilienne No. 5*, 'Chorinho', measures 31–40.[34]

In Villa-Lobos' *Étude No. 10*, a repeated f# played on the low E string of the guitar acts as a pedal through measures 57–63 (Ex. 4.25), again imparting energy and unity to the succession of chords.

Ex. 4.25. Heitor Villa-Lobos, *Étude No. 10*, measures 57–63.[35]

Jobim's approach to the use of pedal technique is well demonstrated in the introduction to 'Surfboard', where the melody and harmonic support are built over a repeated G in the bass (Ex. 4.26). Here the regular, duple pulse of the pedal note contrasts with the syncopated triple-grouping of the chords in the upper staff.

Ex. 4.26. Antônio Carlos Jobim, 'Surfboard', measures 1–4.[36]

Jobim's 'Pois é' is another example of melodic and harmonic construction built over a bass pedal (Ex. 4.27).

Jobim's use of pedal tones in his music is quite extensive and varied. With precedents from most classical composers, Jobim was able to adapt the technique to suit his own idiom, often using pedal notes to impart a rhythmic drive or contrast. A noteworthy example is Jobim's adaptation of Debussy's more harmonically focused pedal treatment found in 'La soirée dans Grenade'. Measures 38–52 of this piece contain a two-note pedal with the bass notes (A and E) sounded a 5th apart repeated at the beginning of each measure (Ex. 4.28). The effect of this pedal, with its thick bass sound from the double notes, is to give the piece

Ex. 4.27. Antônio Carlos Jobim, 'Pois é', measures 15–23.[37]

a sense of solidity and grandeur. This section, however, is not the only part of this piece that uses pedal tones. In the introduction, for instance, Debussy applies pedal tones ranging from C^1 to c^3, over a span of 5 octaves, and from measure 67 he uses double-note pedal tones an octave apart in the bass.

Jobim used a similar two-note pedal technique in his 'Pato preto', evoking a similar grandiose atmosphere with the pedal notes (D and A) at an interval of a 5th. Rather than relying on accented pedal notes sounding at the beginning of each measure, Jobim established a syncopated rhythm repeated for each measure. The pedal is broken at measure 60 for one measure where the two pedal notes are pitched a semitone higher, but it is quickly re-established in the following measure (Ex. 4.29).

In Jobim's 'Two kites' (Ex. 4.30), the alternating pedal notes create a buoyant, carefree lilt to the song by sounding a note outside the octave (in this case at an interval of a 9th), playfully avoiding the expected note-at-the-octave rocking bass pedal.

Melodic Timing

Another rhythmic characteristic of Jobim's work is his allowance for flexibility in interpretation of the rhythmic phrasing of the melody. The subtle shift of the onset timing of melody notes ahead of the beat (especially beat one of the measure) is also characteristic of much Brazilian popular music. This rhythmic shift is very difficult to transcribe or specify using conventional musical notation, and is subject to personal interpretation. Nevertheless, it is essential to convey a sense of energy, 'sway' or what is referred to in Brazil as 'balanço'. For example, the rhythmic interpretation of the melody for Jobim's 'Triste' is specified

Ex. 4.28. Claude Debussy, 'La soirée dans Grenade', measures 38–52.[38]

Ex. 4.29. Antônio Carlos Jobim, 'Pato preto', measures 54–66.[39]

differently in Chediak's *Tom Jobim Songbook* from the same melody in the songbook series *Cancioneiro Jobim*. In Ex. 4.31, from the *Tom Jobim Songbook*, the timing of the melody is generally shown later than in the same passage from *Cancioneiro Jobim* (Ex. 4.32). Also the triplet specification of the beat in measure 19 of the *Tom Jobim Songbook* version has been changed to straight quavers in the *Cancioneiro Jobim* version, an indication of the flexibility of performance (or lack of concern) over strict rhythmic interpretation in Jobim's melodies.

It is significant that Jobim himself authorized both score versions of this song and was obviously not concerned about strict rhythmic performance of his melodies, assuming the allowance for individual stylistic interpretation is necessary to retain a sense of appropriate swing or 'balanço'. The same flexibility in rhythmic interpretation of melody occurs in jazz and in most popular music. However, the accuracy and timing of the rhythmic accompaniment is an entirely different matter.

The existence of swing rhythm and the rhythmic tensions created by playing slightly ahead or behind the beat have been recognized by musicians, teachers and music writers for some time, but the mechanisms of swing have never been fully explained. The appeal of much popular music is often linked to an intangible, undefined emotional response to a particular

Ex. 4.30. Antônio Carlos Jobim, 'Two kites', measures 213–36.[40]

Ex. 4.31. Antônio Carlos Jobim, 'Triste', measures 17–19, *Tom Jobim Songbook*.[41]

Ex. 4.32. Antônio Carlos Jobim, 'Triste', measures 17–19, *Cancioneiro Jobim*.[42]

rhythm of one kind or another. This rhythm may possess a certain visceral attraction that defies conventional analysis in its simplicity, and yet loses its essential character if attempts are made to capture it in score. Rhythmic analyses have revealed small, yet consistent timing discrepancies or rhythmic nuances in selected popular music recordings, indicating that these nuances may play an important part in the individuality and musical appeal of these performances.[43]

Rhythmic nuance and ensemble accuracy are particularly important in jazz, where the literature indicates that swing is somehow embodied in the syntax of a piece of music.[44] At the outset, the definition of the term 'swing' is problematic because 'much of what it gives to music is felt rather than observed and cannot be accurately notated'.[45] Music which is strictly interpreted from a score places the attack of notes at intervals that are either on the beat or at a mathematical fraction of the beat. Swing rhythms, on the other hand, place the notes around the beat, sometimes slightly ahead of the beat sometimes slightly behind, creating a rhythmic tension that has a profound effect on how music is perceived. Middleton states that 'a satisfactory theory of rhythm is one of the things musicology does not possess, and if it did, it would necessarily encompass far more musical parameters than just the obviously rhythmic'.[46] Middleton also suggests that the intra-musical structures of the sounds themselves contain the key to a much more satisfactory rhythmic theory and possibly to an advance in general musical analysis.

Consequently, in order to partially accommodate rhythmic offsets and to indicate that a swing interpretation is required, there is a tendency in many of Jobim's scores to shift forward the onset of melody notes. This is evident in the melodic transcriptions found in the *Tom Jobim Songbooks*, for instance, where the anticipating melody note is notated as a tie across the barline, as demonstrated in Ex. 4.33.

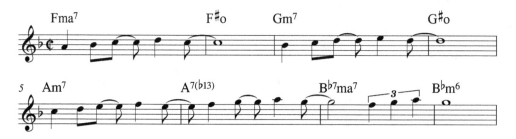

Ex. 4.33. Antônio Carlos Jobim 'Este seu olhar', *Tom Jobim Songbook*.[47]

In most bossa nova recordings it is obvious that the syncopation is not played exactly as indicated. Instead, the attack of the tied note occurs somewhere between what is written and the first beat of the measure. This rhythmic flexibility in phrasing is also related to what Fischer refers to as 'pre-phrasing'. Fischer points out that this is particularly evident in the elastic singing style of João Gilberto who makes a feature of singing well ahead of the beat.[48]

Conclusion

The influence of local musical styles, especially samba, provided Jobim with an extensive rhythmic resource from which he drew much inspiration. Most of the rhythmic accompaniment for his bossa nova songs exhibit the syncopation of samba (clave rhythms in guitar or *surdo* rhythms in the bass for instance), but these rhythms also extend to his melodies that were frequently constructed as sequences of repeated rhythmic cells. The sustained use of contrasting rhythms, typically involving the juxtaposition of binary and ternary rhythms, and the contrast of uneven rhythmic subdivision against an even beat is also prevalent in much of his music. Jobim also used regularly repeated pedal tones as a means of rhythmic propulsion, as harmonic grounding and as a contrast to other irregular rhythms. While not able to be specified accurately in score, the anticipation of the beat in the performance of Jobim's melodies is also a prevalent characteristic of interpretations of his songs.

Notes

1 Béhague, 'Brazil' 274.
2 The accurate notation of these melodies is problematic and can often give rise to several different rhythmic interpretations of the same melody. This problem, as it relates to written scores, is discussed in more detail on page 129.
3 In this example the tamborim rhythm in measures 3 and 4 is an equivalent rhythm to the preceding measures with the third semiquaver in each beat not sounded. In performance this beat would be nowhere near as pronounced as the others as it is played with an upstroke and is subsequently omitted.
4 'D' and 'E' refer to right and left hands, 'direta' and 'esquerda'. Gonçalves and Costa 58.
5 Béhague, 'Bossa Nova' 78.
6 See a discussion of the difficulties of adequate rhythmic transcription in the Introduction, Page 14.
7 Jobim and Jobim, *Cancioneiro Jobim: Obras Completas, 1971–1982*, vol. 4, 69.
8 Jobim and Jobim, *Cancioneiro Jobim: Obras Escolhidas* 287.
9 Runswick 52.
10 Giffoni 13.
11 This is close to what is accepted as 'baião' rhythm.
12 Béhague, 'Bossa Nova' 78.
13 Jobim and Jobim, *Cancioneiro Jobim: Obras Escolhidas* 251.
14 There is considerable debate over the term 'Brazilian clave'. Few Brazilian musicians acknowledge it as such; however, for the purposes of explanation and identification in this text, it is merely a name given to the rhythm(s) outlined in Ex. 4.8.
15 Faria 61.
16 Faria 63.
17 Béhague, 'Brazil'.

18 Jobim, *A Arte de Tom Jobim*.
19 Jobim and Jobim, *Cancioneiro Jobim: Obras Completas, 1971–1982*, vol. 4, 44.
20 Author's transcription from Adnet, *Coração Popular*.
21 Béhague, *Heitor Villa-Lobos* 82.
22 Villa-Lobos, *Choros no. 5*.
23 The term 'pre-phrasing' is used by the composer/arranger Clare Fischer who comments on João Gilberto's singing style in the video *Bossa Nova*, dir. Walter Salles.
24 Author's transcription from Gilberto, 'Chega de Saudade'.
25 Jobim and Jobim, *Cancioneiro Jobim: Obras Completas, 1971–1982*, vol. 4, 24.
26 Chediak, *Tom Jobim Songbook*, vol. 2, 92.
27 Chediak, *Tom Jobim Songbook*, vol. 3, 103.
28 A similar effect of rhythmic displacement is obtained with clave rhythms.
29 Debussy, *Debussy Piano Works*, vol. 1, 35.
30 Jobim and Jobim, *Cancioneiro Jobim: Obras Completas, 1966–1970*, vol. 3, 73.
31 Triplet written as a sextuplet.
32 Jobim and Jobim, *Cancioneiro Jobim: Obras Completas, 1966–1970*, vol. 3, 116.
33 Jobim and Jobim, *Cancioneiro Jobim: Obras Completas, 1983–1994*, vol. 5, 183.
34 Villa-Lobos, *Suite Populaire Brésilienne*.
35 Villa-Lobos, *Étude No. 10*.
36 Jobim and Jobim, *Cancioneiro Jobim: Obras Completas, 1959–1965*, vol. 2, 255.
37 Jobim and Jobim, *Cancioneiro Jobim: Obras Completas, 1966–1970*, vol. 3, 126.
38 Debussy, *La Soirée Dans Grenade*.
39 Jobim and Jobim, *Cancioneiro Jobim: Obras Completas, 1983–1994*, vol. 5, 164.
40 Jobim and Jobim, *Cancioneiro Jobim: Obras Completas, 1971–1982*, vol. 4, 177.
41 Chediak, *Tom Jobim Songbook*, vol. 2, 99. The measure numbering presented here allows for an eight-bar introduction presented in the *Cancioneiro* version.
42 Jobim and Jobim, *Cancioneiro Jobim: Obras Escolhidas* 316. For the purposes of comparison the melody presented in example 4.32 is written an octave above that presented in the reference text.
43 Freeman 548–50.
44 Middleton 177.
45 Gammond, 'Swing'.
46 Middleton 177.
47 Chediak, *Tom Jobim Songbook*, vol. 3, 53.
48 Clare Fischer commenting on the singing style of João Gilberto in the video *Bossa Nova*.

Chapter 5

Thematicism and Structural Design

Self-Referential Attributes of Bossa Nova

Bossa nova developed not only from a combination of many musical styles, but also by employing a form of subtle self-support mechanism in which all its musical elements assisted and referred to each other. This self-referential attribute, a common element in all bossa nova songs, lent itself to the interaction of its musical constituents, melody, harmony, rhythm, lyrics, instrumentation, to the extent that no one particular musical constituent dominated another. Prior to bossa nova, singers generally emphasized a song's melody, using it as a vehicle to promote their individual vocal style, but in bossa nova vocal delivery was subdued. Integration of musical elements was a high priority. Accompanying instruments that traditionally assumed a background role, such as the guitar, were given a higher profile and supplied an important rhythmic as well as harmonic function. The balance and rapport between instruments and the voice also occasionally extended to lyrical content. For instance, in the song 'Samba de uma nota só', the lyric refers directly to the melody of the song itself.

<table>
<tr>
<td>

"Eis aqui este sambinha
feito numa nota só.
Outras notas vão entrar
Mas a base é uma só.
Esta outra é conseqüência
do que a cabo de dizer
Como eu sou a conseqüência
inevitá vel de você."

</td>
<td>

"This is just a little samba
built upon a single note.
Other notes are bound to follow
but the root is still that note.
Now this new one is a consequence
of the one we've just been through.
As I'm bound to be the unavoidable
consequence of you."

</td>
</tr>
</table>

Ex. 5.1. Antônio Carlos Jobim, 'Samba de uma nota só' first verse lyric, with Portuguese lyric by Newton Mendonça and English lyric by Jobim.

In Jobim's 'Vivo sonhando' (Dreamer) both the melody and the harmonic progression remain static for the two opening measures that introduce the main theme of the song

(Ex. 5.2). In this instance neither the melody nor the harmony is particularly outstanding, and both depend on the rhythmic delivery of the words to give them vitality. The interaction of musical constituents is, therefore, essential to bring the song to life. To emphasize the unchanging nature of the melody and harmony, Jobim repeats the two opening measures at measure 13. The listener's attention is drawn to the rhythmic delivery of the words rather than to any sense of development in the melody or harmony.

Ex. 5.2. Antônio Carlos Jobim, 'Vivo sonhando', measures 9–16.[1]

The inter-dependence of melody, harmony and lyric is particularly crucial in 'Soneto de separação' (Separation Sonnet) (Ex. 5.3). This lament, written in 1959 at the birth of the bossa nova era, evidences Jobim's ability to draw as much pathos as possible from a limited set of musical material. As in 'Vivo sonhando', the melody of each phrase is essentially a single note, which is unremarkable in itself. However, with the melody supported by a minimally voiced harmonic progression and Vinicius de Moraes' lyrics, the overall effect of the song is intense and dramatic. The emphatic, on-the-beat rhythmic placement of the chordal accompaniment also adds to the heightened sense of drama and feeling of anguish and despair. The opening twelve measures are a particularly poignant reminder of the power of simplicity. In this instance, the static (repeated) melodic phrases consist merely of the single notes g^1 (measures 1–5), f^1 (measures 5–8) and e^{b1} (measures 9–12) that are contrasted with the sustained descending bassline.

While 'Samba de uma nota só', 'Vivo sonhando' and 'Soneto de separação' are excellent examples of songs that contain static melodies contrasted with changing harmony, in 'Bonita' (Ex. 5.4) the reverse applies. Here the melody changes while the harmony remains

Ex. 5.3. Antônio Carlos Jobim, 'Soneto de separação', measures 1–12.[2]

essentially static and rooted in A minor for fifteen measures. While the harmony does change superficially, the changes are due essentially to a simple chromatic counterpoint.

Juxtaposition of Static and Shifting Musical Material

The juxtaposition of static and shifting (changing) musical material is also common in the music of Villa-Lobos. For instance, in Villa-Lobos' *Prelude No. 1* (Ex. 5.5), the upper (static) E minor triad is repeated with the same rhythmic pattern for the first five measures, while the bass outlines the melody. While the technique (that of extended harmony based on a static tonality) is essentially the same as in 'Bonita', Jobim's harmony is less defined and does not embody the same rhythmic drive as the Prelude.

Another example of Villa-Lobos' use of static and shifting musical material can be found in 'Gavota-Choro', the fourth of his *Suite Populaire Brésilienne*. Here, the crotchet motive b^1–c^2–b^1–e^2 is repeated for five measures while the harmonic progression changes against it (Ex. 5.6).

The juxtaposition of static and shifting musical material is also common in Debussy's work. For instance, in *La Cathedral Engloutie* from his first book of *Preludes*, Debussy contrasts a static (repeated) motive against a descending bass accompaniment. The sequence

Ex. 5.4. Antônio Carlos Jobim, 'Bonita', measures 9–23.[3]

Ex. 5.5. Heitor Villa-Lobos, *Prelude No. 1*.[4]

Ex. 5.6. Heitor Villa-Lobos, *Gavota-Choro*, measures 24–28.[5]

Ex. 5.7. Claude Debussy, *La Cathedral Engloutie*.[6]

of 'crotchet' chords in the opening measure (Ex. 5.7) is repeated in measures 3 and 5, while the left-hand, sustained chordal accompaniment descends on every repeat – from G to F to E.

Other examples of this juxtaposition of static and shifting musical material can be found in Debussy's *Hommage à Rameau* and *Prélude à l'après-midi d'un faune*. Jobim also makes much use of this technique in 'Se todos fossem iguais a você' (Ex. 5.8). In this example the melodic motive in measure 41 (upper treble clef) is repeated in measures 43, 45 and 46 while the bass harmonic accompaniment changes allowing a different harmonic perspective at each repeat, so that the attention on the motive is continually refocused.

Ex. 5.8. Antônio Carlos Jobim, 'Se todos fossem iguais a você', measures 41–48.[7]

Motivic Design Restrictions

The simplicity and restrictions of the repeated motivic design in much of Jobim's music highlights a distinct characteristic of his style and again emphasizes the inter-dependence of melody and harmony. A particularly noteworthy example of restricted motivic design can be found in Jobim's 'Retrato em branco e preto' (Portrait in black and white).[8] Here the melody is constrained to a tight cluster of four semitones and re-appears in this form throughout the piece while the harmony changes.[9] As can be seen in the extract shown in Ex. 5.9, the melody and harmony are inter-dependent and it is their inter-dependence that creates a musical whole.

The development of this restricted melody has counterparts in several of Chopin's piano pieces. In his observations of Chopin's *Étude Op. 10 No. 6* (Ex. 5.10), Cortot describes what he refers to as a 'vital lower part' uniting with 'the passionate lament of the upper voice in the right hand'.[11] This lower part, he maintains, 'must sustain and strengthen the expressive character of the [upper part] while preserving its own timbre and its own freedom of rhythm'. The lower part to which Cortot refers can be seen in Ex. 5.10 as the semiquaver figure in the left hand covering a tight chromatic span of a few semitones, with an occasional excursion outside this melodic 'cluster' at the end of the measure.

Ex. 5.9. Antônio Carlos Jobim, 'Retrato em branco e preto', measures 1–8.[10]

Ex. 5.10. Frédéric Chopin, *Étude Op. 10 No. 6*, opening measures 1–6.[12]

Ex. 5.11. Frédéric Chopin, *Op. 34 No. 3*, measures 8–17.[13]

This repeated figure imparts a dynamic momentum that contrasts with the measured unfolding of the sustained notes of the upper melody and bass. In another example, Chopin's *Op. 34 No. 3*, the unaccompanied motive consists of a similar tight chromatic span of a few semitones (Ex. 5.11).

The combination of dynamic momentum imparted by the repeated motives in both Chopin examples, together with the tight chromatic spacing within the motives, may have provided Jobim with a valuable mechanism for his melodically diverse compositional explorations using a similar technique. As can be seen, 'Retrato em branco e preto' provides a good example of the application of a similarly tightly spaced melody, not as an accompanimental figure, but as the main theme. In the Chopin *Étude*, the chromatic motive does not assume the role of the melody but functions more as a middle-ground, propulsive figure underpinning the higher melody. Its descending bassline is also essentially chromatic (apart from the note f in measure 2 and the tone transition at the end of measure 6), and the voicing of the motive closely parallels the bassline. The harmonic construction in 'Retrato em branco e preto' is also underpinned by a chromatic descending bassline that starts on the root E and ends at measure 4 on the note C. From measures 1–5 the bass is augmented by a secondary note at the interval of a tenth that defines the immediate harmony independent of the four-note motive. Subsequently, the secondary lower notes continue to define the change in harmony allowing the motive to function independently as melody.

Aside from the similarities with Chopin's chromatic clustered motives, Jobim used his motives in a different way to that in either of the Chopin extracts. In the *Étude*, for example, the motive is repeated twice in one measure before it is voiced at another pitch in the next measure, and in *Op. 34 No. 3* the motive is repeated over two measures before it is voiced at another pitch. In 'Retrato em branco e preto' the motive extends over at least three measures before changing and then reappears throughout the piece. The construction of the song using this technique is indicative of the extent of the harmonic flexibility that Jobim saw in using Chopin's tight chromatic motives as melody rather than as an accompanimental figure.[14]

In his orchestral work Jobim used a similar closely spaced motivic technique for an accompaniment figure in 'Tempo do mar', a piece that he included on his self-funded album *Matita Perê* in 1973 (Ex. 5.12). In this piece, a semiquaver motive traces a compact path that encompasses, for the most part, four semitones. It has a similar dynamic effect to the left-hand figure in Chopin's *Étude*, but is used in a more impressionistic context. It is doubled at the interval of a 4th and is the only accompaniment to the melody, whereas in Chopin's *Étude* both an upper (melodic) line and the bass define the harmony independently.

The similarity of these excerpts from Chopin and Jobim is in the form or shape of the motives, not their purpose. Jobim often played Chopin's pieces on the piano and certainly admired Chopin's work, but the influence here seems more reflexively mechanical than premeditated. It would be easy to imagine Jobim arriving at these Chopin-esque phrases, more as his fingers fell on the keys from having practiced Chopin than from any theoretical application of Chopin's style.

'Insensatez'

An example that reveals a more overt emulation of Chopin's musical style, and in fact is modelled on Chopin's *Prelude in E minor, Op. 28. No. 4*, is Jobim's 'Insensatez'. A comparison of these two pieces reveals many similarities, not only in the falling minor 2nd motive that is a feature of both melodies, but also the harmonic progression. Both pieces are presented in their entirety in Exs. 5.13 and 5.14.[16] Despite their obvious similarities, however, a closer analysis uncovers differences between the two pieces that substantiate Jobim's individual and innovative compositional approach.

Aspects of the compositional process of Chopin's *Prelude* are evident from his autograph manuscript.[17] Schachter suggests that the piece was almost complete before it was committed to notation.

> The intricate chromatic counterpoint of the left-hand part seems to have been written at once in abbreviated notation (without the repeated pitches), but already in its final form and without a single correction, except for the last few measures. The lines appear to be improvised on the page, and I should imagine that they were in fact improvised, or at least worked out, at the piano before Chopin wrote them down.[18]

It would appear that Chopin's invention of this harmonic progression was more empirically pianistic than pre-conceived.[19] The movement between successive chords is achieved by comfortable, downward, semitone (or occasionally tone) movements evident in the descending chords of the left-hand accompaniment (Ex. 5.13). The same pianistic approach is

Ex. 5.12. Antônio Carlos Jobim, 'Tempo do mar', measures 8–15.[15]

evident in Jobim's 'Insensatez' (Ex. 5.14), although Jobim does not write his accompaniment as repeated complete chords but rather states them in expanded and arpeggiated form.

The chord voicings in 'Insensatez' shown in Ex. 5.14 are quite comfortably spaced for piano performance and it is likely that Jobim's ideas for 'Insensatez' were worked out at the piano, then later transcribed for guitar. Even in the guitar accompaniment (lower stave, Ex. 5.15), the pianistic, closely grouped chord structure is evident in the highest notes of the harmonic support for the melody.

Both Chopin's *Prelude* and Jobim's 'Insensatez' use the $\hat{6}$–$\hat{5}$ neighbour-note motive as a prominent feature.[23] In Chopin's *Prelude* (Ex. 5.13) the right-hand melodic neighbour-note motive, b¹–c²–b¹, appears in measures 1–2 and is repeated three times in as many measures. Schachter refers to the abbreviated form of this motive, c²–b¹, as 'winding through the piece like a chorus of sighs'.[24] This sentiment, suggested by the melody, is described by Ashton Jonson as '[seeming] literally to wail, and its sadness is exquisite'.[25] Schachter notes that the

Ex. 5.13. Frédéric Chopin, *Prelude in E minor, Op. 28 No. 4.*[20]

Ex. 5.14. Antônio Carlos Jobim, 'Insensatez'.[21]

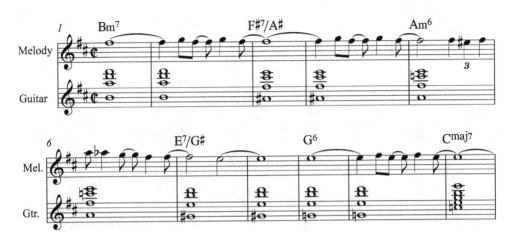

Ex. 5.15. Antônio Carlos Jobim, 'Insensatez', measures 1–11, melody and guitar accompaniment.[22]

emotional connotations of this falling semitone interval, usually with the rhythmic accent on the second note, had been well-known by composers for centuries.

> The $\hat{5}$–$\hat{6}$–$\hat{5}$ and $\hat{6}$–$\hat{5}$ neighbor-note figures in minor have a long association with the affect of grief (inherited from Phrygian compositions of the Renaissance); and minor-mode basses descending chromatically to $\hat{5}$ (also embodying Phrygian characteristics) have been lament figures since the seventeenth century. Semitonal intensity combined with downward motion seems an appropriate musical analogue to actions and feelings associated with loss, sadness, and death. These stylistic features could hardly be given greater prominence than in this Chopin *Prelude*, and they occur in a setting of intense pathos.[26]

For the purposes of comparison, the right-hand (melodic line) of Chopin's *Prelude* is outlined in Ex. 5.16. In this example it can be seen that the melodic motive c^2–b^1 leads into measures 3, 4, 5, 15, 16 and 17 (i.e. the motive spans the measureline), with variations of the same motive (at different pitches) occurring at the start of measure 6 and in measure 24.

In 'Insensatez', a similar neighbour note motive, beginning g^2–$f\#^2$, is used as the fundamental element from which the melody evolves. Following essentially the same format as the *Prelude*, the melody starts on scale degree $\hat{5}$ in measure 1, and is repeated on every successive, descending scale degree, until arriving at scale degree $\hat{1}$ in measure 32 as the final note and nadir pitch.[28] Ex. 5.17 shows the melody of 'Insensatez' in the same isolated form as shown for the *Prelude* above.

In Ex 5.17, while the melodic motive g^2–$f\#^2$ (which is centred on scale degree $\hat{5}$) starts at the same scale degree as the *Prelude*, it does not follow exactly the same path. Jobim's melodic structure follows what is essentially a repeated motive pattern built on

Ex. 5.16. Frédéric Chopin, *Prelude in E minor, Op. 28 No. 4*, right-hand (melodic line).[27]

Ex. 5.17. Antônio Carlos Jobim, 'Insensatez', melody.

consecutive descending scale degrees ($\hat{5}$ $\hat{4}$ $\hat{3}$ $\hat{2}$ $\hat{1}$) with minor alterations. For instance, at measure 21 the melody rises to f#² instead of following an anticipated trend to d², and the eight-measure phrase (measures 17–24) ends on the note d² in measure 23, not the expected scale degree $\hat{2}$.

Overall, the melody of the *Prelude* (Ex. 5.16) reveals a similar descending line ($\hat{5}$ $\hat{4}$ $\hat{3}$ $\hat{2}$ $\hat{1}$) but with important interruptions to the expected melodic contour. Chopin's structural intent is plainly different to Jobim's. The melodic line in 'Insensatez' is more lyrical and uninterrupted, whereas the melodic line in the *Prelude* is more segmented and follows a more contrapuntal approach. The *Prelude*, for example, is in two halves, antecedent and consequent, with an interruption to the descending melodic line ($\hat{5}$ $\hat{4}$ $\hat{3}$ $\hat{2}$ $\hat{1}$) occurring between the antecedent and consequent at measure 13, after the melody has reached scale degree $\hat{2}$. At that point the melody returns to $\hat{5}$ and continues its descent through $\hat{4}$, $\hat{3}$ and $\hat{2}$ before finally reaching $\hat{1}$ as the final note of the piece. The melodic descent, however, is not as straightforward as it appears, and is not always confined to the notes of the right hand. In his analysis of the *Prelude*, Schachter indicates that the arrival at scale degree $\hat{4}$ at the end of measure 19 is anticipated and strengthened by the left-hand tonic note of the A minor (IV) chord at the start of measure 19, giving credibility to its rather transitory appearance.[29] Also, scale degree $\hat{3}$ does not occur in the right-hand part but instead is presented as a constituent note of the C major (VI) chord in the left hand at measure 22. Scale degree $\hat{2}$ is also presented as an inner voice, f#, the 5th note of the V⁺⁴ chord in measure 25. These last three scale degree readings suggest a rather contrived interpretation, but they do indicate, at least, a difference in melodic structure between the two pieces. Therefore, although the neighbour-note motive and the initial opening measures are remarkably similar in both pieces, the overall melodic intent is quite different.

Another constraint that would have effected the development of 'Insensatez' in a different manner from the *Prelude* is the fact that it is a song, not an instrumental piece. Its melodic line is thus constrained to be more lyrical and regular with none of the large leaps such as those that occur in measures 10, 13 and 17–19 of the *Prelude*. Also, Schachter considers the first nine measures of the *Prelude* as an orderly progression of 6/3 chords (Ex. 5.18).[30] 'Insensatez', however, shows very little correlation with this familiar technique of parallel 6/3 chords, although there is, nevertheless, an occasional similarity in falling 3rd figures.

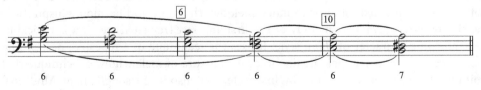

Ex. 5.18. Frédéric Chopin, *Prelude in E minor, Op. 28 No. 4*, measures 1–11, reduction.

Another difference between the two pieces is apparent in Jobim's embellishment of the fundamental harmony. Although Chopin opens the *Prelude* with an unembellished minor chord and generally refrains from extending the harmony beyond tonic, 3rd and 5th, apart from occasional suspensions. Jobim, however, adds a flattened 7th note to his opening minor chord and generally extends the harmonic structure of his accompaniment beyond the triad form with the addition of 9ths, 11ths, flat 5ths, etc.

There are, nevertheless, striking resemblances between the two pieces. The similarity of the initial harmonic progression, which is essentially I–V7–(VII)–IV7, can be seen in the unfolding of this progression over the first eight measures of 'Insensatez', and the first four measures of the *Prelude*. Suspensions occur at the downbeat of measures 2 and 3 of the *Prelude*, but both suspensions resolve within the measure to the appropriate chord for the progression I–V7–(VII)–IV7. Another similarity is found in the functionally identical harmonic support for the first melody note on scale degree $\hat{5}$ (chord I) and in the harmonic support for the melody note on scale degree $\hat{4}$ (chord IV7). Also, from the beginning of both pieces the bass descends by semitones for at least the first five note transitions, representing a distinctive feature of both pieces.

Flexibility of approach, an important characteristic of Chopin's style, is mentioned by Abraham in his book *Chopin's Musical Style*: 'If Chopin had favourite devices he never, or very seldom, lapsed into routine. The more clearly one recognises his basic formulae, the greater is one's delight in his variations of them'.[31] Jobim also tended to follow this belief, but developed it to enhance the vitality of his musical variations in a more methodical and idiosyncratic way. Jobim's music can often appear to 'lapse into routine' by the repetition of a musical phrase or idea once or occasionally twice (such as the repeat of the first eight measures a tone lower in measures 9–16), then, perhaps halfway through a subsequent repeat, he may introduce an unexpected twist and lead the listener down a different musical path (as occurs with the introduction of the f# in measure 21 and the delayed arrival at scale degree $\hat{2}$). The melodic and harmonic structure of 'Insensatez' is an excellent example of this.

Descending Minor Second Motive

Two pieces that exhibit a strong sense of *saudade* similar to the effect of the descending minor 2nd motive in 'Insensatez' are Villa-Lobos' *Choros No. 5* and Jobim's 'Falando de amor'.[32] The *Choros No. 5* for piano, *Alma Brasileira*, demonstrates a compositional style that may have provided Jobim with much melodic, rhythmic and harmonic inspiration. The slowly moving *saudade* melody of the first and last (repeated) section is typical of the serenading character of *choro* style. It uses the technique of a repeated, descending minor 2nd motive in the melodic line to evoke an aura of melancholy, a technique that Jobim used to great effect not only in 'Insensatez' but also in the song/lament 'Modinha'.

Ex. 5.19. Heitor Villa-Lobos, *Choros No. 5*, measures 3–8.[33]

Ex. 5.20. Antônio Carlos Jobim, 'Falando de amor', measures 11–19.[34]

In Ex. 5.19, the descending minor 2nd motive can be seen in the melody (treble clef) in measures 3 and 4 with the step from c^2 to b^1, and in measures 6 and 7 with the step from g^1 to $f\#^1$.

'Falando de amor' is another example of Jobim's use of the descending minor 2nd motive (Ex. 5.20). In this instance, the motive appears as $e^{\flat 1}$ to d^1 in measures 11, 12, 13, 14 and 15, and in measure 19, the step from g to f# also evokes a similar response.

Musical Inter-dependence and Understatement

The strong inter-dependence of repeated (often simple) motives and complex (often chromatic) harmonic progressions in Jobim's work highlights an important feature of his style. According to Reily, however, the overall effect of this inter-dependence of musical elements:

> [...] led to a style of little contrast, as no musical feature was allowed to over-ride the others. Consequently, bossa nova neutralised the centrality of the singer, who, in becoming integrated into the ensemble rather than accompanied by it, lost prominence. In bossa nova the piece took precedence over the performer; what was valued was the group effort, both in terms of composition and interpretation, rather than the 'star'.[35]

The assertion that the style had little contrast seems at odds with historical and musical reality. On the contrary, the contrast of musical elements highlighted their individual powers. The fact that one musical element may have been particularly subdued, or subtle, or static in any particular song ultimately worked in favour of a particularly effective ensemble result. This subtle and collaborative approach distinguished bossa nova from American jazz where almost the reverse philosophy applied, individuality and virtuosity being highly prized. Solo improvisation is possibly the most recognized characteristic of jazz, but this aspect is nowhere near as important in bossa nova. Musical inter-dependence and understatement are two of the essential ingredients that made bossa nova initially so appealing and ultimately so malleable in the hands of skilled interpreters.

Transposed Motive Repetition

A more elaborate variation on motive repetition that involves transposition and less restricted melodic shapes can be seen in the works of Villa-Lobos and Debussy. The principles developed by these composers in particular were adopted by Jobim to form one of the most definitive characteristics of his style.

Composed in Paris in 1949, Villa-Lobos' *Hommage á Chopin* exhibits several characteristics found in many of Jobim's songs. As can be seen in Ex. 5.21, a prominent characteristic of this section of the piece is the repeated, single-measure melodic motive that is transposed downwards by step (one or two semitones) in successive measures for five measures (2–7).

Each successive appearance of the melodic motive outlines a diminished chord, with the last (in measure 7) outlining an F7 chord.[37] The motive is accompanied by a rhythmically active right-hand pattern that articulates the harmony and parallels its sequential transposition.[38] This type of structure, where a repeated melodic motive

Ex. 5.21. Heitor Villa-Lobos, *Hommage á Chopin*, measures 1–8.[36]

moves in parallel with a descending bassline,[39] can be found, for instance, in Jobim's 'Eu te amo' (Ex. 5.22). Here the melodic motive occupies two measures and is transposed a whole tone on every repeat while the harmony is structured so that the bass descends chromatically by one semitone for every measure over an eight measure passage.

Jobim's 'Dinheiro em penca' (Ex. 5.23) is another example of parallel motion of melodic motive and descending bassline.

Variants of this form of song construction, where a repeated melodic motive is superimposed over a descending bassline but without necessarily following the bassline transposition, are more characteristic of Jobim's songs – 'Insensatez', 'Brigas nunca mais' and 'Olha Maria' are other examples.

Ex. 5.22. Antônio Carlos Jobim, 'Eu te amo', measures 9–18.[40]

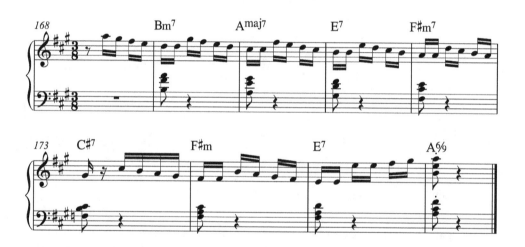

Ex. 5.23. Antônio Carlos Jobim, 'Dinheiro em penca', measures 168–173.[41]

'Águas de março' (Waters of March)

The song 'Águas de março' is another excellent example of the juxtaposition of simple motive(s) against complex harmonic progression. The jazz critic Leonard Feather proclaimed 'Águas de março' as 'among the top ten songs of all time'[42] and wrote that: 'It's one of those songs that turn out to have an extremely complex structure when analysed, but that sound incredibly spontaneous and natural when heard and felt'.[43] 'Águas de março' is also remarkable because Jobim wrote not only the music but the English and Portuguese lyrics for the song.

The complexity of harmony in 'Águas de março' is counterbalanced by a simple melody built on a two-note motive. Jobim dealt with this self-imposed restriction – to write a song with a melody based on essentially two notes – with considerable flair and ingenuity. The essence of his compositional strategy was to simply vary the rhythm and phrasing of the melody, relating this closely to the lyrical content of the song, and setting this within a repetitive, four-measure harmonic structure. Even without musical accompaniment, Jobim's text constitutes an impressive and skilful piece of poetry. His words fall effortlessly into a constantly changing rhythmic architecture and evoke compelling images of day to day life such as 'a truckload of bricks in the soft morning light' and unexpected events such as 'the sound of a shot in the dead of the night'.[44] Before considering Jobim's musical approach to this song, however, it is worth considering the circumstances surrounding its creation and the development of its lyrical content.

'Águas de março' was composed in March 1972, in the rainy season at the end of summer. Jobim was building a wall along the limits of his family farm, *Poço Fundo* (Deep well), in the middle of Rio de Janeiro State. It was raining everywhere, and the roads had turned to mud. As Jobim recounted, 'the whole scene was a big mess'.[45] Some time before the onset of the rain he had been walking in the forest with his wife, Thereza.

> The song was literally born in the forest. I was on *Poço Fundo* with Thereza, looking at the water rushing in a brook, and it just began to pour forth. Incredibly enough, Thereza had paper and pencil. I began to say: 'É pau, é pedra, é o fim do caminho [...]'. And the lyrics came out almost complete, crystal-clear. The final touches were added at home in the afternoon.[46]

Jobim was very particular with the words he chose for this song and spent considerable effort ensuring they were well integrated with the animated rhythm of the melody. He chose words that were concise, stark and evocative and used these words to suggest rather than describe familiar events, items and ideas. Sentence construction and phrasing were short and economic. Adjectives, subjunctive tenses and participles were avoided, and the song was built using a series of short lyrical and musical statements complete in themselves.[47] Water was referred to in all its forms – from rain drops to a river – the words and music described the extent of nature's transformation as the song developed.

In the series of publications *Cancioneiro Jobim*, Jobim's son, Paulo, recalls that the title 'Águas de março' and the sentiment of the song were inspired by the poet Olavo Bilac who had written the poem 'O caçador de esmeraldas' (The emerald hunter).[48]

Foi em março, ao findar da chuva, quase à entrada.	It was in March, after the rainy season.
Do outono, quando a terra em sede requeimada	Nearly autumn, when the parched land Had drunk deep from the waters of the season
Bebera longamente as águas da estação	That with his band of sturdy backwoodsmen
Que, em bandeira, buscando esmeraldas e prata	In search of emeralds and silver
À frente dos peões, filhos da rude mata Fernão Dias Paes Leme entrou pelo sertão.	Fernão Dias Paes Leme strode into the wilderness.

Jobim was keen to finish both a (Brazilian) Portuguese and an English lyric version of 'Águas de março'. The sounds of the words, their rhythms and individual meanings were very important – so important that he was meticulous in presenting a separate melody for each version. It wasn't an easy task, as Jobim recounted before the release of the song in the United States, yet it is a measure of Jobim's genius that the results are just as effective in either language.

> Although the record was made specifically for Brazil, I wrote the English lyrics because translation is always a painful thing to me. I've never been satisfied with American versions of my lyrics, because they weren't exactly translations. People just wrote them without knowing what they were talking about. So I decided to write the English lyrics myself, and they're going to be included, together with the original, in the US release of the album. When I wrote the lyrics on that piece of wrapping paper there was a tune that came along with them which I thought of as a provisional thing. I intended to write something more complex later, but eventually realised that that was the right tune. It would have been a mistake to complicate the melody.[49]

Not content with entrusting the translation of the lyrics to anyone, Jobim decided to restrict the selection of English words to those with Anglo-Saxon roots, avoiding as much as possible any words with Latin roots. In an interview with writer Bob Blumenthal, Jobim said later that 'I avoided all English words derived from Latin when I translated that [the original lyric in Portuguese]. It is eminently an Anglo Saxon lyric, lots of one-syllable words'.[50] For a musician whose first language was not English to undertake such a task is indeed remarkable. Much of the song could not be translated directly without destroying the rhythmic integrity of the original, so Jobim re-wrote the lyrics, substituting suitable words and phrases to fit difficult passages, but making sure that the sentiment and images were true to his original intentions. It is a measure of Jobim's genius that, not only was he successful in translating his original Portuguese lyrics and fitting new words to the song structure, but that, having done so, the English version became as much a stand-alone piece of poetry as the original Portuguese version.

Jobim had created complete sentences in the original Portuguese lyric – 'É pau, é pedra, é o fim do caminho'. However, in translation Jobim's English lyric shows an understanding of poetic artistic licence by simply stating the article and leaving out the verb from the original Portuguese – 'A stick, a stone. It's the end of the road'. Occasionally, in being beholden to the rhythm, Jobim's selection of words necessitated a search for rather abstruse Anglo-Saxon words such as 'a must' in measure 48, or contextually remote words such as 'A float' and 'a drift' in measure 56, but it is their sound rather than their meaning that is important here.

Jobim, like his compatriot Villa-Lobos, was fond of ornithological allusions and references in his songs, and 'Águas de março' is no exception. In measure 15, Jobim makes reference to a bird that obviously held a strong fascination for him – 'matita pereira'. He named his 1973 album, and also a song that appeared on this album, after the bird. In the series *Cancioneiro Jobim,* the bird (spelt slightly differently) is described as follows:

'Matita Perê' is the name of a mysterious bird that sings facing the trunks of trees, so that the sound spreads and you can hear the song without seeing the bird. It is also known as 'saci' (or 'saci-perere'), the name of a hobgoblin in Brazilian folklore with which it is associated.[51]

There are many spellings of the name of this bird – 'matintapereira', 'matintaperera' and 'martim-pererê' are three alternatives. The footnote to Jobim's 1973 album *Matita Perê* reveals one of the characteristics of the bird that he would no doubt have found attractive.

Matita Perê – elusive bird of the Brazilian backlands. Pursue his song and you shall never find him. In summer he also sings at night. This fabled bird has many legends and over fifteen different names. A kind of striped cuckoo who also puts his eggs in the nests of other birds. When he calls and his mate answers, their song forms a mysterious chromatic scale, and then, when they get together, the song ceases and you can hear the silence.[52]

In another description from producer, musician and historian Luiz Roberto Oliveira, Matita Perê is described as a 'one-legged, red-hatted, pipe-smoking spirit of the forest, dark-skinned, riding an animal called a "capibara"'.[53]

The conductor and arranger for many of Jobim's recordings, Claus Ogerman, said this of 'Águas de março':

Antônio's lyrics (he did the English translation for this song himself) are serious poetry. Here he uses basically a sequence of keywords in one's life. Antônio actually had in mind to write another, more tuneful melody to these lyrics, he considered the music we now have to be merely a 'dummy', a rhythmic skeleton while he worked on the words, later to be replaced by a different composition. But he never got around to do it. This recording is the only time I ever suggested to him to overdub his voice in unison over his first vocal track. I felt that the twin-voice effect added to the 'projection' of the song.[54]

Águas de março

É pau, é pedra, é o fim do caminho
É um resto de toco, é um pouco sozinho
É um caco de vidro, é a vida, é o sol
É a noite, é a morte, é o laço, é o anzol
É peroba do campo, é o nó da madeira
Caingá, candeia, é o matita pereira
É madeira de vento, tombo da ribanceira
É o mistério profundo, é o queira ou não
queira
É o vento ventando, é o fim da ladeira
É a viga, é o vão, festa da cumeeira
É a chuva chovendo, é conversa ribeira
Das águas de março, é o fim da canseira
É o pé, é o chão, é a marcha estradeira
Passarinho na mão, pedra de atiradeira
Uma ave no céu, uma ave no chão
É um regato, é uma fonte, é um pedaço
de pão
É o fundo do poço, é o fim do caminho
No rosto o desgosto, é um pouco sozinho
É um estrepe, é um prego, é uma ponta, é
um ponto
É um pingo pingando, é uma conta, é um
conto
É um peixe, é um gesto, é uma prata
brilhando
É a luz da manhã, é o tijolo chegando
É a lenha, é o dia, é o fim da picada
É a garrafa de cana, o estilhaço na estrada
É o projeto da casa, é o corpo na cama
É o carro enguiçado, é a lama, é a lama
É um passo, é uma ponte, é um sapo,
é uma rã
É um resto de mato, na luz da manhã
São as águas de março fechando o verão
É a promessa de vida no teu coração

Waters of March

A stick, a stone, it's the end of the road
It's the rest of a stump, it's a little alone
It's a sliver of glass, it is life, it's the sun
It is night, it is death, it's a trap, it's a gun
The oak when it blooms, a fox in the brush
A knot in the wood, the song of a thrush
The wood of the wind, a cliff, a fall
A scratch, a lump, it is nothing at all
It's the wind blowing free, it's the end of the
slope
It's a beam, it's a void, it's a hunch, it's a
hope
And the river bank talks of the waters of
March
It's the end of the strain, it's the joy in your
heart
The foot, the ground, the flesh and the bone
The beat of the road, a slingshot stone
A fish, a flash, a silvery glow
A fight, a bet, the range of a bow
The bed of the well, the end of the line
The dismay in the face, it's a loss, it's a find
A spear, a spike, a point, a nail
A drip, a drop, the end of the tale
A truck load of bricks in the soft morning
light
The shot of a gun in the dead of the night
A mile, a must, a thrust, a bump,
It's a girl, it's a rhyme, it's a cold, it's the mumps
The plan of the house, the body in bed
And the car that got stuck. It's the mud, it's
the mud
A float, a drift, a flight, a wing,
A hawk, a quail, the promise of spring
And the river bank talks of the waters of
March
It's the promise of life, it's the joy in your
heart

Instrumental

É uma cobra, é um pau, é João, é José
É um espinho na mão, é um corte no pé
São as águas de março fechando o verão
É a promessa de vida no teu coração
É pau, é pedra, é o fim do caminho
É um resto de toco, é um pouco sozinho
É um passo, é uma ponte
É um sapo, é uma rã,
É um belo horizonte, é uma febre terçã,
São as águas de março fechando o verão
É a promessa de vida no teu coração
É pau, é pedra, é o fim do caminho
É um resto de toco, é um pouco sozinho
É um caco de vidro, é a vida, é o sol
É a noite, é a morte, é o laço, é o anzol
São as águas de março fechando o verão
É a promessa de vida no teu coração

Instrumental

A snake, a stick. It is John, it is Joe
It's a thorn in your hand and a cut in your toe
A point, a grain, a bee, a bite
A blink, a buzzard
A sudden stroke of night
A pin, a needle, a sting, a pain
A snail, a riddle, a wasp, a stain
A pass in the mountains, a horse and a mule
In the distance the shelves rode three
shadows of blue
And the river bank talks of the waters of
March
It's the promise of life in your heart, in your
heart
A stick, a stone, the end of the load
The rest of a stump, a lonesome road
A sliver of glass, a life, the sun
A night, a death, the end of the run
And the river bank talks of the waters of
March
It's the end of all strain, it's the joy in your
heart.

Ex. 5.24. Antônio Carlos Jobim, 'Águas de março' (Waters of March), Portuguese and English lyrics. Text translation from Jobim, *Cancioneiro Jobim: Obras Escolhidas, 1971–1982*, 330.

The overall structure of the song does not follow the typical strophic ballad structure of verse, chorus, verse, but is instead through-composed and exists as one complete entity without any obvious major sections. However, there are short musical phrases or building blocks that are repeated throughout the song, and these Jobim constructed to evoke the effect of a continuously flowing stream of water. Just as a stream of water changes direction in an almost random, unpredictable fashion, so too do the appearances of melodic phrases. Each melodic phrase represents a certain momentary direction. In keeping with the 'block' structure of the song, much of the text is simply a sequence of very short sentences or ideas. The Portuguese and English texts are outlined in Ex. 5.24. The complete score can be found online.[55]

The melody, imitating the lyric, consists of a set of short phrases, based on the two-note motive e^1 to c^1, with each phrase outlining a distinctive melodic path that ends on the first beat of the measure on the tonic note, c^1 (Ex. 5.25). Often there is a passing note between the upper note e^1 and the home note c^1. These constituent phrases are set out in order of

Ex. 5.25. Antônio Carlos Jobim, 'Águas de março', the set of constituent melodic phrases.

appearance in the song, not in any hierarchical order. In fact, because of the nature of the architecture of this song these phrases could appear in almost any order and still make sense.[56] The phrases are designed to be inter-changeable and all (with the possible exception of phrase 3) can be linked in any order without melodic (or harmonic) discontinuity.[57] In other words, the musical phrases act as autonomous building blocks that go together to create the song. Despite the independence of these phrases, the strong musical connection with the lyric is maintained because the lyric itself is segmented and consists of descriptive single words and short phrases that allude to the overall sentiment rather than tell a story.[58]

All phrases begin on the second beat of the measure, except for phrase 6, syncopation being introduced with the note c^1 (and other accented melody notes) tied across the bar line. The song begins with phrase[1] followed by phrase 2 repeated seven times (in the Portuguese version), then followed by phrase 3, then phrase 1, phrase 2, phrase 3 (extended), phrase 4 (extended) and so on. Ex. 5.26 shows this particular sequence.

Ex. 5.26. Antônio Carlos Jobim, 'Águas de março', opening sequence of melodic phrases (Portuguese version).

Ex. 5.27. Antônio Carlos Jobim, 'Águas de março', measures 40–43.[59]

5 1	2	2	2	2	2	2	2	12 3	3x	1	2	3	3x	3x	3x
20 4x	4x	4x	4x	4x	4x	4x	2	28 1	2	2	2	3x	3x	3x	3x
36 4	2	2	2	1	2	2	2	44 3x	3x	3x	3x	4	2	2	2
52 (2)	(4)	4	4	1	2	2	2	60 4x	4x	4x	4x	(1)	(2)	(3)	(3)
68 (3)	(3)	(3)	(3)	(2)	(2)	(2)	(1)	76 (2)	(2)	(2)	3x	3x	3x	3x	4x
84 4x	4x	4x	1	2	2	2	3x	92 3x	3x	3x	4	5	4x	4x	1
100 2	2	2	2	2	2	2	4	108 5	4	5	6	6	6	6	6
116 6	6	6	6	6	6	6	(1)	124 end							

Ex. 5.28. Antônio Carlos Jobim, 'Águas de março', overall sequence of melodic phrases.

An indication of the flexible architecture of this song, and a suggestion that the development of the song is not based on the melody, can be seen by comparing the Portuguese and English versions. Jobim made two recordings of this song in 1972 on the album simply entitled *Jobim*. On the first track ('Águas de março'), he sang (overdubbed) the Portuguese version of the lyric, while on the second track ('Waters of March') he overdubbed the English version. Both tracks used exactly the same instrumental accompaniment. However, Jobim selected different melodic phrases where the English and Portuguese text demanded a different rhythmic interpretation, as seen in Ex. 5.27 for instance.

The entire song can be represented as a sequence of selected melodic phrases as defined in the table shown in Ex. 5.28. This diagram shows the sequence of melodic phrases for the song in table form where each block containing a phrase number represents a measure of the song.[60] The sequence is read from left to right and there are 16 measures in every row. Phrase 3 (extended) and phrase 4 (extended) are designated as 3x and 4x respectively. Phrase numbers in parenthesis indicate slight variations of the designated phrase. The small numbers in the upper left-hand corner of some blocks are measure numbers.

The appearance of this chart suggests there is little sense of development throughout the song because of the seemingly arbitrary selection of melodic phrases. In the first part of 'Águas de março', melodic phrases are often repeated, giving an almost minimalist impression. Any sense of development is sustained more by the continuity of text than by musical devices, but the awareness of progression is not always obvious. Towards the end of the song, however, the situation is transformed as a slowly descending chromatic melodic line builds the song to a conclusion as it unfolds over the last twelve measures (phrase 6). Jobim made much of the chromaticism of these final measures in several recordings of 'Águas de março' by singing each descending note sustained for the full measure as a counter line against the final melodic phrase 6.[61]

Despite the irregularity of the melodic phrases shown in Ex. 5.28, the harmonic plan is not as unpredictable. In fact, for most of the piece, the chord $C^{6/9}$ cyclically returns every four measures. The return to $C^{6/9}$ is usually preceded by an Fm6 chord.[62] By means of this chordal repetition, the song is constructed using a sequence of four-measure structural harmonic blocks assembled independently of the melody. The simplicity of the melodic phrases supports this compositional method. Almost any of the four-measure harmonic blocks harmonize with any combination of the six melodic phrases. The four-measure harmonic blocks are outlined in Ex. 5.29.

Block A: $\text{I}^{9/6}$	$\mid \text{I } 7$	$\mid \text{VIm}^{6}$	$\mid \text{IVm}^{6}$
Block B: $\text{I}^{9/6}$	$\mid \flat\text{V}^{7\#11}$	$\mid \text{IVma}^{7}$	$\mid \text{IVm}^{6}$
Block C: $\text{I}^{9/6}$	$\mid \text{Vm}^{7\,(9)}$	$\mid \#\text{IVm}^{7\,(\flat5)}$	$\mid \text{IVm}^{6}$
Block D: I^{6}	$\mid \text{Vm}^{7}, \text{I}^{7}$	$\mid \text{II}^{7}$	$\mid \text{IVm}^{6}$
Block E: I	$\mid \text{Im}^{7}$	$\mid \text{II}^{7}$	$\mid \text{IVm}^{6}\ (\text{or } \flat\text{IIma}^{7})$

Ex. 5.29. Antônio Carlos Jobim, 'Águas de março', chord sequences comprising four-measure, structural harmonic blocks.

The layout of the four-measure harmonic blocks as they appear throughout the song is outlined in Ex. 5.30. In this diagram each cell represents four measures of the song. Each is labelled A, B, C, D or E according to the chord sequence within each four-measure block, as defined in Ex. 5.29. The sequence is read from left to right and there are 16 measures (4 lots of four-measure blocks) in each row. The layout is essentially the same as in Ex. 5.28 except that individual measures are not indicated as separate cells. There is also a group of three-measures starting at measure 64 that does not follow any of the chord sequences shown in Ex. 5.29 and consequently offsets the measure count.

5 A	8 B	12 C	16 C
20 C	24 C	28 A	32 C
36 C	42 A	44 C	48 A
52 D	56 A	60 C (+ 3 measures)	67 (A)
71 B	75 A	79 C	83 A
87 A	91 E	95 E	99 A
103 C	107 C	111 D	115 D
119 E	123 end		

Ex. 5.30. Antônio Carlos Jobim, 'Águas de março', the sequence of four-measure, structural harmonic blocks throughout the complete song.[63]

A comparison of this structure with the arrangement of melodic phrases shown in Ex. 5.28 indicates clearly that the melody is constructed virtually independent of the harmonic accompaniment.

Jobim's understanding of melodic and harmonic inter-dependence is evident at measure 13 where he writes a chord constructed of 3rds (designated Gm7(9)/C in the score) shown in Ex. 5.31. In this chord the root G is not part of the chord but is supplied by the melody preceding the chord. This is typical of the 'open' sound of Jobim's chord voicings in many of his songs. The melody often supplies the important note of the chord – the root or 3rd – thereby eliminating doubled notes in the accompaniment and the melody. This very

Ex. 5.31. Antônio Carlos Jobim, 'Águas de março', measures 12–13.[64]

economic approach to harmonization imparts an extra sonic dimension and importance to melodic and harmonic inter-dependence.

Sergio Cabral, Jobim's biographer, states that the song 'Águas de março' was written originally on guitar. It was in 1972 when Jobim was building a new house on the family farm in the country and there was no piano. One effective guitar technique that Jobim used throughout the song to evoke 'strain' is the repeating of the unusually voiced C major 7th chord. In this chord the major 7th note (b^1) is sounded a semitone below the root (c^2) as shown in Ex. 5.32. The dissonant juxtaposition of these two notes a semitone apart within the same chord in such a prominent rhythmical position heightens the feeling of tension and movement within the song – a feeling that is perpetuated when the chord is repeated every four measures. For some reason this voicing sounds much less dissonant on guitar than it does on piano. It may be for that reason that this voicing was not included in the

Ex. 5.32. Antônio Carlos Jobim, 'Águas de março', C major 7th guitar chord voicing.[66]

piano score in the series *Cancioneiro Jobim*, but rather the relevant chord was changed to a C6/G or C(9)6.[65]

In many ways it is the last thirteen measures (111–123) that give greater insight into the mechanism of the song than anything that is revealed within the song itself. From measure 112 there is a falling chromatic line that extends almost an entire octave from bb^1 to c^1, voiced in the upper notes of the chords at the start of each measure.

The existence of this chromatic line from bb^1 to c^1 may have been a determining factor in Jobim's choice of chords for the whole song at the outset. For instance, the chromatic line B♭–A–A♭–G–G♭–F appears at the start of the song in the bass (Ex. 5.34).

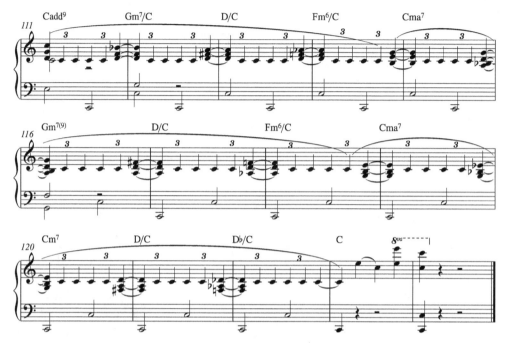

Ex. 5.33. Antônio Carlos Jobim, 'Águas de março', final measures 111–24.[67]

Ex. 5.34. Antônio Carlos Jobim, 'Águas de março', measures 5–11.[68]

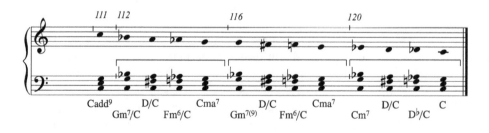

Ex. 5.35. Antônio Carlos Jobim, 'Águas de março', harmonic reduction final measures.

An analysis of the complete score reveals that the sequence of chromatically descending notes, bb–a–ab–g, can be found in every four-measure block throughout the song.[69] It would appear, therefore, that Jobim used this sequence of notes to determine the nature of the harmonization for every chord within each four-measure block. The repeated sequence of notes, bb–a–ab–g, when offset (or cycled) by one reads g–bb–a–ab. These notes are constituent notes of every corresponding chord in Ex. 5.29. It would seem, therefore, that this chromatic sequence of notes is the key to the structure of the whole song.

The notes of the chromatic motive g–f#–f–e, a minor 3rd below bb–a–ab–g, are also found in almost all of the chords within the four-measure blocks of the song. Their harmonic context is most obvious in the final twelve measures. This is shown in the harmonic reduction of the final twelve measures (Ex. 5.35) where both four-measure chromatic sequences are shown relative to the longer chromatic line from bb^1 to c^1.

The chromatic motive bb–a–ab–g (and the motive g–f#–f–e harmonized a minor 3rd-below) can be seen as occupying four-measure blocks in the above example as indicated by the horizontal brackets at measures 112, 116 and 120. However, as the chord names (below the bass staff) suggest, these four-measure blocks are offset relative to the four-measure harmonic blocks as shown in Ex. 5.29.[70]

Jobim's harmonization of the long, descending chromatic line from bb–c reveals the melodic orientation of his approach to composition. Generally, given a repeated melodic phrase, Jobim would choose appropriate chords so that the melody note was part of the chord. Of course with highly chromatic chords the range of choices for an appropriate chord becomes quite extensive, but here the choice of chord is fixed because of the four-measure blocks. This fact necessitates a repeat of the note g1 at measure 116 in order to maintain a chromatic descending melodic line.[71] In measure 120 the derivation of the four-measure harmonic Block E: C–Cm^7–D^7–Dbma^7, mentioned in Ex. 5.29 can be seen. Here the more common second chord in the sequence, Gm7 would not harmonize well with the eb in the upper chromatic line. Instead Jobim uses a Cm7 chord which is more-or-less defined by the notes in the sequence as it stands. Also, the choice of Dbma7 for the second last chord is all but defined by the notes in the sequence at that point.

The attraction of the melody to the tonic note c is also very strong and obvious from the outset. The note c appears nearly always at the beginning of each measure and harmonizes throughout in virtually every measure. Also, the phrases always descend to the note c – they never ascend (c–d–e for instance).

Jobim uses a c pedal note in the last thirteen measures to underscore a slowly descending melodic line. The song, however, remains framed by the simple two-note motive e^1–c^1 that appears at the start and is restated at the conclusion of the song as two single, exposed, notes repeated in a higher octave – a programmatic reminder of the origins of the 'Waters of March'.

Melodic Tributes

As has been seen in previous chapters, the influence of Debussy on Jobim's work is subtle but far reaching. Jobim was happy to discuss his musical influences in interviews and even occasionally revealed, or paid tribute to, specific influences in his music. An unmistakeable direct melodic tribute to Debussy was paid by Jobim in 'Chovendo na roseira' written for the film *The Adventurers*.[72] Jobim's opening melodic line is almost a direct quotation from Debussy's 'Rêverie' (Exs. 5.36 and 5.37).

Ex. 5.36. Claude Debussy, 'Rêverie', measures 3–5.[73]

Ex. 5.37. Antônio Carlos Jobim, 'Chovendo na roseira', measures 23–28.[74]

'Chovendo na roseira' also reveals harmonic influences from Villa-Lobos. The song 'Abril' (Seresta No. 9) was written by Villa-Lobos in 1926 and, as well as providing a model for guitar accompaniment that contrasts duple and triple rhythms, it almost certainly provided Jobim with the harmonic foundation for 'Chovendo na roseira'.[75] Following the polyrhythmic guitar introduction shown in Ex. 4.14, the same rhythmic figure continues with the addition of harmonium and bass (Ex. 5.38). Here every measure is based upon a tonic chord (with the root e in the bass) and an alternate added 6th or 7th.

The same alternate measures of tonic 6th and 7th chords in 3/4 time can be found in the first eighteen measures that introduce the main melody in 'Chovendo na roseira' (Ex. 5.39).

Ex. 5.38. Heitor Villa-Lobos, 'Abril', measures 5–12.[76]

This regular alternation of chords adds to the 'macro' rhythm of the piece – in effect the chord changes create a repeated rhythmic pattern that spans a greater time scale than that set up by individual notes within the measure.

Jobim also included a musical acknowledgement of Villa-Lobos in his instrumental 'Stone Flower'. Towards the end of Villa-Lobos' 'Abril', after a vocal section, there is a repeated short, but distinct, three-measure motive in the guitar part (Ex. 5.40).

The same motive (without the lower 3rds) can be heard in 'Quebra pedra (Stone Flower)', again towards the end of the piece, this time played on flute and in the key of D major (Ex. 5.41). So obvious is the statement it can only be construed that Jobim was deliberately evoking the spirit of Villa-Lobos by quotation.

Ex. 5.39. Antônio Carlos Jobim, 'Chovendo na roseira', measures 23–34.[77]

Ex. 5.40. Heitor Villa-Lobos, 'Abril', three-measure phrase played on the guitar.[78]

Ex. 5.41. Antônio Carlos Jobim, 'Quebra pedra (Stone Flower)', measures 87–90, three-measure phrase played on flute.[79]

Melodic Contour

The characteristics of bossa nova melody and form had their counterparts in previous styles, most notably *choro* and *modinha* (as has been discussed). Jobim's acknowledgement of the *modinha* influence in his work can be heard in his song simply entitled 'Modinha'. This was originally included in the 1980 *Terra Brasilis* album, but was also included on the 1987 album *Tom Jobim Inédito*, where it was placed immediately after Villa-Lobos' 'Modinha'

Ex. 5.42. Antônio Carlos Jobim, 'Modinha', measures 5–12.[81]

(Seresta number 5). It is typical of most Brazilian *modinhas*: with its initial octave melodic leap and its dramatic repeated descending melodic motive it exemplifies the form (Ex. 5.42). Béhague describes the form as having 'elaborate melodic lines' with lyrical qualities similar to those found in operatic arias.[80]

Aside from the many obvious musical influences in Jobim's work and his ability to create his own idiosyncratic voice, there have been many commentators who have singled out Jobim's melodic invention as his most important musical ability. Composer Henry Mancini, for instance, was entranced by the melody of Jobim's 'Wave' when he first heard it and commented: 'My favourite song, not only of his but of all songs, is "Wave". That's another one I couldn't believe when I first heard it. It shouldn't work. It goes all over the place, but it does it so beautifully'.[82] Example 5.43 shows the melody of the first twelve measures of 'Wave' (after the introduction).

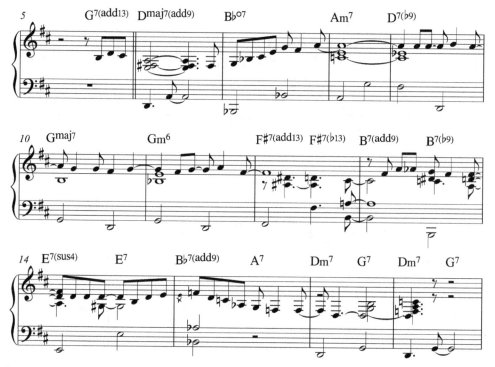

Ex. 5.43. Antônio Carlos Jobim, 'Wave', measures 1–17.[83]

Whole-Tone Scales

Perhaps the most widely known musical technique associated with Debussy is his use of the whole-tone scale. Examples of its use can be seen throughout Debussy's work, but it is well illustrated in pieces such as 'Voiles' (*Preludes*, Book I), 'Feuilles Mortes' and 'Jimbo's Lullaby' and in his two sets of *Images*. Although Jobim did not take to the whole-tone scale with any degree of extended purpose, he did use it in the introduction to 'As praias desertas'. The opening

Ex. 5.44. Antônio Carlos Jobim, 'As praias desertas' (Deserted beaches), introduction, measures 1–5.[84]

whole-tone arpeggio and the following richly coloured chords create an 'open' sonic atmosphere and evoke a sense of fluidity, much as Debussy had done with his whole-tone creations. Jobim, however, soon reverts to a more tonal passage leading to the body of the song and does not sustain the aura he created to introduce the song as Debussy did in many of his pieces.

Choro **Structural Form**

The form and harmonic structure of the *choro* 'Chega de saudade' (discussed on pages 66–67) is testament to Jobim's ability to compose a truly remarkable, harmonically rich, and appealing song. Jobim's 1970 album *Stone Flower* contains an instrumental track simply entitled 'Choro', his direct acknowledgement of the influence of this style. Reproduced in Ex. 5.45 is the melody of the piece showing its form and melodic construction. It departs from the common form of the *choro* (A–B–A–C–A), in that the first 'A' section is repeated, with the repeat of the B section (featuring flutes and strings in place of an otherwise ubiquitous piano melody) equivalent to a 'C' section. Jobim's melody also has the momentum normally associated with *choro* (it features long sequences of short quaver notes) although the wide

Ex. 5.45. Antônio Carlos Jobim, 'Choro' (Garoto).[85]

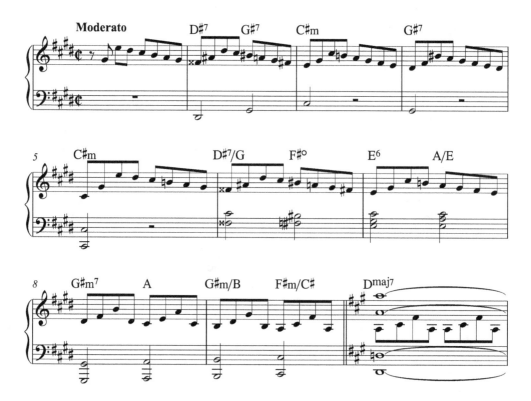

Ex. 5.46. Antônio Carlos Jobim, 'Meu Amigo Radamés', measures 1–10.[86]

arpeggiated opening phrase is atypical. Grace notes, trills and ornamentations common in *choro* are also heard in this recording.

The *choro* 'Meu Amigo Radamés' is Jobim's tribute to his mentor Radamés Gnattali. In contrast to the syncopations and rhythmic complexities of much of Jobim's music, the opening measures of this piece show an almost Baroque rhythmic regularity in the momentum of the quaver melody and in the harmonic construction, a possible recognition and tribute to Gnattali's classical background and influence.

'Dindi'

There have been many recordings and arrangements of this particularly eloquent love song since it was written in 1959. On the original recorded version Silvia Telles sang the (Brazilian) Portuguese lyrics, but subsequently 'Dindi' became one of Jobim's better-known songs when Jobim himself recorded an English version in a session with the Nelson Riddle Orchestra in 1965.[87]

A cursory glance at the score of this song reveals a somewhat banal and directionless melody that essentially parallels the harmony a 3rd above the root of each accompanying chord.[88] The melody's simplicity might even indicate that it was written by a novice, but on hearing 'Dindi' performed it becomes obvious that interest is sustained not in the melody but in the unusual chord progression. The song introduces the technique of alternating major 7th chords a tone apart – a technique that was later embraced and used to great effect by the songwriter Jimmy Webb in his 1968 song 'Wichita Lineman'. Webb acknowledges his debt to Jobim in his book *Tunesmith*.[89]

Ex. 5.47. Antônio Carlos Jobim, 'Dindi', opening measures 1–4.[90]

Ex. 5.48. Claude Debussy, 'Les collines d'Anacapri', measures 62–65.[91]

A precedent for the sonic effect of alternating major 7th chords a tone apart was established by Debussy in his 'Les collines d'Anacapri', *Prelude V*, Book 1. Example 5.48 shows the passage in measures 62–65 where alternating B major and A major chords (with the melody playing the major 7th and 9th notes of the A major chord) suggest a sense of detachment and tranquil contemplation.

Several different conclusions to Jobim's song 'Dindi' reveal an interesting aspect of his compositional method. Two interpretations of 'Dindi' are outlined in the *Tom Jobim Songbook,* vol. 3, while another (different) version is presented in the *Cancioneiro Jobim* series (Ex. 5.49).[92] The first of the two versions in the *Tom Jobim Songbooks* is an arrangement with an English lyric, and the second is an arrangement with a Portuguese lyric.[93] Both these versions are essentially the same throughout the body of the song, except for the phrasing of the melody to suit the lyric, but Jobim presents a quite different and more harmonically inventive conclusion for the Brazilian/Portuguese version. The *Cancioneiro Jobim* conclusion to 'Dindi' is even more harmonically elaborate while catering for both English and Portuguese lyrics simultaneously. All three conclusions for 'Dindi' are presented in Exs. 5.49(a), (b) and (c).

The English version (Ex. 5.49a) is relatively straightforward.[94] However the Portuguese ending (Ex. 5.49b), instead of returning to a Cma7 chord after the end of the 3rd measure (as in the English version), changes to a D7(9) chord to harmonize the same melody. In the next measure Jobim not only changes the upper melody note from e^2 to eb^2, but also harmonizes the two melody notes (eb^2 and c^2) first with an Fm7 chord then with a Dbma7(9) chord, eventually finishing with the original C7 chord. This suggests that not only is Jobim prepared to change a melody from major to minor merely to break a pattern, but that he will also change harmonization for an alternative effect if the original harmonic design becomes somewhat repetitive or predictable. The third conclusion to 'Dindi' from *Cancioneiro Jobim* bears this out (Ex. 5.49c). Here the complexity of harmonic design is increased even further, especially in the D–Db–C transition, the arpeggiation in the final two measures and the highly coloured final chord.

Ultimately, these alternative conclusions to 'Dindi' demonstrate Jobim's flexible, open-ended approach to composition and his relentless experimentation with melody and harmonic structure. Jobim would have developed an experimental sensibility in his early career as a popular-music performer by introducing a melody from another song over the accompaniment to the song being played, a common practice in jazz. A classic example from his recorded performances is his singing the melody to 'Take the A-Train' over the chord changes to 'Garota de Ipanema' from his last concert in Brazil in 1993.

Alternative Melody

An extension of this playful technique is the creation of a new, alternative melody to fit the chord changes for a given song, as distinct from mere on-the-spot improvisation. Improvisations are never repeated in exactly the same way, whereas an alternative melody can be, and usually is, repeated. Jobim's repeated alternative melody for 'Garota de Ipanema', for instance, can be heard on several recordings such as *A Arte de Tom Jobim* and *Terra Brasilis.* Jobim also extended this practice of melodic substitution to other compositions.

Ex. 5.49. Antônio Carlos Jobim, 'Dindi', alternative conclusions to the song, from *Tom Jobim Songbook, vol. 3,* and *Cancioneiro Jobim.*[95]

Ex. 5.50. Antônio Carlos Jobim, 'Retrato em branco e preto', normal melody (upper staff) and alternative melody (middle staff).[96]

For instance, the chord progressions for 'Wave' and 'Tide' are essentially identical, yet the melodies are quite different. Another of his outstanding 'alternative' melodies can be heard in the substitute melody he composed for the recording of 'Retrato em branco e preto' (Ex. 5.50). In this instance the alternative melody has as much strength and attraction as the original and could have formed the basis for a completely different piece.

Jobim's alternative melodies do not have the on-the-spot awkwardness of many improvised jazz solos that can often develop into mere showpieces for technical dexterity. His melodies are pre-conceived and remembered – his alternative melody for 'Garota de Ipanema', for instance, cannot be regarded as merely an improvisation because it has been the same in many subsequent recordings. This highlights a fundamental difference between Jobim's approach to music performance and the approach taken to jazz performance. Jobim's method is more measured, specific and pre-prepared. His broad musical influences are more apparent, especially in his melodies, yet his music is economical and 'to-the-point' without losing any of its emotional or dynamic impact. Understatement is indeed his musical strength.

Conclusion

Melodically Jobim's compositions exhibit broad variety in structure and form. His melodies range from single repeated notes and simple sequential phrases to complex phrases with wide tessitura. The juxtaposition of static and changing musical material is a common means of mitigating the overriding effect of any particular musical element. This type of approach to composition can be found in the work of Villa-Lobos and Debussy and highlights the inter-dependence of melody and harmony in Jobim's work. Taking a lead from Chopin's use of chromatic clustered motives, Jobim changed their function from middle-ground figures to components of independent melody. The flexibility of this technique also offered him a valuable mechanism for harmonic exploration.

Jobim's debt to his musical forebears is shown in 'Insensatez', which bears more than a passing resemblance to Chopin's *Prelude in E minor Op. 28 No. 4*, 'Chovendo na roseira', which reproduces melodic fragments from Debussy's 'Rêverie', and 'Stone Flower' that quotes a three-measure melodic motive from Villa-Lobos' 'Abril'. Far from merely reproducing the style and intent of these 'borrowed' fragments, Jobim places these in highly original contexts while at the same time acknowledging his inspiration. His recognition of local Brazilian folk styles is apparent in the *choros* 'Chega de saudade', 'Choro' and 'Meu amigo Radames' and also in the *modinha* simply entitled 'Modinha'. Many of Jobim's recordings contain alternative melodies that are not improvised but carefully created to match existing harmonic structures. This is indicative of Jobim's meticulous approach to composition and highlights one of the major differences between Jobim's music and jazz.

Notes

1   Jobim and Jobim, *Cancioneiro Jobim: Obras Completas, 1959–1965*, vol. 2, 229–30.
2   Jobim and Jobim, *Cancioneiro Jobim: Obras Completas, 1959–1965*, vol. 2, 94.
3   Jobim and Jobim, *Cancioneiro Jobim: Obras Completas, 1959–1965*, vol. 2, 262.
4   Villa-Lobos, *Prélude No. 1*.
5   Villa-Lobos, *Gavota-Choro*.
6   Debussy, *La Cathedral Engloutie*.
7   Jobim and Jobim, *Cancioneiro Jobim: Obras Escolhidas* 223.
8   This piece was originally entitled 'Zingaro' and was released in America in 1968 on the album *A Certain Mr. Jobim*. It later became known as 'Retrato em branco e preto' (Portrait in black and white) when lyrics were written by Chico Buarque de Holanda.
9   The complete score for 'Retrato em branco e preto' can be found online at: http://www2.uol. com.br/tomjobim/download.htm.
10 Jobim and Jobim, *Cancioneiro Jobim: Obras Escolhidas* 304.
11 Alfred Cortot, Performance notes, in Chopin, *12 Studies Op. 10*, 40.
12 Chopin, *12 Studies Op. 10*, 42.
13 Chopin, *Oeuvres Pour Le Piano*.
14 An interesting aspect to the recording that Jobim made for the album *A Certain Mr. Jobim* (1967) was the inclusion of a different melody to the repeat of the first 4 measures and the repetition of this 'new' melody at the repeat of measure 9. The melody he played was not merely improvised at the time, but it represented another fully prepared and entirely acceptable melodic solution to the original harmonic progression – an indication of Jobim's irrepressible melodic inventiveness. The alternative melody can be seen on page 176.
15 Jobim and Jobim, *Cancioneiro Jobim: Obras Completas, 1971–1982*, vol. 4, 72–73.
16 The complete 'Insensatez' score showing vocal melody, Portuguese and English lyrics and chord designations is presented online at http://www2.uol.com.br/tomjobim/download. htm.
17 See Schachter, 'The Prelude in E Minor' 164.
18 Schachter, 'Prelude in E Minor' 162.
19 … at least at the detailed level defining the transitions between successive chords. The overall structure fits a more considered form.
20 Chopin, *Prélude Op. 28, No. 4*.
21 Jobim and Jobim, *Cancioneiro Jobim: Obras Escolhidas* 262; also available as a pdf downloadable file at http://www2.uol.com.br/tomjobim/mp_insensatez.htm.
22 Chediak, *Tom Jobim Songbook*, vol. 3, 69.
23 The use of carets above numerals denote scale degree in the prevailing key. For instance $\hat{6}$ is the note g in the key of B minor. For more information see Forte 43.
24 Schachter, 'Prelude in E Minor' 169.
25 Ashton Jonson 175.
26 Schachter, *Unfoldings* 163.

27　At the end of the piece, Schachter refers to the 'stretch $\hat{3}$-$\hat{2}$-$\hat{1}$ of the *Prelude*'s fundamental line' as 'unfold[ing] in the lower octave'. He also adds that '[a]lthough the structure is fulfilled, the sense of melodic resolution is made somewhat obscure, adding to the improvisatory, quasi-fragmentary character of the piece'. Schachter, 'Prelude in E Minor' 168.

28　Chopin initially omits the neighbour note motive on scale degree $\hat{3}$.

29　Schachter, 'Prelude in E Minor' 167.

30　Schachter, 'Prelude in E Minor' 175.

31　Abraham 91.

32　The term *saudade* is discussed on page 39.

33　Villa-Lobos, *Choros No. 5*.

34　Jobim and Jobim, *Cancioneiro Jobim: Obras Completas, 1971–1982*, vol. 4, 166.

35　Reily 13.

36　Villa-Lobos, *Hommage Á Chopin*.

37　The first statement of the melodic motive in measure 2 is based on an A# arpeggiated half-diminished chord with the note c# in the bass. In measure 4 the highest note of the triplet figure does not form part of the diminished sequence (d#^{1} would be the expected note). However, its inclusion does not detract from the overall diminished sonority of the motive established by the notes A, f# and b#. The notes a^2, f#^{2} and c^2(b#) also appear in the right-hand accompaniment further strengthening the diminished sonority.

38　This is true except for measure 4 where two extraneous suspended notes (b^2 and e^2) are introduced.

39　Another Villa-Lobos example is his *Prelude No. 3*.

40　Jobim and Jobim, *Cancioneiro Jobim: Obras Completas, 1971–1982*, vol. 4, 178.

41　Jobim and Jobim, *Cancioneiro Jobim: Obras Completas, 1971–1982*, vol. 4, 159.

42　Holston, 'Saying Goodbye to Antônio Carlos Jobim' 56.

43　Jobim and Jobim, *Cancioneiro Jobim: Obras Escolhidas* 146.

44　Chediak, *Tom Jobim Songbook*, vol. 2, 27.

45　Oliveira, *Clube do Tom*.

46　Jobim and Jobim, *Cancioneiro Jobim: Obras Completas, 1971–1982*, vol. 4, 25.

47　Jobim and Jobim, *Cancioneiro Jobim: Obras Escolhidas* 147.

48　Jobim and Jobim, *Cancioneiro Jobim: Obras Completas, 1971–1982*, vol. 4, 25. Both the Portuguese and its English translation appear in this text.

49　Jobim and Jobim, *Cancioneiro Jobim: Obras Escolhidas* 147.

50　Blumenthal, 'Cover Notes'.

51　Jobim and Jobim, *Cancioneiro Jobim: Obras Completas, 1971–1982*, vol. 4, 25.

52　Giacomelli, *Águas de março*.

53　Cohen, *Águas de março*.

54　Claus Ogerman, quoted in *Remembering Antonio Carlos Jobim*, 24 May 2001, http://bjbear71.com/Jobim/tom-ogerman.html.

55　It can be downloaded as a pdf file at http://www2.uol.com.br/tomjobim/mp_aguas_de_marco.htm.

56　Notes in parenthesis represent the most likely note to lead into the melodic phrase (usually this is the final c^1 of the preceding phrase).

57 The extended version of phrase 3 can be seen to be used more for contrast, helping to delineate a larger scale form.

58 According to Tinhorão, 'Águas de março' uses a folklore theme named 'Aqua de ceu' (or 'Águas do céu') recorded originally by Leny Eversong in 1956. The track appeared on the record *Cinco Estrelas Apresentam Inara* (Inara presents five Stars), but had been in existence well before. 'It is based on a *macumba* (African-Brazilian religious ritual) beat collected in 1933 by J. B. Carvalho. It featured the lines "É pau, é pedra, é seixo miúdo/roda baiana/por cima de tudo", Tinhorão claimed. Barbosa, 'Suspicion of Plagiarism involves *Águas de março*'.

59 Jobim and Jobim, *Cancioneiro Jobim: Obras Escolhidas* 334.

60 Except for measure 5, which is in 3/2 spanning two blocks and contains phrases 1 and 2 (Portuguese version).

61 Jobim and Regina, 'Águas de março'.

62 Except for measures 98 and 122, where a D$\flat$/C chord is used as a substitute.

63 As in Ex. 5.28, measure 5 is in 3/2 spanning two 'blocks' or measures.

64 Jobim and Jobim, *Cancioneiro Jobim: Obras Escolhidas* 331.

65 Jobim and Jobim, *Cancioneiro Jobim: Obras Escolhidas* 330.

66 Chediak, *Tom Jobim Songbook*, vol. 2, 26.

67 Jobim and Jobim, *Cancioneiro Jobim: Obras Escolhidas* 339.

68 Jobim and Jobim, *Cancioneiro Jobim: Obras Escolhidas* 330.

69 Apart from the modulation that occurs in the three-measure introduction to the instrumental interlude, measures 64–66.

70 To be perfectly correct, the chromatic sequence mentioned as being the key to the song's construction would be g–b$\flat$–a–a$\flat$ instead of b$\flat$–a–a$\flat$–g, but the distinction becomes less significant when each four-measure block is repeated throughout the song.

71 At measure 111, the melody note c^2 is the root of its accompanying chord, C major (with added 9th). Four measures later, at measure 115, the accompanying chord is again C major (with added major 7th) and the melody note g^1 is the 5th note of the chord. In order to harmonize with the four-measure block structure, Jobim repeats the melody note g^1, and, by so doing, avoids disrupting the chromatic downward flow while at the same time maintaining the four-measure block structure. At measure 119 the melody note e^1 is the 3rd of the chord C major (7). Finally at measure 123 the melody has reached c^1 which is the root of the final C major chord.

72 Even in the alternative title of this piece, 'Children's Games', there is an oblique reference to Debussy's *Children's Corner*. This piece was later given an English lyric by Gene Lees and was sebsequently re-named 'Double Rainbow'.

73 Debussy, *Rêverie*.

74 Jobim and Jobim, *Cancioneiro Jobim: Obras Completas, 1966–1970*, vol. 3, 96.

75 Rhythmic discussion on page 115.

76 Author's transcription from Adnet, 'Abril'.

77 Jobim and Jobim, *Cancioneiro Jobim: Obras Escolhidas* 320.

78 Author's transcription from Adnet, 'Abril'.

79 Jobim and Jobim, *Cancioneiro Jobim: Obras Completas, 1966–1970*, vol. 3, 105.

80 Béhague, 'Modinha'.

81 Jobim and Jobim, *Cancioneiro Jobim: Obras Escolhidas* 218.

82 Henry Mancini quoted in *Bossa Nova*.

83 Jobim and Jobim, *Cancioneiro Jobim: Obras Escolhidas* 310–11.

84 Jobim and Jobim, *Cancioneiro Jobim: Obras Completas, 1947–1958*, vol. 1, 166.

85 Jobim and Jobim, *Cancioneiro Jobim: Obras Completas, 1966–1970*, vol. 3, 100–01. The subtitle 'Garoto', which appears as the main title in *Cancioneiro Jobim*, is a reference to the famous *choro* composer/guitarist Annibal Augusto Sardinha (1915–55), better known as Garoto.

86 Jobim and Jobim, *Cancioneiro Jobim: Obras Completas, 1983–1994*, vol. 5, 170.

87 The English version of 'Dindi' with translation by Ray Gilbert was first released on the album *The Wonderful World of Antonio Carlos Jobim* in 1964.

88 The complete score of 'Dindi' is available online at http://www2.uol.com.br/tomjobim/download.htm.

89 Webb 73 and 217.

90 Jobim and Jobim, *Cancioneiro Jobim: Obras Completas, 1959–1965*, vol. 2, 249.

91 Debussy, *Piano Works* 21.

92 Jobim and Jobim, *Cancioneiro Jobim: Obras Escolhidas* 293.

93 Chediak, *Tom Jobim Songbook*, vol. 3, 43, 44.

94 The C9sus4 chords in the last five measures could be interpreted as B♭9 over a C pedal.

95 The melody in the *Cancioneiro* example has been transposed up an octave for comparison with the other examples.

96 The normal melody and accompaniment are shown as written in Jobim and Jobim, *Cancioneiro Jobim: Obras Escolhidas* 305–06. The alternative melody is the author's transcription from Jobim, *Antônio Carlos Jobim: Composer*.

Chapter 6

Conclusion

In many respects Jobim's musical output was a product of circumstance. In his youth, Jobim had wanted to become a concert pianist but, through circumstance, was forced to change his focus to composition. This decision, together with the cultural environment of the optimistic post-war years of the 1950s that supported diversity in broad artistic endeavours such as poetry, theatre, architecture and writing, was fundamental in creating an environment in which Jobim's compositional talents could develop.

Brazilian nationalism had been a motivating force in the development of musical styles such as samba and *choro* since the early part of the twentieth century, and these local styles were valuable to art-music composers such as Villa-Lobos, who sought to compose in a nationalist manner. The 1930s 'witnessed a surge of cultural nationalism and a flourishing in popular music', and samba subsequently gained 'its status as the premier genre of Brazilian popular music [...]. Musicians from black working-class neighborhoods in Rio benefited from the growing popularity of the genre among the middle-classes and often participated in efforts to legitimise it and institutionalise it'.[1] The realization that nationalism was a powerful agent of cultural unification became entrenched as a fundamental ideology from that point in time. Essential to this ideology was a wide-ranging sense of cultural eclecticism and a subsequent acceptance of popular musical styles that was not apparent at the same time in other countries. Consequently, it is this inclusive philosophy of cultural eclecticism that characterizes the work of both Jobim and his greatest musical inspiration and role model, Heitor Villa-Lobos.

The broad appeal of bossa nova (of which Jobim could be called the greatest composer) was due in large part to its inclusion of local samba rhythms, popular themes, sentiments, aspirations, traditions and folklore into its content and structure, but these were not by themselves sufficient to guarantee widespread recognition.[2] Classical art-music elements also gave the style, and indeed all of Jobim's music, an air of sophistication and authority that rendered it as reflective of a more educated, privileged and sought-after lifestyle. The Brazilian 'respectable' middle class, who had before the 1930s considered samba a primitive, lowly musical form, found in bossa nova's samba rhythms further elements of respectability to which they could relate, and in turn bossa nova found it had an expanded audience that reached beyond the carnival sambistas and unrecognized practitioners of the home-grown samba style.[3]

The appeal of Jobim's music to most social levels reflects the acknowledgement of a broad stylistic heritage, an attribute also found in the music of composers as diverse as W. A. Mozart and Charles Ives. Despite obvious stylistic differences to Jobim, Mozart's unity of purpose within a variety of colours and textures, his maintenance of a balance between high and low forms of music, and also between solo and orchestral performance, is similar to the eclectic influences in Jobim's use of both the vernacular and classical in his popular songs and orchestral works. Ives' eclecticism was profoundly influenced by his environment, his music including colloquial elements such as folk songs and hymns. Their use as a means of revitalization and Ives' deployment of eclecticism as an agent for reconciliation between high art and the vernacular are strategies common to Jobim's musical convictions. In a further historical comparison, Jobim, like Mahler, created his own voice by contrasting derivative musical elements against others foreign to their original setting – by distortions of the context of musical associations. This technique was not, however, without its detractors. In the case of both composers, this juxtaposition of familiar musical material from different sources was sometimes derided as mere affection for the banal.

The acceptance and use of other musical genres, regardless of their immediate appeal, heritage or likely critical reaction is also a conviction shared by the popular music composer Jimmy Webb. Unlike Mozart, Ives and Mahler, the vernacular has most often been the basis of his work, yet he has actively pursued unfamiliar musical territory, from classical art music to hip hop and techno, regarding his discoveries as an 'antidote to ignorance'.[4] His compositional philosophy, however, not only outlines his belief in eclecticism but also highlights a significant impediment to the widespread acceptance of eclecticism as a compositional strategy and a fundamental principle. Acceptance of this philosophy entails a broad subjugation of individual taste, and not only an openness to widely varying musical styles but also an acceptance of the cultural baggage that is part of the identity of every style. More often than not it is the baggage, not the music, that hinders any further investigation. To accept eclecticism as a beneficial strategy for musical composition, therefore, one must be prepared to listen critically to many different musical styles so that appropriate choices can be made. Choice implies selection, but it also implies that an attempt has been made to listen, regardless of how repellent the listening experience may have been in the first instance.

The response of a composer to the slurs and innuendos that come with the assimilation of disparate musical styles into their own, including the cultural assumptions associated with those styles, necessarily effects the reception of their work. Conviction and solidarity of purpose are traits frequently in evidence in the character of celebrated composers. Meyerbeer's 'music of society', for instance, was criticized in its day for its blatant techniques and obvious orchestration, harmony and texture, yet his use of wide-ranging stylistic resources was also equated with cultural virtues. For instance, his inclusion of different musical styles to which different social groups could relate meant that his music became a means of cultural reconciliation, as was also the case with Ives' music.

Erik Satie was also misunderstood in his time for his self-effacing attitude towards his own musical creations. His music was variously described as 'poor and simple – raving proletarian music' and as possessing 'banal musical clichés'.[5] Far from denying or retaliating against these condescending opinions, however, Satie indifferently continued his exploration of the latest trends in French music, working under the assumption that by so doing his followers would be confused and that, consequently, 'an artist could not become a pedant or a founder of a school.'[6] Underlying Satie's philosophy was his desire to use as many different musical styles and techniques as possible, an eclectic drive that he knew would provide, if not widespread recognition, then at least some form of credible artistic fulfilment and sense of achievement independent of the assessment of his peers.

As the spiritual catalyst for the avant-garde, Satie used sound in a surreal and abstract way that was different to the structured methods of conventional tonal form and development. The avant-garde movement, which developed at the start of the twentieth century, had at its heart Satie's experimental, open and eclectic philosophical outlook. Through the passage of time and increasing acceptance, this ideology became virtually the *raison d'être* of mid-to-late twentieth-century art-music composition of a modernist caste. Excluding accepted and traditional techniques for the sake of the new, avant-gardism created such a climate of philosophical uniformity that it became 'the typical chronic condition of contemporary art' by the latter part of the twentieth century.[7] Gillmor laments the about-face of the avant-garde ideal and the condition into which it had developed by the mid-1980s.

> In a curious reversal of established trends, the twentieth century has witnessed the ultimate triumph of the avant-garde and has seen the eclectic paradoxically become the iconoclast. Certainly in the West where the artist works in relative freedom from aesthetic dictates, it takes a great deal of courage to adhere to traditional values and to utilise established idioms and procedures. Avant gardism, in becoming very nearly the norm in the West, has become an established way of life for increasing numbers of young composers, and so commonplace has this activity become since World War II that the term 'avant-garde' has ceased to carry the more or less distinctive connotations it enjoyed in the *fin de siècle* and early twentieth century. If there is an avant-garde in the 1980s, it consists only of those who feel sufficiently at ease with the past not to compete with it or duplicate it.

> Today's composer, supported in large part by the university or the state, is expected to create in an advanced idiom, to avoid duplicating the past, especially his own past, to continue the search – as befits the scholar – for new and startling forms of artistic expression. Indeed there seems to be a direct correlation between the uniqueness of a composer's musical language and his stature in the eyes of his colleagues. Hermeticism has carried the day, and a highly original musical vocabulary has become the *sine qua non* for artistic success in academia.[8]

It is not difficult to see, then, why Jobim's music has not been more widely studied or discussed in academic circles, nor written about in serious musicological detail. Jobim's music is eclectic, not hermetic, and appeals unashamedly to past musical idioms and techniques. As well, any revelations of new forms of artistic expression are subtle, not overt, and rely more on contextual novelty than autonomous formulae. In this context Jobim would share the same reaction from the critics of high culture as did Erik Satie – 'a problem', a 'strange case' and a 'fascinating enigma'. The fact that this has not occurred may be a consequence of the fact that Jobim did not overtly promote himself as a 'serious' music composer (although he wrote 'serious' orchestral music) and would not have been considered a problem to western art music, especially living for the most part in Rio de Janeiro, away from the eyes and ears of the western critical press.[9]

Poggioli identifies several characteristics inherent in the theory of the avant-garde ideal – activism usually motivated by antagonism towards someone or something, leading to nihilism and eventually agonism.[10] The sense of novelty for novelty's sake is then limited to those aspects towards which one is not antagonistic. The eclectic sphere of musical possibilities is reduced the moment an avant-gardist accepts these premises and adopts the characteristics that Poggioli identifies. In a sense, Jobim surpassed the avant-garde ideology by accepting everything, even pedestrian musical styles and characteristics that were not startlingly new. The outcome of Jobim's eclectic principles and those of the avant-garde represents in many respects a trumping of the avant-garde ideal.

Thus, although Jobim may not have broken new ground in any singular theoretical or practical way, what remains unique about his style is his original juxtaposition and idiosyncratic incorporation of existing techniques. The identification of technical features of his music reveals aspects that, by themselves, may not be unique, may very often be fundamental and would inevitably contain either a conventional characteristic of western tonal music or a well-documented African influence. It was, however, Jobim's command of existing techniques that made his music successful. Diversity and eclecticism had everything to do with this success. He was able to take the best from many different styles and techniques to synthesize his own compositional method. To demonstrate Jobim's eclecticism is to point to many mundane and ordinary musical characteristics – the point is that they are 'many', not that they are 'mundane and ordinary'. It is the fidelity of choices constituting Jobim's style that was the key to the success of his music.

The overt sentimentality in much of Jobim's music may be another cause for its lack of status and avoidance by the critical music press. Recalling a situation where the derogative term 'Hollywood' was used by conservatorium staff to describe the sentimental nature of Korngold's Piano Trio, Koehne writes:

Classical musicians often use this term to express their unease with music that is openly sentimental, or that uses some trace of the language we associate with either classical or contemporary Hollywood scoring. Demon Hollywood has become the personification of the forces in modern life which have undermined, if not destroyed, the classical establishment's faith in its own superiority. The Hollywood composer is by definition a failure, because he has succumbed to the lure of popularity, or relinquished his proper ambition to stand above the commercial and common world.[11]

As the above indicates, much the same negative reaction to sentimentality has also occurred to those who have acquired popular success. In their book *Bad Music: The Music We Love to Hate*, Washburne and Derno point out that, according to the cultural critics Walter Benjamin and Susan Sontag, 'anything with mass appeal has typically been regarded as culturally suspect'.[12] As well, in the late twentieth century, exclusion of popular forms of jazz from critical literature is due to, according to Deveaux, the assumption that the 'progress of jazz as art necessitates increased distance from the popular'.[13] Washburne laments this exclusion and suggests that 'we should aspire to refine and adapt our historical conceptual lens through which we deal with these phenomena and in the process align jazz scholarship with more cutting-edge popular music/cultural studies'.[14]

The widespread perception of overt sentimentality and banality in much of Jobim's music applies not only to English translations of many of his lyrics, but also to the simplicity of many of his melodies, especially when taken out of context from their accompaniment. In a (rather defensive) comment about the melody or 'big tune' in John Adams' *Grand Pianola Music*, Koehne also recalls the New York Director Peter Sellars remark that '[...] one of the things about official High Art twentieth century music is that you weren't allowed to have a tune'.[15] Sellars went on to describe Beethoven's compositional mechanism in the *Ode to Joy* as '[taking] a really, really tacky tune and [repeating] it over and over again until it becomes transcendent'. Far from denigrating the effect of this intrusion from the everyday world, Sellars delights in its boldness as he does with Adams' 'big tune' in the final movement of *Grand Pianola Music* and rejoices in its connection with the vernacular. Koehne also points out:

> This elaboration of the everyday, transforming the banal by means of aesthetic and technical sophistication – yet without sacrificing or disrespecting the qualities which give the music its immediate appeal – has long been an important element in classical composition, from Haydn to Tchaikovsky.[16]

Another difficulty encountered in defining Jobim's style arises from the fact that specific ethnic idioms and stylistic characteristics, identifiable as common to other composers, do not occur across the whole of his oeuvre. For instance, the bossa nova rhythm, a characteristic that is strongly associated with Jobim, occurs in only a relatively small percentage of his songs.[17] Other 'broadly' characteristic traits, such as a tendency for chromatic, descending linear relationships in his accompaniments, or his propensity for using minor-2nd motives, or his use of *choro* forms, are not endemic. Any single identified stylistic characteristic, therefore, should not be thought of as being 'essential' to Jobim's style. The fact that these stylistic characteristics are present at all is important because they demonstrate Jobim's eclecticism. If there is any identifiable and fundamental characteristic of Jobim's musical style, it is diversity.

The extent of Jobim's eclecticism is well demonstrated in his popular songs, for which he achieved widespread international acclaim, but his ability to assimilate influences from recognized art-music composers in all his music, both popular and 'serious', not only extended his eclectic standing but also enhanced his musical credibility. His scores and recordings demonstrate his undoubted ability, even though he had chosen to finance a good proportion of them himself in the absence of interest from the western art-music world.

This book deals primarily with the understanding of how Jobim assimilated external musical influences to create his musical innovations. It has attempted to reveal some of the many musical influences that Jobim absorbed and made his own. The appeal of Jobim's music lies in its flexibility – in its ability to be played at different tempos, for the phrasings of its melody to be dramatically pulled and stretched, in its ability to assimilate altered harmonies and to be played by different instrumental ensembles, yet always retain its identity. Jobim's inclusive and eclectic philosophy towards musical composition – his openness to diverse stylistic influences and his willingness to use them – is the key to his musical success. Not only was Jobim able to transform Brazilian national and folk music idioms into his own musical style, but he also embraced both the classical and popular musical worlds, an accomplishment that few, if any, popular music composers have been able to emulate with such success.

Another factor that sets Jobim apart from most other popular music composers is that his music was innovative and compelling in all of the four fundamental characteristics of music – melody, harmony, rhythm and form. Jobim took each to a level of sophistication unprecedented in popular music, managing to do this without losing the attraction of simplicity. He knew and understood the difference between sophistication and complexity. Although Jobim's eclecticism may not have been a conscious effort on his part, but more of an absorption of the abundant musical influences surrounding him, there was, however, an unknown source of inspiration that put him apart from his contemporaries. As he admitted:

'Minha composição também é misteriosa. Não sei de onde vem.'
(Composition for me is so mysterious. I've no idea where it comes from.)

Antônio Carlos Jobim.[18]

Notes

1   Perrone and Dunn 11.
2   Moreno 140.
3   Moreno 133.
4   Webb 418.
5   Gillmor 105 and 107.
6   Gillmor 105.
7   Gillmor 117.
8   Gillmor 118.
9   Gillmor 114.

10   Poggioli 60.
11   Koehne 154.
12   Washburne 2.
13   Deveaux 553, quoted in Washburne and Derno 137.
14   Washburne 137.
15   Koehne 157.
16   Koehne 158.
17   Jobim himself said that 'ninety percent of my songs cannot be considered part of Bossa Nova'. See page 33.
18   Jobim 167.

Bibliography

Abraham, Gerald. *Chopin's Musical Style*. Oxford University Press, 1960.

Adnet, Mario. 'Abril'. *Coração Popular: Villa-Lobos*. Indie Records, 2000.

———. *Mario Adnet: 2 Kites: Para Gershwin e Jobim*. Indie Records, 2000.

Adorno, Theodor Wiesengrund. *Philosophy of Modern Music*. Translated by Anne G. Mitchell and Wesley V. Blomster, Seabury Press, 1973.

Aldwell, Edward, and Carl Schachter. *Harmony and Voice Leading*. Vol. 1, Harcourt, Brace, Jovanovich, 1978.

Andriessen, Louis, and Elmer Schönberger. *The Apollonian Clockwork: On Stravinsky*. Translated by Jeff Hamburg, Oxford University Press, 1989.

Ankeny, Jason. 'Brian Eno'. *All Music Guide to Rock*. Edited by Chris Woodstra, Vladimir Bogdanov and Stephen Thomas Erlewine, Backbeat Books, 2002.

Apel, Willi, editor. *Harvard Dictionary of Music*. 2nd ed., Heinmann Educational Books, 1976.

Appleby, David P. *Heitor Villa-Lobos: A Bio-Bibliography*. Greenwood Press, 1988.

———. *The Music of Brazil*, University of Texas, 1983.

Araújo, Samuel. 'The Politics of Passion: The Impact of Bolero on Brazilian Musical Expressions'. *Yearbook for Traditional Music*, vol. 31, 1999, pp. 42–56.

Ashton Jonson, G. C. *A Handbook to Chopin's Works*. 2nd ed., William Reeves, 1908.

Banfield, Stephen. 'Rev. of *The American Popular Ballad of the Golden Era: 1924–1950* by Allen Forte'. *Journal of Music Theory*, vol. 44, 2000, pp. 236–49.

Barbosa, Marco Antonio. 'Suspicion of Plagiarism Involves Águas de março'. *AllBrazilianMusic*, 2001, accessed 25 May 2004, http://www.allbrazilianmusic.com/en/Artists/Artists.asp?Status=ARTISTA&Nu_Artista=667.

Bartlett, Rosamund. 'Stravinsky's Russian Origins'. *The Cambridge Companion to Stravinsky*, edited by Jonathan Cross, Cambridge University Press, 2003, pp. 3–18.

Béhague, Gerard. *The Beginnings of Musical Nationalism in Brazil*, Information Coordinators Inc., 1971.

———. 'Bossa and Bossas: Recent Changes in Brazilian Urban Popular Music'. *Ethnomusicology*, vol. 17, 1973, pp. 209–25.

———. 'Bossa Nova'. *The New Grove Dictionary of Music and Musicians*. Edited by Stanley Sadie and John Tyrrell, 2nd ed., Macmillan, 2001.

———. 'Brazil'. *The New Grove Dictionary of Music and Musicians*. Edited by Stanley Sadie and John Tyrrell, 2nd ed., Macmillan, 2001.

———. *Heitor Villa-Lobos: The Search for Brazil's Musical Soul*. Institute of Latin American Studies, University of Texas, 1994.

———. 'Jobim, Antônio Carlos [Tom] (Brasileiro De Almeida)'. *The New Grove Dictionary of Music Online* ed. Stanley Sadie and John Tyrrell, accessed 8 February 2004, <http://www.grovemusic.com>.

———. 'Latin America'. *The New Grove Dictionary of Music and Musicians*. Edited by Stanley Sadie and John Tyrrell, 2nd ed., Macmillan, 2001.

———. 'Modinha'. *The New Grove Dictionary of Music and Musicians*. Edited by Stanley Sadie and John Tyrrell, 2nd ed., Macmillan, 2001.

———. *Music in Latin America: An Introduction* Macmillan, Prentice-Hall, 1979.

———. 'Samba'. *The New Grove Dictionary of Music and Musicians*. Edited by Stanley Sadie and John Tyrrell. 2nd ed., Macmillan, 2001.

Block, Geoffrey, and J. Peter Burkholder, editors. *Charles Ives and the Classical Tradition*. Yale University Press, 1996.

Blumenthal, Bob. 'Cover Notes'. *Antonio Carlos Jobim: Terra Brasilis*, Warner Brothers, 1995.

Boilès, Charles L. 'Processes of Musical Semiosis'. *Yearbook for Traditional Music*, vol. 14, 1982, pp. 24–44.

Borim, Dário. 'Pride and Prejudice'. *Brazzil,* 1 Apr. 2000, http://www.brazzil.com.

Bossa Nova. Directed by Walter Salles, SBS Brisbane, 27 Jul. 1996.

Brackett, David. *Interpreting Popular Music*. University of California Press, 2000.

Brooks, William. 'Music in America: An Overview'. *The Cambridge History of American Music*, edited by David Nicholls, Cambridge University Press, 1998, pp. 30–48.

Bullock, Alan, and Oliver Stallybrass, editors. *The Fontana Dictionary of Modern Thought*. Fontana Books, 1983.

Bush, John. 'My Life in the Bush of Ghosts'. *All Music Guide to Rock*, edited by Chris Woodstra, Vladimir Bogdanov and Stephen Thomas Erlewine. 3rd ed., Backbeat Books, 2002.

Butler, Christopher. 'Stravinsky as Modernist'. *The Cambridge Companion to Stravinsky*, edited by Jonathan Cross, Cambridge University Press, 2003, pp. 19–36.

Byrd, Charlie. *Jazz 'n' Samba for Guitar: The Music of Antonio Carlos Jobim*. Ludlow Music Inc., 1965.

Cabral, Sérgio. *Antônio Carlos Jobim: Uma Biografia*. Lumiar Editora, 1997.

———. 'The Bossa Nova'. *Bossa Nova Songbook*, edited by Almir Chediak. Vol. 1, Lumiar Editora, 1990, pp 18–21.

———. 'The Pathway of the Master'. *Tom Jobim Songbook*, edited by Almir Chediak. Vol. 1, Lumiar Editora, 1990, pp. 38–45.

———. 'Tom: Revolution with Beauty'. *Bossa Nova Songbook*, edited by Almir Chediak. Vol. 4, Lumiar Editora, 1990, pp. 14–17.

Carrasqueira, Maria José, editor. *O Melhor De Pixinguinha*. Irmãos Vitale, 1997.

Castro, Ruy. *Bossa Nova: The Story of the Brazilian Music That Seduced the World*. Translated by Lysa Salsbury, A Capella Books, 2000.

———. *Chega de Saudade: A História e as Histórias da Bossa Nova*. 2nd ed., Editora Schwarcz Ltda, 1998.

Cezimbra, Márcia, Tessy Callado and Tárik de Souza. *Tons Sobre Tom*. Revan, 1995.

Chediak, Almir, editor. *Bossa Nova Songbook*. 5 vols, Lumiar Editora, 1990.

———. *Tom Jobim Songbook*. 3rd ed., 3 vols, Lumiar Editora, 1990.

Chopin, Frédéric. *Chopin Album: Eine Sammlung De Ausgewähltesten Compositionen*. Bosworth & Co., n.d.

———. *Sämtliche Klavier Werke*. 3 vols, Edition Peters, n.d.

———. *Fantasy in F Minor, Barcarolle, Berceuse and Other Works for Solo Piano*. Dover Publications, 1989.

———. *Oeuvres Pour Le Piano*. Augener, n.d.

———. *Prelude Op. 28, No. 4*. G. Schirmer, 1915.

———. *24 Preludes Op. 28*. Lea Pocket Scores, n.d.

———. *12 Studies Op. 10*. Edited by Alfred Cortot, Éditions Salabert, 1930.

Cohen, Ken. *Águas de março*, newsgroup posting, 10 Sep. 1997, rec.music.brazilian.

Cook, Nicholas. *A Guide to Musical Analysis*. J. M. Dent & Sons, 1992.

Copland, Aaron. 'Tradition and Innovation in Recent European Music'. *Music and Imagination*, Harvard University Press, 1952.

Cross, Jonathan. 'Composing with Stravinsky: Louis Andriessen in Conversation with Jonathan Cross'. *The Cambridge Companion to Stravinsky*, edited by Jonathan Cross, Cambridge University Press, 2003, pp. 251–59.

———. *The Stravinsky Legacy*. Cambridge University Press, 1998.

Dassin, Joan. 'Cultural Policy and Practice in the Nova Republica'. *Latin American Research Review*, vol. 24, 1989, pp. 115–23.

de Schloezer, Boris. *Igor Stravinsky*. Claude Aveline, 1929.

de Souza, Tárik. 'O Arquiteto Da Utopia'. *Tons Sobre Tom*, edited by Márcia Cezimbra Tessy Callado and Tárik de Souza, Editora Revan, 1995, pp. 143–56.

———. 'The Tides of a Modernist Maestro'. *Tom Jobim Songbook*, edited by Almir Chediak. Vol. 3, Lumiar Editora, 1990, pp. 14–18.

de Ulhoa Carvalho, Martha. 'Cancão Da America: Style and Emotion in Brazilian Popular Song'. *Popular Music*, vol. 9, 1990, pp. 321–49.

Deveaux, Scott. 'Constructing the Jazz Tradition: Jazz Historiography'. *Black American Literature Forum*, vol. 25, 1991, pp. 525–560.

Debussy, Claude. *Claude Debussy: Piano Music (1888–1905)*. 2nd ed., Dover Publications, 1973.

———. *Debussy Piano Works*. 3 vols, Lea Pocket Scores, 1968.

———. 'Jardins sous la pluie'. *Estampes*, United Music Publishers, 1903.

———. *La Cathedral Engloutie*. Broekmans & Van Poppel, 1968.

———. *La Soirée Dans Grenade*. Durand-Costallat, 1985.

———. *Oeuvres Completes De Claude Debussy*. Durand-Costallat, 1985.

———. *Rêverie*. Éditions Jobert, 1952.

———. *Sirènes*. Paris, 1999.

Delfino, Jean-Paul. *Brasil Bossa Nova*. Édisud, 1988.

Elbling, Peter, and Steve Muscarella. *Rolling Stone Presents 20 Years of Rock & Roll*. Straight Arrow Productions, 1987.

Elson, Howard. *McCartney Songwriter*. W. H. Allen, 1986.

Emerson, Ralph Waldo. 'An Address'. *Ralph Waldo Emerson: Essays & Poems*, The Library of America, 1996.

————. 'The American Scholar'. *The Collected Works of Ralph Waldo Emerson*, edited by Alfred R. Ferguson. Vol. 1, Belknap Press of Harvard University Press, 1971.

————. 'Self Reliance'. *The Works of Ralph Waldo Emerson*. Vol. 1, G. Bell & Sons, 1913.

Enciclopédia Música Brasileira. Edited by Marcos Antônio Marcondes, PubliFolha, 2003.

Faria, Nelson. *The Brazilian Guitar Book*. Sher Music, 1995.

Fink, Robert. 'Elvis Everywhere: Musicology and Popular Music Studies at the Twilight of the Canon'. *American Music*, vol. 16, 1998, pp. 135–79.

Fisk, Eliot. 'King of the Bossa Nova: Spotlight on Antonio Carlos Jobim'. *Guitar Review*, vol. 55, 1983, pp. 1–7.

Flanagan, David. 'Antônio Carlos Jobim'. *The New Grove Dictionary of Jazz*, edited by Barry Kernfield, Macmillan, 1988.

Fletcher, Peter. *World Musics in Context: A Comprehensive Survey of the World's Major Musical Cultures*. Oxford University Press, 2001.

Fornäs, Johan. 'The Future of Rock: Discourses That Struggle to Define a Genre'. *Popular Music*, vol. 14, 1995, pp. 111–25.

Forte, Allen. *The American Popular Ballad of the Golden Era, 1924–1950*. Princeton University Press, 1995.

Freeman, Peter. 'Swing and Groove: Contextual Rhythmic Nuance in Live Performance'. *7th International Conference on Music Perception and Cognition*, Causal Productions, 2002, pp. 548–50.

Fryer, Peter. *Rhythms of Resistance*. Wesleyan University Press, 2000.

Fulcher, Jane. 'Meyerbeer and the Music of Society'. *The Musical Quarterly*, vol. 67, 1981, pp. 213–29.

Gammond, Peter. *The Oxford Companion to Popular Music*. Oxford University Press, 1991.

Giacomelli, E. F. *Águas de março*, newsgroup posting, 5 Sep. 1997, rec.music.brazilian.

Giffoni, Adriano. *Música Brasileira Para Contrabaixo*. Irmãos Vitale Editores, 1997.

Gilberto, João. 'Chega de Saudade'. *Bossa Nova: João Gilberto Desafinado*, Saludos Amigos, 1992.

Gilliam, Angela, and Onik'a Gilliam. 'Odyssey: Negotiating the Subjectivity of Mulata Identity in Brazil'. *Latin American Perspectives*, vol. 26, 1999, pp. 60–84.

Gillmor, Alan M. 'Erik Satie and the Concept of the Avant-Garde'. *The Musical Quarterly*, vol. 69, 1983, pp. 104–19.

Gloag, Kenneth. 'All You Need Is Theory? The Beatles' "Sgt. Pepper"'. *Music & Letters*, vol. 79, 1998, pp. 577–84.

Gonçalves, Guilherme, and Odilon Costa. *O Batuque Carioca*. Groove, 2000.

Grasse, Jonathon. 'Conflation and Conflict in Brazilian Popular Music: Forty Years between "Filming" Bossa Nova in Orfeu Negro and Rap in Orfeu'. *Popular Music*, vol. 23, 2004, pp. 291–310.

Grout, Donald Jay. *A History of Western Music*. 3rd ed., J. M. Dent & Sons, 1985.

Harding, James Duffield. *The Principles and Practices of Art*. London, 1845.

Harvard Dictionary of Music. Edited by Willi Apel, 2nd ed., Heinemann, 1976.

Hebdige, Dick. *Subculture: The Meaning of Style (New Accents)*. Methuen, 1979.

Helland, Dave. 'The End of Three Vocal Eras: Farewell to Cab Calloway, Antonio Carlos Jobim, and Carmen Mcrae'. *Down Beat*, vol. 62, no. 3, 1995, p. 6.

Hodel, Brian. 'The Choro'. *Guitar Review*, vol. 73, 1988, pp. 31–35.

———. 'Concerts in Review: Antonio Carlos Jobim Carnegie Hall'. *Guitar Review*, vol. 62, 1985, p. 35.

———. 'Villa-Lobos and the Guitar'. *Guitar Review*, vol. 72, 1988, pp. 20–27.

Holden, Stephen. 'Jazz: Jobim and Bossa Nova'. *Guitar Review*, vol. 72, 1988, p. 32.

Holston, Mark. 'Jobim's Living Artistry'. *Americas (English Edition)*, 55, Mar. 2003, p. 1.

———. 'Saying Goodbye to Antônio Carlos Jobim'. *Americas (English Edition)*, 47, Mar. 1995, p. 56.

Homem, Wagner, and Luiz Roberto Oliveira. *Historias de Cançoes: Tom Jobim*. Vol. 4, Leya, 2012.

Huey, Steve. 'Absolutely Free'. *All Music Guide to Rock*, edited by Chris Woodstra, Vladimir Bogdanov and Stephen Thomas Erlewine, Backbeat Books, 2002.

Iger, Arthur L. *Music of the Golden Age, 1900–1950 and Beyond: A Guide to Popular Composers and Lyricists*. Greenwood Press, 1998.

Ives, Charles. *Essays before a Sonata*. Edited by Howard Boatwright, W. W. Norton, 1964.

Jacob, Gordon. *Orchestral Technique*. 3rd ed., J. W. Arrowsmith, 1991.

Jobim, Antonio Carlos. *Tide*. A&M Records, n.d.

———. *Antônio Brasileiro*. Sony Discos, 1995.

———. *Antônio Carlos Jobim*. Verve, n.d.

———. *Antônio Carlos Jobim & Miucha*. Iris Musique, 1993.

———. *Antonio Carlos Jobim and Friends*. Polygram, 1996.

———. *Antônio Carlos Jobim: Composer*. Warner Bros., 1995.

———. *Antônio Carlos Jobim: Meus Primeiros Passos e Compassos*. Revivendo, 2000.

———. *Antônio Carlos Jobim: The Composer Plays*. Verve Records, 1985.

———. *Ao Vivo: Tom Canta Vinicius*. Jobim Music, 2000.

———. *A Arte De Tom Jobim*. Polygram do Brasil, n.d.

———. *Echoes of Rio*. RCA, 1989.

———. *Elis & Tom*. Verve. Polygram, n.d.

———. *Inédito*. CPBO, 1987.

———. *Matita Perê*. Polygram do Brasil, n.d.

———. *O Pequeno Principe*. Festa Irineu Garcia, n.d.

———. *Passarim*. Verve, n.d.

———. *Sinfônico*. Biscoito Fino, 2003.

———. *Stone Flower*. Columbia Jazz Contemporary Series, 1990.

———. *Terra Brasilis*. Warner Archives, n.d.

———. *The Wonderful World of Antonio Carlos Jobim*. Discovery Records, 1964.

———. *Urubu*. Warner Music Brazil, 1987.

———. *Wave*. A&M Records, 1986.

Jobim, Antônio Carlos, and Elis Regina. 'Águas de março'. *Compact Jazz: Antonio Carlos Jobim*, Verve, 1990.

Jobim, Antônio Carlos, and Paulo Jobim. *Cancioneiro Jobim: Obras Completas*. 5 vols, Jobim Music, 2000–2001.

———. *Cancioneiro Jobim: Obras Escolhidas*. Jobim Music, 2000.

Jobim, Antônio Carlos and Vinícius de Moraes. *Polêmica e Orfeu da Conceicão*. Odeon, 2002.

Jobim, Helena. *Antônio Carlos Jobim: Um Homem Iluminado*. Editora Nova Fronteira, 1996.

Jonson, G. C. Ashton. *A Handbook to Chopin's Works*. 2nd ed., William Reeves, 1908.

Keller, Hans. 'National Frontiers in Music'. *Tempo*, vol. 33, 1954, pp. 23–30.

Kelly, Barbara L. 'Maurice Ravel'. *The New Grove Dictionary of Music and Musicians*, edited by Stanley Sadie and John Tyrrell. 2nd ed., Macmillan, 2001.

———. *Tradition and Style in the Works of Darius Milhaud 1912–1939*. Ashgate, 2003.

Knapp, Raymond. 'Suffering Children: Perspectives on Innocence and Vulnerability in Mahler's Fourth Symphony'. *19th-Century Music*, vol. 22, 1999, pp. 233–67.

Koehne, James. 'The Flight from Banality'. *Bad Music*, edited by Christopher J. Washburne and Maiken Derno, Routledge, 2004, pp. 148–72.

Kopplin, Dave. 'Rev. of *Listening to Classic American Popular Songs*, by Allen Forte'. *Echo: A Music-Centered Journal*, vol. 3, no. 2, 2001, Los Angeles: UCLA, http://www.echo.ucla.edu/Volume3-issue2/reviews/kopplin.html#top

Laird, Paul. 'Leonard Bernstein: Eclecticism and Vernacular Elements in *Chichester Psalms*'. *The Society for American Music Bulletin*, vol. 25, no. 1, 1999, p. 7.

Laloy, Louis. *Louis Laloy (1874–1944) on Debussy, Ravel and Stravinsky*. Translated by Deborah Priest, Ashgate, 1999.

Landow, George P. 'J. D. Harding and John Ruskin on Nature's Infinite Variety'. *The Journal of Aesthetics and Art Criticism*, vol. 28, 1970, pp. 369–80.

Lanza, Joseph. *Elevator Music*. Picador, 1994.

Larkin, Colin. *The Encyclopedia of Popular Music*. 3rd ed., Muze, 1998.

Lawn, Richard J., and Jeffrey L. Hellmer. *Jazz Theory and Practice*. Alfred Publishing Co., 1993.

Lees, Gene. *Singers and the Song*. Oxford University Press, 1998.

———. 'Um Abraço No Tom Antonio Carlos Jobim'. *Singers and the Song II*, Oxford University Press, 1998, pp. 217–51.

Lesure, François. 'Debussy, Claude: Orchestration and Timbre'. *The New Grove Dictionary of Music and Musicians,* edited by Stanley Sadie and John Tyrrell. 2nd ed., London: Macmillan, 2001.

Lind, Michael. *The Next American Nation: The New Nationalism and the Fourth American Revolution*. Free Press, 1995.

Lockspeiser, Edward. *Debussy: His Life and Mind*. Vol. 2, Cassell, 1965.

Major, Barbara J. *Remembering Antonio Carlos Jobim*, 24 May 2001, http://bjbear71.com/jobim/tom-ogerman.html.

Mammi, Lorenzo, Arthur Nestrovski and Luiz Tatit. *Três Canções De Tom Jobim*, Cosac Naify, 2004.

Mandel, Howard. 'Rio on the Hudson'. *Ear Magazine*, vol. 11, no. 5, Feb. 1987, pp. 8–9.

Macquarie Dictionary. 3rd ed., Macquarie Library, 1997.

Marcondes, Marcos, editor. *Enciclopédia Da Música Brasileira: Erudita*. Publifolha, 2000.

———, editor. *Enciclopédia Da Música Brasileira: Samba e Choro*. Publifolha, 2000.

Mawer, Deborah. *Darius Milhaud: Modality & Structure in Music of the 1920s*, Ashgate, 1997.

McGowan, Chris, and Ricardo Pessanha. *The Brazilian Sound: Samba, Bossa Nova, and the Popular Music of Brazil*. Temple University Press, 1998.

Michaelis Dicionário Ilustrado. Vol. 2, Melhoramentos, 1961.

Middleton, Richard. 'Popular Music Analysis and Musicology: Bridging the Gap'. *Popular Music*, vol. 12, 1993, pp. 177–89.

Milhaud, Darius. *Notes without Music*. Translated by Donald Evans, Dennis Dobson, 1952.

———. 'Polytonalité et Atonalité'. *La Revue Musicale*, vol. 4, 1923, pp. 29–44.

Moore, Allan. *Analyzing Popular Music*. Cambridge University Press, 2003.

Moreno, Albrecht. 'Bossa Nova: Novo Brasil the Significance of Bossa Nova as a Brazilian Popular Music'. *Latin American Research Review*, vol. 17, 1982, pp. 129–41.

Morgan, Robert P. 'Ives and Mahler: Mutual Responses at the End of an Era'. *19th-Century Music*, vol. 2, 1978, pp. 72–81.

Morwood, James, editor. *A Dictionary of Latin Words and Phrases*. Oxford University Press, 1998.

Murphy, John. 'Self-Discovery in Brazilian Popular Music: Mestre Ambrósio'. *Brazilian Popular Music and Globalisation*, edited by Charles A. Perrone and Christopher Dunn, Routledge, 2001.

Mussorgsky, Modest Petrovich. *Tableaux d'une Exhibition*. arr. *Kartinki S. V.*, Deutsche Grammophon, 1980.

Napolitano, Marcos. '"Ja Temos Um Passado": 40 Anos do LP *Chega De Saudade*'. *Latin American Music Review*, vol. 21, 2000, pp. 59–65.

Navegador, Caro. 'Rev. of *A Pré-História do Samba*, by Bernado Alves', translated by James Sera. *Discos Raros*, Jan. 2001, http://www.historiasamba.hpg.ig.com.br/text.htm.

Neto, Jovino Santos. 'Brazilian Piano Styles'. *2003 Annual Conference of the International Association of Jazz Education*, Jan. 2003, Toronto, www.jovisan.net/iaje_2003.htm.

Nicholls, David, editor. *The Cambridge History of American Music*. Cambridge University Press, 1998.

O Melhor Do Choro Brasileiro: 60 Peças Com Melodia E Cifras. 3 vols, Irmãos Vitale, 1997.

Oliveira, Luiz Roberto. *Clube do Tom*, Aug. 2003, http://www.clubedotom.com.br.

Orledge, Robert. 'Satie, Koechlin and the Ballet "Uspud"'. *Music & Letters*, vol. 68, 1987, pp. 26–41.

Paddison, Max. 'The Critique Criticised: Adorno and Popular Music'. *Popular Music*, vol. 2, 1982, pp. 201–18.

Paiano, Enor. 'Jobim Recalled as One of Century's Great Composers'. *Billboard*, vol. 106, 1994, p. 3.

Pascall, Robert. 'Style'. *The New Grove Dictionary of Music and Musicians*, edited by Stanley Sadie and John Tyrrell. 2nd ed., Macmillan, 2001.

Peppercorn, Lisa M. *The World of Villa-Lobos in Pictures and Documents*. Ashgate, 1996.

Perrone, Charles A. 'An Annotated Interdisciplinary Bibliography and Discography of Brazilian Popular Music'. *Latin American Music Review*, vol. 7, 1986, pp. 302–40.

———, editor. *Brazilian Popular Music & Globalization*. Routledge, 2002.

———. 'From Noigandres to "Milagre Da Alegria": The Concrete Poets and Contemporary Brazilian Popular Music'. *Latin American Music Review*, vol. 6, 1985, pp. 58–79.

Perrone, Charles A., and Christopher Dunn. '"Chiclete Com Banana": Internationalisation in Brazilian Popular Music'. *Brazilian Popular Music and Globalisation*, edited by Charles A. Perrone and Christopher Dunn, Routledge, 2002.

Peyser, Joan. 'The Bernstein Legacy'. *Opera News*, vol. 65, 2000, pp. 22–29.

Poggioli, Renato. *The Theory of the Avant-Garde*. Translated by Gerald Fitzgerald, Harvard University Press, 1968.

Rathert, Wolfgang. 'The Idea of Potentiality in the Music of Charles Ives'. *Ives Studies*, edited by Philip Lambert, Cambridge University Press, 1997.

Ravel, Maurice. *Album De Six Morceaux Choisis, Pour Piano Seul*. Durand, 1913.

———. *Ballade De La Reine Morte D'aimer*. Salabert, 1975.

———. *Gaspard De La Nuit*. Alfred Publishing, 1990.

———. *Ma Mere L'oye*. Durand, 1910.

———. *Maurice Ravel. 1875–1937*, Calliope, 1990.

———. *Menuet Antique*. Enoch, 1898.

———. *Miroirs*. B. Schott's Söhne, 1906.

———. *Pavane Pour Une Infante Défunte*. Schott, n.d.

———. *Rapsodie Espagnole*. Durand, 1908.

———. *Sérénade Grotesque*. Editions Salabert, 1975.

———. *Sonatine, Pour Le Piano*. Durand, 1905.

———. *Trio Pour Piano, Violon Et Violoncelle*. Durand, 1915.

Raynor, Henry. 'The Necessity of Eclecticism'. *The Music Review*, vol. 20, 1959, pp. 282–88.

Redlich, Hans F. 'The Creative Genius of Gustav Mahler'. *The Musical Times*, vol. 101, 1960, pp. 418–21.

Reily, Suzel Ana. 'Tom Jobim and the Bossa Nova Era'. *Popular Music*, vol. 15, 1996, pp. 1–16.

Reising, Russell. *Every Sound There Is: The Beatles' Revolver and the Transformation of Rock and Roll*. Edited by Russell Reising, Ashgate, 2002.

Reynolds, Joshua. 'The Sixth Discourse'. *The Literary Works of Sir Joshua Reynolds*. Vol. 1, London, 1852.

Ricoeur, Paul. *Hermeneutics and the Human Sciences: Essays on Language, Action, and Interpretation*. Translated by John B. Thompson, Cambridge University Press, 1981.

Rogers, Robert M. 'Jazz Influence on French Music'. *The Musical Quarterly*, vol. 21, 1935, pp. 53–68.

Rosado, Ana Maria. 'A Conversation with Sharon Isbin'. *Guitar Review*, vol. 72, 1988, pp. 14–18.

Runswick, Darryl. *Rock, Jazz & Pop Arranging*. Faber Music, 1992.

Ruskin, John. 'Of Unity, or the Type of the Divine Comprehensiveness'. *Modern Painters*. 5th ed., Vol. 2, George Allen, 1908.

Sabaneyeff, Leonid. *Modern Russian Composers*. Martin Lawrence, 1927.

Samson, Jim. *The Music of Chopin*. Routledge & Kegan Paul, 1985.

Satie, Erik. *Je Te Veux*. Salabert, 1904.

Schachter, Carl. 'The Prelude in E Minor Op. 28 No. 4: Autograph Sources and Interpretation'. *Chopin Studies*, edited by Jim Samson and John Rink. Vol. 2, Cambridge University Press, 1994, pp. 161–82.

———. *Unfoldings: Essays in Shenkerian Theory and Analysis*. Edited by Joseph N. Straus, Oxford University Press, 1999.

Schreiner, Claus. *Musica Brasileira: A History of Popular Music and the People of Brazil*. Marion Boyars, 1993.

Sève, Mário. *Vocabulário do Choro: Estudos e Composições*. 2nd ed., Lumiar Editora, 1999.

Shera, F. H. *Debussy and Ravel*. Oxford University Press, 1925.

Sinatra, Frank. *Francis Albert Sinatra & Antonio Carlos Jobim*. Reprise, n.d.

Slonimsky, Nicolas. *Music of Latin America*. George G. Harrap & Co., 1946.

Souster, Tim. 'Notes on Pop Music'. *Tempo*, vol. 87, 1968, pp. 2–6.

Stroud, Sean. '"Musica e Para o Povo Cantar": Culture, Politics, and Brazilian Song Festivals, 1965–1972'. *Latin American Music Review*, vol. 21, 2000, pp. 87–117.

Tadeu, Acácio, and Camargo Piedade. 'Brazilian Jazz and Friction of Musicalities'. *Jazz Planet*, edited by E. Taylor Atkins, University Press of Mississippi, 2003, pp. 41–58.

Tarasti, Eero. *Heitor Villa-Lobos: The Life and Works, 1887 to 1959*. McFarlane, 1995.

Taruskin, Richard. *Stravinsky and the Russian Traditions*. Vol. 2, University of California Press, 1996.

Thompson, Daniella. 'Choro, Inc.' *Brazzil*, Apr. 2000, http://www.brazzil.com/pages/musapr00.htm.

———. 'Let's Hear It for Jobim'. *Brazzil*, Jun. 2002, http://www.brazzil.com/pages/p47jun02.htm.

———. 'The Man Who Invented Bossa Nova'. *Brazzil*, May 1998, http://joaogilberto.org/daniella.htm.

———. 'More Than Jobim's Alter Ego'. *Brazzil*, May 2003, http://www.brazzil.com/p113may03.htm.

———. 'O Encontro Au Bon Gourmet: The Disc That No-One Reviewed'. *Musica Brasiliensis*, 2004, p. 7.

Tick, Judith. 'Rev. of *The Cambridge History of American Music*, Ed. David Nicholls'. *Journal of the American Musicological Society*, vol. 56, 2003, pp. 721–35.

Tinhorão, José Ramos. *Música Popular: Um Tema Em Debate*. Editóra Saga, 1966.

Treece, David. 'Guns and Roses: Bossa Nova and Brazil's Music of Popular Protest, 1958–68'. *Popular Music*, vol. 16, 1997, pp. 1–29.

Ulhôa, Martha Tupinambá de. 'Chiclete Com Banana: Us and the Other in Brazilian Popular Music'. *Musical Cultures of Latin America: Global Effects, Past and Present*, edited by Steven Loza, Ethnomusicology Publications, University of California, 1999.

Vallas, Léon. *The Theories of Claude Debussy*. Translated by Maire O'Brien, Oxford University Press, 1929.

van der Lee, Pedro. 'Sitars and Bossas: World Music Influences'. *Popular Music*, vol. 17, 1998, pp. 45–70.

Veloso, Caetano. *Tropical Truth: A Story of Music and Revolution in Brasil*. Translated by Isabel de Sena, Alfred A. Knopf, 2002.

Veloso, Caetano and Christopher Dunn. 'The Tropicalista Rebellion'. *Transition*, vol. 70, 1996, pp. 116–38.

Vianna, Hermano. *The Mystery of Samba: Popular Music and National Identity in Brazil*. Translated by John Charles Chasteen, University of North Carolina Press, 1999.

Villa-Lobos, Heitor. *Bendita Sabedoria*. Editions Durand, 1958.

———. *Choros No. 5*. Max Eschig, 1955.

———. *Etude No. 4*. Max Eschig, 1953.

———. *Étude No. 10*. Max Eschig, 1953.

———. *Gavota-Choro*. Max Eschig, 1955.

————. *Hommage Á Chopin*. Max Eschig, 1955.

————. *Prélude No 1*. Max Eschig, 1954.

————. *Suite Populaire Brésilienne: No. 5 Chôrinho*. Max Eschig, 1923.

Washburne, Christopher J. 'Does Kenny G Play Bad Jazz? A Case Study'. *Bad Music,* edited by Christopher J. Washburne and Maiken Derno, Routledge, 2004, pp. 123–147.

Washburne, Christopher J. and Maiken Derno, editors. *Bad Music*. Routledge, 2004.

Webb, Jimmy. *Tunesmith: Inside the Art of Songwriting*. Hyperion, 1998.

Wheaton, Jack W. 'Antônio Carlos Jobim: Melodic, Harmonic and Rhythmic Innovations'. *Jazz Research Proceedings Yearbook,* 2001, pp. 136–44.

Winckelmann, Johann Joachim. 'Essay on the Beautiful in Art'. *Writings on Art,* edited by David Irwin, Phaidon, 1972.

CPSIA information can be obtained
at www.ICGtesting.com
Printed in the USA
FSHW011632191019
63107FS